THE BLACK STAR MURDERS

THE BLACK STAR MURDERS

Dale L. Gilbert

St. Martin's Press
New York

THE BLACK STAR MURDERS. Copyright © 1988 by Dale L. Gilbert. All rights reserved. Printed in the United States of America. No part of this book may be used or reproduced in any manner whatsoever without written permission except in the case of brief quotations embodied in critical articles or reviews. For information, address St. Martin's Press, 175 Fifth Avenue, New York, N.Y. 10010.

Design by Jaye Zimet

Library of Congress Cataloging-in-Publication Data

Gilbert, Dale L.
    The black star murders / by Dale L. Gilbert.
      p.   cm.
    ISBN 0-312-01391-4 : $17.95
    I. Title.
PS3557.I338B5 1988
813'.54—dc 19   87-29911

First Edition

10 9 8 7 6 5 4 3 2 1

DEDICATION

This one is for Pat: my best friend, my most loyal supporter, and severest critic. Without her, this book wouldn't exist. Nor, I think, would I. Our love is here to stay.

PROLOGUE

Sometimes things just get out of hand. It all began as just a small favor for a sometimes friend. Gus, the perpetually morose little guy who operated the Portola, my favorite restaurant on Michigan Avenue, cornered me in the bar one night. I knew he was grinding axes when he signaled for a second refill on the house. One on rare occasions, maybe, but two—never! He tiptoed around until I finally told him to get to the point before either he went broke or I turned into a lush.

It was one of the oldest chapters in the book. They'd come around about a year ago. There were three that first time. Cold men with cat's eyes, Gus said. They made him feel like a bug. Every week from then on it had cost him three hundred to stay in business and remain healthy. One of the original trio would come by to collect, always the same man and always Wednesday night right around ten. Gus wrote it off as one more cost of doing business in a top location in uptown Chicago.

Six months ago the push had gone up to five hundred and things began to tighten up. He'd had to let a busboy go and the house labels behind the bar had slipped a notch here and there. Last week word had come down that it was going to be a grand a pop from now on. Gus said he couldn't absorb it and still keep the Portola a quality operation. His back was against the wall. So he sweated bullets and finally made a decision. The decision was to come to me. We'd talked a little—too much, maybe. Enough for him to know that I was the kind of private cop that wasn't afraid to get my hands dirty. Also I loved the place and he knew it.

He'd made it into a class act. His obvious concern about compromising struck a sympathetic chord. In a world of indifferent service and mediocre goods, the Portola was a refreshing change. So good old Matt Doyle clapped him on the back and told him to be of good cheer.

Talk is cheap. Before very long I'd be wishing I'd opted to just switch hangouts.

The following Wednesday I hung around from eight on, waiting for Gus to give me the high sign. My man walked into the bar at 9:50; I didn't need any help spotting him. He moved with that special economy of motion found only among top athletes and highly disciplined hunters. FBI agents get the look if they manage to avoid all the purges and hang on long enough. Criminal pros have it in spades; it's how you tell them from the swaggering amateurs. Something Gus had failed to mention: The guy's complexion was faded olive, maybe two generations removed from that charming island of stone in the Mediterranean noted for its export of terror and silence. I felt a sudden chill and suspected Gus of forgetting accidentally on purpose.

The guy walked directly toward the bar, surveying the room without conscious thought. Resting his hands on the red leather pad at the edge, he continued a wary surveillance via the mirror behind the bar. I did my best to blend into the woodwork, wearing the glazed smirk of a barfly.

Gus hurried over to the register, withdrew an unmarked envelope, and rushed half the distance toward the hood. There he stopped and slid the envelope savagely along the bar top the rest of the way.

Hood's hand flicked out and intercepted it, but his eyes

riveted Gus's. I could almost hear the little alarm bells going off. There'd been a tiny change in a year-old ritual and it was enough. Gus was right about the cat's eyes. The extortionist's eyes were incurious, totally devoid of human emotion, but they weren't likely to miss much, and he didn't seem to believe in blinking very often. The money disappeared inside his topcoat. He spun around and headed for the door, looking around now as if trying to memorize every face in the dimly lighted room. I actually felt his gaze and thought it rested on me a fraction longer, but I freely admit it may have been a simple case of paranoia. The guy's presence in the room was a feral, palpable thing. I was surprised that no one else seemed to notice. The level of idle chatter, punctuated with the clank of glasses, remained constant.

The short hairs at the nape of the neck really do rise in times of great fear and danger. At least mine do. Every one of them was standing at attention. I felt like a clown. That gambit with the envelope along the top of the bar had been dumb. I'd taken the whole thing entirely too lightly, preparing a trap for some form of lowland gorilla with an I.Q. maybe twice his chest size, tops. But, instead I was getting up to follow a guy who looked as if he could take his choice between playing halfback for the Bears and running Chrysler.

He got cute a couple of times. Paused in full stride halfway out the door, then pulled a reverse and backtracked quickly just to see who'd be caught leaning. It didn't do him any good because I'm relatively cute myself. I hung on and made the rounds with him that night, and I'm willing to bet he thought he was doing a solo. He finished up a little after 1:00 A.M. at a grimy office in the corner of a warehouse down on the South Side. The lack of traffic made me feel like a nudist at a meeting of the D.A.R., so I called it a night.

Two weeks later I was appalled to find myself pulling up in front of a pair of very substantial iron gates just off Lake Shore Drive. The house was set well back, and the grounds covered a minimum of ten acres. Quite an extravagance, considering a hundred thousand an acre in that neighborhood would qualify as a distress sale. The man I'd been summoned to meet would never need a distress sale, but it was common knowledge that he'd caused quite a few.

A whip-thin young man in black stepped out of the shadows of the shrubbery and beckoned to me. He did a thorough job of checking both me and the car before punching the code numbers into the control box mounted on one of the great stone pillars. The gates swung open in silence. Not a syllable had passed between us. I watched him slip my automatic into his right coat pocket. I considered asking for a claim check but thought better of it. Taking a deep breath, I vowed to keep a damper on my usual urge to agitate; this whole program would be dicey enough without that.

There were two more men waiting in front of the two-story colonnaded portico. As I pulled closer, I recognized Gus's delivery boy. Given sufficient time, the intensity of his gaze might well have produced at least first-degree burns. His companion merely looked bored as he motioned me into position and proceeded to shake me down mechanically. Satisfied, he nodded toward the front door. One fell in on either side of me, close enough to make me appropriately edgy. Amateurs would have placed themselves fore and aft, but these two knew the ropes.

Our tight little trio broke up inside an oak-paneled room, which I took to be either an office or a study. Two walls were lined solidly with books. At the far end there was a massive and yet ornate Empire desk easily the size of a regulation pool table. On the wall behind it hung a three-foot cross featuring a dying Christ. Seated behind the outsized desk was my host for the evening. His name was Dominic Nuncio. He was known by other names around town, but to his face it was never anything but a respectful, Mr. Nuncio. If he took orders from anyone, which I doubted, it wasn't anyone in town. Chicago was his fiefdom in many dark and dirty ways, and he ruled it with an iron fist.

Huge though the desk was, it was barely big enough. His big, dark face rested directly atop a bloated sausage body without the apparent benefit of a neck. His complexion was mottled with age and wine, oily-looking under the muted lighting. If it's true that eyes are the windows of the soul, his soul must have been an unspeakably ugly thing.

"Why have you concerned yourself with my private affairs, Mr. Doyle?" His voice was a painfully thin rasp, as if he suffered from acute bronchitis. His large swollen hands were folded on the desk; he aimed his eyes at me over bulging cheeks like snipers atop adjoining hills.

"You know how it is. A friend asks a favor. I imagine you've already heard the one about 'A friend in need is a pest'? It's sure as hell true, but what can you do?"

He sucked in a deep whistling breath, and it came back out as a sigh. "I received the package you sent. It made me very upset." He made it sound as if his being upset were a worldwide disaster. "It annoys me that you found it so easy to provide a partial but reasonably accurate schedule of one of my enterprises. It annoys me even more that you were able to include photographs. They aren't very good, by the way. You really should invest in a better camera. I'm not sure just what you think the photos prove, but it certainly shows malicious intent on your part. And the worst thing of all was the tape. I would have sworn that would have been impossible to get. Just to think that you'd go to all that trouble to assemble such a file on *me!*"

No gesture was used to emphasize the final pronoun, but none was needed. The tone clearly conveyed the message that we were talking mortal sin here, not venial.

For a moment the relentless eyes switched their focus up to Gus's mailman. It was an incredible relief to be out from under that gaze even for a few seconds. "Adjustments will have to be made. Won't they, Joseph? It would seem we're getting a little sloppy in our work habits, aren't we?"

A muted, "Yes, Mr. Nuncio," emanated from my right rear.

"Just for the record, it wasn't all that easy," I told the eyes as soon as they resumed their lock on me.

He gave the slightest backward wave of his right hand, as if dismissing the subject as too trivial for discussion. "Get to the point, Mr. Doyle. What exactly is it you think you can get from me?" He had the ability to say my name in such a way that it sounded like an obscenity.

"It's really very simple." I knew I could never bring myself to call him Mr. Nuncio, and I damn sure wasn't dumb enough to call him anything else. "A friend of mine named Gus owns the Portola Restaurant. You've just about quadrupled the juice on him this last year. He can't make it, not and keep the place as it is. I eat there a lot and I'd really hate to see the place go down. The way I see it, you don't interfere in my life, I don't interfere in yours."

The caliber of the eyes diminished slightly. "I'd advise you to speak seriously, Mr. Doyle. What . . . do . . . you . . . want?"

"Just what I said. Lay off the Portola. You do that and there's no reason we can't be buddies."

He made that throwaway motion with his hand again. I sensed an added degree of tension in the room. "Let me pose a question to you, Mr. Doyle. I assure you it is not rhetorical. What do you think your chances are of walking out of this room alive?"

I licked my lips. That's bad because I have a theory about lip-lickers and it isn't complimentary. "Damn good, considering I've stashed enough material in a very safe place to put you away for a lot more years than you've got to spare."

The awful parody of a face rearranged itself into what it thought was a smile. "Such a situation would never be acceptable. To allow you to walk around free, holding a loaded gun to my head? Not possible."

I grinned right back. It may have been a poor attempt, but I tried. "No, you misunderstand me. My white horse got shot out from under me years ago, and my armor is all rusted out. I didn't set out to clean up the town and ride off into the sunset. It can't be done; I have no illusions left about that. I'm here to do a small favor for a sad little man whose only gift is his devotion to his customers. Maybe you can appreciate how rare that is these days. Drop Gus from your rolls. What the hell; it's not as if I'm asking you to take a vow of poverty. It's a reasonable request. Thirty days from now, if you do this small thing for me, everything I have in your file comes back to you."

Nuncio's outsized head tilted slightly to one side as if he needed to get a different perspective on me. "That was smart. Putting it as a favor to you like that. As you probably know, I am noted for doing favors for those I think deserve them. But it doesn't change the fact that you're trying to blackmail me. You must understand how that would look. Things get around. A small thing perhaps, but enough to cause some doubts in certain quarters maybe. A man like me can't afford that."

"Don't you remember? You hired me to check out some of your operations for soft spots. I've done the same for lots of businessmen. It's what I do for a living; I'm damn good at it, as you can see. So I found a few. Now I'm entitled to get paid."

He erupted with a series of staccato gasps. Either he was laughing or having a seizure. "You impress me, Mr. Doyle. You really do. You strike me as a man who might almost be believed when he gives his word to a deal. Are you willing to make a sacred oath to turn over everything—and I do mean *everything*—on the terms you've suggested? What do you hold dear enough to make such an oath sacred?"

"This!" I placed my right hand on top of my head and improvised a pledge. "That should be good enough—my life is my bond. My mother didn't raise any stupid children, and I'd be a real dunce to cross you. I'll ask you to take your oath to reprieve Gus on that big Bible on the shelf behind you." I'd done my homework; the word was he was a deeply religious man. It's not so unusual. One of his forebears—Al Capone—practically supported the church right here in Chicago not so many years ago. "Mother church" and "omertà" seemed somehow to coexist comfortably in the minds and hearts of such men.

He nodded ever so slightly. Joseph rounded the desk with a good turn of speed and fetched the Bible. "An excellent choice. This Bible is signed by four—no, five—generations of Nuncios. My word will be forged of steel."

After saying the words, he remained looking down at the worn leather cover, tracing his finger along the hand-tooled designs. "If your figures are correct, Mr. Doyle, you may have done me more of a favor than you know. Such an increase would be unprecedented. The first rule of my modest little insurance business is never increase the client's premium more than twenty-five percent in any one year. And then only if his increased prosperity warrants. All such decisions must be made here in this room."

The eyes glanced briefly above and behind me again. It took every bit of self-control I could muster to ignore the fact that Joseph was an arm's length behind me. If I had inadvertently put a noose around his neck, he was undoubtedly dying to kill me where I sat.

Nuncio studied me reflectively. He looked relaxed and almost avuncular now, but I could only think of all the evil and ugliness those dead eyes had watched impassively.

"This may surprise you, but it would not be unheard of for a bright young man of, I assume, Irish descent to be welcomed into our little group. An organization like this is no different from any *Fortune* 500 company. Everything depends on talent. With the right man in the right place you turn a nice profit. There have never been enough good men. I'm referring to something in middle management, of course. It may also surprise you to know that the vast majority of my enterprises are entirely legitimate."

I waited until I got it right. The one thing in all the world I didn't want to do now was insult the man, because fat as he was, he would be thin-skinned. It was going to be like telling Santa to stick the toys back in the bag and beat it.

"I'm flattered, but it wouldn't work. I'm strictly a maverick. Never been a team player. Tell me to go north, I'll head south every time. My loss, but I know my limitations."

"You are right to decline, I think. It hasn't escaped my notice that you cannot bring yourself to call me Mr. Nuncio, as much as you desired my good graces tonight. I believe you are what is called a romantic, Mr. Doyle. You consider yourself a qualified judge of what is right and what is wrong in the world. A man of ideals. Such people thrive in books and old movies. Children have a great need to believe in that sort of hero when they are very young. But a grown man living in Chicago? Doing the sort of work you do? The odds are terrible for you. And it must get very confusing for you at times."

A shake of the head and another tiny wave of the hand. "It's your affair, Mr. Doyle." He reached into the top drawer of the desk and pulled out a red leather checkbook. "I'll pay you for your services now. I don't like being billed. How much?"

"You don't owe me a dime."

"But I hired you. Remember? You turned in a very satisfactory report. Let me make this perfectly clear. I do not want to be in your debt when you leave this house. I won't be."

"Same problem here. If I took the money I'd be a hired hand. You might get the idea I could be called back into active duty someday. Look, we've just made a nice little gentlemen's agreement. Full value given and received both ways. Let's just call it even."

The friendly atmosphere, such as it was, evaporated. "No tainted money for the sainted Matthew Doyle? That's what you're telling me, isn't it?"

"Not at all. It's just like you said—I'm a romantic. If I

took your money it would smack of extortion. You called it blackmail yourself. This is the only face I've got to shave every morning, so I have to like it. Besides, with any luck, Gus will supply me with the best meals in town for life. That adds up to one hell of a fee. I'm satisfied."

"May you live long enough to collect," Nuncio said flatly. The hand moved a centimeter, and I felt a nudge at my left shoulder. The meeting was over.

As I slid behind the wheel of my car, I got one last look at Joseph's face. Adjustments were going to have to be made, the old man had said. Joseph was going to owe me. I'd heard discipline in his outfit made marine boot camp seem like a picnic in the park. In spite of my agreement with his boss, I knew it was a debt Joseph would be dying to collect.

The gates were open by the time I arrived. The same guy handed my automatic back to me, shells intact, as if he were selling tickets for a movie. I didn't relax until I was well out of sight. I'd been like a clenched fist the entire time. Now the reaction was setting in. A not-so-faint tremor of hands. Foot a little uneven on the pedal. A river of sweat gushed from under both arms. But I felt great. I'd entered the den of the dragon, stuck my head in its maw, and gotten away with it. It had been close: If I'd caught that hellish old man on an off night, or failed to rein in my mouth. . . . He'd wished me a long life. Or had he? I wondered if his blessing was anything like the kiss they're supposed to give you just before they shove a shotgun in your ear.

Gus was properly jubilant in his own dour way. If I'd wanted to become a boozer I could have made out fine. But I continued to enforce my strict limit of two Scotch-waters; something told me it wasn't a real good time to get sloppy. The minute it became obvious that Gus was really off the hook I wanted to deliver the package, but experience told me to stick with the letter of the agreement. On the thirtieth day I dropped the goods off at the gate on Lake Shore Drive. No offense to the post office, but I wouldn't trust them with my life. And that's exactly what was involved.

It happened two nights later. He was waiting in the gloom of the entrance to my apartment building. The first thing I heard was the grunt of effort a fighter makes when he throws his Sunday punch, immediately followed by the unforgettable sound a knife makes scraping across your own precious ribs. It's an incredibly ugly, personal sound. Sometimes I still wake up in the wee hours hearing it. If my overcoat hadn't ruined his angle, he would have no doubt succeeded in guiding the thin blade between my ribs. He certainly didn't fail for lack of effort.

I frantically grabbed the wrist wielding the knife and proceeded to go berserk. Joseph was dressed for it, I wasn't. He wore chinos and a heavy sweater, giving him good mobility. I was trussed up in a buttoned overcoat fast becoming sodden with blood. Fortunately he had a one-track mind. If he'd discarded the knife he would probably have had me, but he seemed determined to bury it in some vital part of my anatomy. The gun under my left armpit may as well have been in Europe, with my coat sealed all the way up and both hands somewhat occupied.

He had maybe twenty useful pounds on me. And time was certainly in his corner because I wasn't going to be feeling all that chipper in another few minutes. With that in mind, I suddenly began spinning around madly out there in the middle of the sidewalk. The stubborn clown had no choice but to join in my maniacal game of crack-the-whip. After achieving proper momentum, I went for trajectory. His skull cracked like a green melon dropped from the second-floor window when I ran him full-tilt into the brick wall of my building. I never gave him another glance. The sound had been evidence enough. It may not have been the way Bruce Lee would have handled it, but maybe he was never assaulted by a professional, dressed for it, armed with a knife, while he was bound up in a tight-fitting overcoat. And with his chest sliced open just for openers. I was just glad to be alive—and more than a little surprised.

* * *

Five long, dreary days in a hospital give you a lot of time to think. Much too much. Joseph had jumped the track and gone after me on his own. Of that much I was certain. But blood had been spilled. He was bound to have family and friends who would right now be experiencing a sudden pressing need to meet me. It's absurdly easy to kill someone if you're serious about it. If his wits had been intact, Joseph could have done it in any of a hundred ways. Chances are the next one would go about it in a more detached and professional manner. The odds, as Nuncio had warned me, were lousy. Chicago suddenly seemed like enemy territory. I watched the snow swirling crazily outside my window, mixing with the grime on the sill to form a dark, greasy sludge.

More and more I found myself thinking about the letter that had been lying somewhere around my tiny office for weeks. It was from some old fart of a politician in San Diego wanting to talk to me about a job. San Diego. The travel magazines always referred to it as America's Finest City. It sure looked good in the "Simon and Simon" episodes I'd tuned in to chuckle at. Maybe it was and maybe it wasn't the finest, but one thing it certainly was, and that's two thousand miles away. And I wouldn't even have to replace the expensive overcoat Joseph had ventilated.

I got a friend on the police force to arrange for the hospital to keep me on the books a few extra days in case anyone asked. Strictly no visitors. Seemed I'd taken a turn for the worse and gone back to Intensive Care. I beat it straight to my office and started making calls. The first guy who showed got to clean out the whole place for four hundred bucks. Minus the files, which I burned. That night at home I packed, then told my landlady she could do whatever she wanted with everything that wouldn't fit into my two bags. She wanted to know where I was going in such a hurry. To get a tan, I told her without thinking. Then I realized it wasn't too bright to be giving out freebies, so I added, "Saudi Arabia. I got this great job with an oil company."

CHAPTER 1

"Maybe I should get a job as a playground supervisor at La Jolla Elementary."

Win and I were in the midst of our morning confrontation. It had become all too predictable lately. It had been eight weeks since we'd wrapped up our last case, which had turned out to be a phony. The son of a local fast-food magnate had kidnapped himself. When he found out, the old man was so proud he made the kid vice president of the corporation. Up until then he'd been afraid the boy had no initiative.

Win, short for Carter Winfield, sat frail but erect behind his desk, reading a book and pointedly ignoring me. The history books claim he was the most brilliant and capable secretary of state this country ever had. I've also been told, and not by him, there was a time when his party begged him on bended knee to run for president. They say it would have been a cinch, but he didn't want any part of it. Said it was demeaning for a man to campaign for public office. I can believe it. Think of all those books he'd have had to pass up. At one time I guess he must have been good with people—hell, he'd had to be. But those days were long gone. Sure, he could still pour on the charm when he had to, but now it was a strain. Except in interviews with reporters and journalists. Then he'd have gladly expounded all day long, given half a chance. In a way he was a paradox: He loved his fellow man in theory, but most days it was all he could bear to see even me. Today was like that.

I run on the beach every morning with Dirk. He's my trainer, as well as gardener, handyman, and general factotum.

Louis Charbonneau hangs around the kitchen and pretends to cook. He's one of the charity cases Win brought with him when he left Washington. Louis is several cards short of a full deck, but he's usually capable of scrambling some eggs and sometimes the toast isn't even burned. Beyond that, it's better not to say. Simple things elude Louis, like remembering to bathe, and half the time his shirt is buttoned such that one side hangs longer than the other and the opposite collar sticks up under his ear. He's like the big old shaggy dog that's become incontinent in his old age but everybody loves him too much to do anything about it. Besides, there's always about a fifty-fifty chance whatever comes out of the kitchen will be edible. When it's not, Dirk keeps a good supply of yogurt, cottage cheese, and other unexciting foods stashed in his apartment over the garages. Nothing is ever said; we'd all rather take a beating than hurt Louis's feelings. Besides, he works as hard as any of us, keeping the big house spotless in addition to his kitchen chores. Remarks about him to Win fall upon deaf ears. None of us is really sure whether this is due to devotion on Win's part or lack of interest, since he doesn't eat much of anything produced in the kitchen anyway.

The only other member of our motley little family is Randy, known to the medical world as Dr. Randolph Bruckner: resident whiz kid who divides his time between keeping Win healthy and dreaming up God-knows-what in the big lab that occupies the entire basement. He's forever sending Dirk off to fetch esoteric little things like 2 mm platinum wire. He seldom complains about Louis's cooking for two reasons: He's a chow hound of the first water and he's so preoccupied I doubt he knows what the hell he's putting in his mouth anyway.

So all the other residents of the sprawling Spanish manse overlooking the Pacific north of La Jolla are kept more or less occupied. Except me. I'm a detective—I know because it says so on my license. The only thing I've detected lately is the shine on the seat of my pants.

"I doubt you possess the proper qualifications. I would imagine patience and tact are required, as an example." Win fielded my jibe with maybe one-tenth of his attention while continuing to concentrate on his book. The maddening thing was that one-tenth was more than adequate. I couldn't even begin to get him to think about taking on a case. He was much too busy corresponding with half the leaders of the free world, and keeping up with the steady flow of new books from publishers who prayed he'd respond with a word of praise they could use on the jacket.

I glared at the handsome old poop. "I'm not going to spend the rest of my life typing letters to your pen pals. How about if I set up a little agency in town? Take on an interesting client now and then. Nothing fancy, just . . ."

"Certainly not! You know very well I need you here. If you're agitated go down to Mission Bay and rent a boat again. Sailing seems to pacify you when you become overwrought."

"Two things. As for needing me here, you don't need me—you need a Kelly Girl. As for the boat, you know I just got back from a week in Catalina, and there's nowhere else to go around here in a boat unless you want me to head out for Cabo San Lucas and up into the Gulf. Which is just what I might do if you don't pry your face out of that damn book!"

Without looking up, Win replied, "I advise against it; the hurricane season is not yet over in Baja. It is neither comfortable nor secure in the Sea of Cortez prior to December."

I was stiff as a board with fury. Even as I stood there rehearsing my resignation speech, he sighed and looked up at me. Those intensely alive gray eyes regarded me with tolerant amusement.

"What sort of investigation are you proposing, Matt? I should think divorce cases are by the board these days. There's scarcely enough left in that quarter to salve the greed of the attorneys, much less the detectives. Lost pets may remain a fertile field, but I fear it may not be appropriate for us. Climbing trees is difficult for me these days, and you're such a Beau Brummel the wear and tear on your extraordinarily extensive wardrobe might prove prohibitive. Have you any suggestions?"

"You serious?"

"Quite! I'll confess to a certain sense of ennui as well. We make claim to being working detectives; I suppose we really ought to espy something occasionally. My only prerequisite is that we select something truly worthy of our time and talents. In view of all the fuss you're making, I'm assuming you have a suitable case in mind. If not, this discussion is academic, if not entirely puerile."

He lowered his eyes again toward the book with his finger sandwiched inside to mark his place. I'd gotten him to surface long enough to get a shot at him, and I wasn't about to waste the opportunity.

"I do have a case in mind, sure. Now that I know you're as anxious as I am to sink your teeth into something, I'll get right on it."

The head came back up. The eyes narrowed. "'Anxious' means fearful. I doubt that is the meaning you sought to convey by means of your little simile."

He was playing for time. Of course he knew I was lying. But the question was how to handle it. "Very well—tell me about this intriguing case you have in mind."

I'd seen it coming but there was no way to duck it. The sad truth was there wasn't a single major crime of interest in all of San Diego currently. Which, I suddenly realized, is why he chose that day to let me get to him. The choice was between a

7-Eleven store robbery, a busy cat burglar, and a guy who'd burned down his house with his wife still inside. And the police had arrested him across the street, watching the fire, still clutching the gas can in his hand. Some choice.

"The truth is, I've become fascinated with those cat burglaries up in Del Mar. If I can scare up a client, why don't we take a crack at that?"

He smiled without notifying his eyes. "How interesting! Please tell me what you've found so compelling about three random cases of breaking and entering. Or perhaps you made your selection solely on the basis of financial demographics."

"That's not entirely wrong. I admit there's a spicier selection of crimes to choose from in the inner city, but well-heeled clients are scarce in the ghetto areas. But that's not the main reason. I've just got a hunch there's more to these thefts than anybody realizes."

"This office doesn't pander to the rich to the exclusion of more interesting challenges elsewhere."

"This office better start pandering to somebody. You forget I'm the guy who does the books. Randy and Louis between them can make money disappear like a sheik in Las Vegas."

Win shrugged his shoulders. "As you know, I am offered a large number of speaking engagements routinely. The stipends are ridiculously large oftentimes. We are scarcely faced with penury."

"Yeah; you'd really love that, too, wouldn't you? We both know you'd starve to death first." This was a myth I did my best to foster. The truth was he'd have loved to give speeches. Hell, he did it all day long. But a big part of my job was to act as a buffer between him and promoters and reporters and journalists. Depending on his mood, he could come across as anything from a disciple of nihilism to a demented druid. (He has this thing about trees.) Anyway, interviewers usually ended up painting him as a nut, so I played it safe and headed them all off. His place in the history books was secure, and I wanted to keep it that way. So I kept a lid on him.

"Look, I hired on here three years ago because you said you were bored with the *Times* crossword puzzles. You said you had a knack for processing data but you needed a legman. You called me your paladin, but it means the same thing. This isn't a civil service job; if it was I wouldn't be here. As you know, I've got my full share of pride to worry about, too. If the day ever comes when I can't produce enough income to pay my own way plus show you a profit, we'll have to scrap the whole deal. Personal rules—not negotiable."

"Very well." Huge sigh. "But why an interest in these inconsequential random acts? If the burglar were inept, the police would have him in custody. Apparently they don't. There are only two possible ways in which he may be apprehended. He might eventually be caught in the act due to the action of an alert citizen. Or he may finally be traced through some stolen article. We have nothing whatever to contribute in either case. Such crimes respond only to diligent effort by a horde of officers employing routine procedures. It isn't for us."

"New rules, huh? We only pick easy jobs now?"

Win glanced wistfully at his book. "Very well, go ahead," he groused. "Perhaps you'll stumble across Judge Crater while you're at it. If you're doing this merely to annoy me, which I suspect, I congratulate you upon your success."

"Don't get too shook up, boss," I grinned. "What chance do I have of scaring up a client anyway?"

As I rushed out the door, it occurred to me I hadn't won much of a victory. The truth was I didn't give a rat's behind about the robberies in Del Mar. But at least I was sprung from the office and that pleased me. Small victories were to be cherished; with Win, they were something of a rarity.

CHAPTER 2

I took my time rolling north along Pacific Coast Highway. The road married itself to the contours of the nearby sea. Pewter-hued swells turned to white lace all along the ragged demarkation line between the elements.

Torrey Pines was a lousy place for surfing. There were no bars offshore to break the backs of the big rollers. By noon the coastal haze would burn off and the water would turn to azure except over the inshore shallows. The astringent scent of the sea became more pronounced as the road dropped from the height of the big twin golf course to just a few feet above sea level. Thirty yards away, ecstatic snowbirds from up north worshiped the sea gods in spite of the sixty-three-degree temperature of the water. Tonight they'd arrange schedules to watch the national weather forecast on the news, hoping record cold marks were being set wherever home was.

It was all a very long way from the bitter blasts of Chicago in winter. It's true the homes along the lake are very nice there as well, but the lake itself didn't bear close inspection. It usually smelled like a tramp steamer's bilge.

I'd decided to take the cat burglar's victims in calendar

order. The first theft had occurred on October twenty-second—eight days previously. The Dwight Long home would have been impressive in most places, but in Del Mar it was only average. It stood clinging to a low hill several blocks back from the beach. The contours of the lot had forced the architect to face the house north, and the neighboring home to the west effectively blocked off any view of the sea. But they'd cleverly contrived to remedy that by tacking on a wedge-shaped bay window which jutted from the front of the house like the prow of a glass-hulled ship. The effect was ludicrous, but probably added about thirty thousand to the value of the house by adding the claim of an "ocean view."

I rang the bell. A squat dumpling of a woman with electric-blue hair answered. She was on the wrong side of fifty.

"Yes?"

"Mrs. Long?" I gave her my patented grin as if she were young and adorable.

"So?"

"My name is Matt Doyle, Mrs. Long. I'm a detective. I'd like to ask you a few more questions about the robbery. It won't take long. Do you mind?"

Her jaw unclamped a little. "Police again? I thought we'd seen the last of you people. The other two last week didn't seem to take much of an interest."

She stepped back and opened the door with an obvious lack of enthusiasm. A short entry opened up into a large living room with a vaulted ceiling. The glass appendage didn't look as inappropriate from inside. The reason for her reluctance was obvious; there was a blaring idiot box in one corner. A tearful screaming match was taking place on one of the daytime soaps.

I saw no reason to correct her misconception about me being a policeman. It wasn't my fault she was a conclusion-jumper. "What makes you say that they didn't seem interested?"

"Oh, I can't blame you people. Considering what was taken." She walked over and lowered the volume, but wasn't about to turn the program off. Her eyes kept darting back to the screen. It was obvious that the wildly improbable figures on the tiny screen were far more real and important to her than I was.

"And just what was that?"

"Well, all he took was . . . you mean to tell me you don't even know?" She glared at me with suspicion. I had the awful feeling she was about to ask to see a badge.

"That's the best way, Mrs. Long. Fresh start, see? I stand here with no preconceived notions about the crime. Reading somebody else's report would program me. Destroy my objectivity. Sometimes it works."

She nodded, doubling her already numerous chins. "I made out a list and gave the only copy to one of the other officers. But I'm sure I can remember."

"You should have kept a copy for your insurance company."

"Insurance! Funny man! It wouldn't even add up to half of the deductible. You want to know what that nut took? I'll tell you: a handful of costume jewelry, a travel alarm clock, an old wrist watch of my husband's that hasn't run in years, and some golf trophies. About half a dozen, I believe. That's it."

I was amazed. "Are you sure? Who would be crazy enough to risk a felony rap for that? Sounds more like a prank to me."

"Don't ask me," she replied with disgust. "I just live here. I didn't even want to *report* it. But when the Falwells down the way were robbed a few days later my husband made me. It was almost embarrassing—as if all my very nice things weren't worth taking. But my husband insisted because it was the same man."

"How can you be so sure?"

She shook her head at my ignorance. "By the white carnation, of course. There it was, lying right on the coffee table when we got home that night. I guess it's his calling card."

The cops had withheld that little tidbit from the press.

They like to sit on unique little details like that. It's not just pettiness on their part; sometimes it helps if they come across someone who knows things they aren't supposed to. "You'll have to bear with me just another minute, Mrs. Long. Remember, this is all news to me. May I see where the thief got in?"

She removed her eyes reluctantly from the TV, and led me to the back of the house. Double sliding glass doors opened onto a minuscule patio off a plant-infested breakfast room. A length of one-inch wooden dowel rested in the track of the opening door.

"We added that piece of wood afterward," she explained. "One of the other policemen had us lock him outside. He stuck some little piece of plastic between the frame and the door, lifted the catch, and waltzed right in. I couldn't have gotten in any faster with my key."

As we retraced our way back through the house I eyed the portable contents. She was right—there was plenty. In the formal dining room I paused in front of a massive oak hutch, which appeared to be built-in. An impressive array of silver was attractively displayed behind glass doors. They yielded freely when I touched them.

"The price of silver may be down right now, but I can't believe he passed all this up."

"I told you I had some nice pieces." She pouted. "Just one of those spoons would bring forty dollars. And there are over a hundred pieces of flatware alone. Lord knows what some of the larger pieces of sterling are worth. The man must have been an idiot. Don't you people have any idea who might have done this yet?"

"Right now I'm a whole lot more interested in why," I told her honestly.

"The thing I guess I really resent is the knowledge that some unknown person entered my home . . . broke in while I was out. It's difficult to explain, but somehow I feel violated.

My lovely home just doesn't seem the same. Not . . . not nice anymore."

Her petulant expression demanded that I make it "nice" again. Sew up the tiny tear in the curtain around her—quickly—before she had to take another peek at the terribly harsh reality of the world around her. She and a lot of others preferred the nasties to be one step removed, controlled by the switch on her TV. Sorry dear—I've tried making it better for a few people. Sometimes I've even succeeded. But I've never been able to put Humpty Dumpty back together again—it can't be done.

I thanked her and let myself out. She rubbed the air once with a puffy hand, her vapid face already seeking the screen like a compass needle homing in on magnetic north.

The Falwell place was three blocks away, slightly higher up the low ridge which paralleled the coastline. It was covered with unfinished vertical boards, rough and full of knots. No two pieces matched in width. The wood was unpainted, allowed to suffer the bleaching effects of sun and salt air. The result was a silvery gray barn so decrepit looking I suppose it was considered chic.

If I thought the same approach was going to work again, I was quickly disillusioned. Dean Falwell responded to the bell. I gave him my pitch. The first words out of his thin little scar of a mouth were, "Let's have a look at your I.D., officer."

Oops! I flipped open my wallet and displayed my private operator's license. "You may have misunderstood, Mr. Falwell—I'm not a policeman. I'm a private investigator working out of La Jolla. My boss—Carter Winfield—has taken an interest in these robberies. He asked me to drive up and have a look around."

"Matt Doyle, is it? Come right in. Call me Dean." His handshake was clammy, which is a sure sign of something—don't ask me what. He'd soon get a sore neck looking up to talk to me, and he was lugging around enough excess poundage to build a husky three-year-old. He had me by about twenty-five years, I guessed. His narrow skull and close-set eyes made him look a little like the world's largest ferret.

He steered me into a phony leather chair in a small room just off the entry hall. The walls were completely book-lined. Opposite me in a twin chair, he demanded, "Well, did you bring me the check or not?"

"Check?"

"No, I don't suppose you did. You'd just be the company investigator—right? So do whatever it is you're here to do, Mr. Doyle, because I want this matter expedited in every way possible. My wife and I are anxious to get started replacing the stolen items."

It just slipped out. "You and your wife are frightened?"

"What!" His face couldn't decide whether to pale or flush. It settled for a blotchy compromise. "Of course we're not frightened. Why should we be? We haven't done anything. . . ."

"That's what 'anxious' means. You meant . . . sorry; forget it." It was appalling to find myself acting as pedantically as Win. Even so, it was interesting the way he'd overreacted. Mr. Falwell was beginning to interest me.

"Dean, as I told you, Mr. Winfield has taken an interest in this series of break-ins. We are not working for your insurance company. But it sounds as if you've got quite a claim. Must have taken everything that wasn't nailed down."

"Damn near!" he agreed, waving his arms. "And the hell of it is, a lot of it is irreplaceable. See, where I get screwed, the limit on contents coverage is based directly on the amount of the structure insurance. We had the maximum allowable, but it wasn't half enough." He tried looking properly tragic.

"How much are we talking about, Dean?"

"We were only covered for seventy-five thousand."

"That's really strange. The house that was hit three days before yours—the Long's—isn't missing anything more than a small handful of worthless junk."

"Lucky them!" He swept his arms around the room to indicate the crowded shelves. "Not many people get as carried away with the collecting bug as me. See all these books? Mostly rare first editions. A lot of them are signed. There's an easy hundred and fifty thousand sitting on those shelves. Thank God the guy didn't know his books or I'd have been completely ruined."

"So tell me what he did get."

"What he got was my coin collection, which included everything from four-thousand-year-old Byzantine specie to sixteenth-century pieces of eight. Plus he copped thirty-five Krugerrands I'd just bought. We're already well over the total amount of my coverage before we even begin to get into my wife's stuff. She lost a diamond pendant and matching earrings totaling more than ten carats, and one hell of a lot more besides."

I shook my head, making appropriate sounds of sympathy, and doing my best to avoid staring at his elaborately contrived hairdo. Combing it all forward like that had probably worked for a long time, but now it looked for all the world as if he were wearing one of those combs carried by people with Afros. Too few surviving hairs tried valiantly to cover his brick-red scalp. Like the Maginot Line, they were too few and far between to do the job.

"That's really rough, Dean; but what I don't understand is why you kept all those things around, knowing you weren't covered."

"What the hell does that mean? This is Del Mar, for Christ's sake, not East San Diego. Considering the taxes they stick me for on this place, I should rate a full-time cop right on the property. What do you guys expect me to do? Stuff everything worthwhile in a vault somewhere and visit it only on my birthday?"

Dean was beginning to annoy me. "I don't know who the 'you guys' are you're referring to, but as far as I'm concerned you can take all your toys out and play with them on the freeway."

He leaped to his feet. Normally it makes me nervous to have someone standing over me when they're blowing, but this time I remained seated. Dean didn't look as if he could do me much damage with anything less than a fire ax. "I don't have to swallow that crap from you," he shrieked. "I've been waiting for you ever since I filed my claim and the agent started giving me the old runaround. Should have had a formal appraisal done, he said. If you clowns wanted an appraisal, it was up to you to pay the sixty bucks an hour those crooks charge to do it. I didn't need it—I know what the stuff was worth. And everybody knows it was all here. You try skating around this claim, buddy, and I'll sue your ass for a lot more than my lousy seventy-five grand and you can damn well hustle right back and tell them that for me."

The guy had strictly a one-track mind; I gave up and decided to let him have it his way. "Okay, relax. If anybody asks me, I'll give them your message. Now how about showing me where this thief got in?"

Satisfied that he'd put me in my place, Dean became the gracious lord of the manor once again. I took a quick inventory as we worked our way toward the rear of the house. The decor was early Motel 6. Three or four of his imaginary Krugerrands would've replaced the lot. We ended up at another sliding glass door overlooking a thoroughly neglected backyard.

"He came in here. The door was still open when my wife and I got home."

There was one difference. Dean hadn't even bothered to lay a wooden dowel in the track of the door.

"Where was the white carnation found?"

He pointed at the cheap formica table in the kitchen-cum-dining room. It was littered with vivid travel brochures. We made the return journey to the front door. I stopped at the entrance to the little room where we'd talked and asked his permission to have a quick glance at the books. He didn't look happy about it, but shrugged it off.

It happens I know a little about collectible books. How could I not? Win's shelves at home were loaded with everything from signed limited editions of contemporary authors he admires to antiquarian beauties going back as far as the seventeenth century. What I saw on Dean's shelves were largely book club editions worth a cool fifty cents at your local Salvation Army thrift store. It wasn't even necessary to pick them up; the cheap shiny cardboard spines were easy to spot. There was hardly a dust jacket in the lot. If the entire library was worth more than a few hundred dollars retail, I'd eat my shoes.

"Mighty impressive, Dean," I lied. "And thanks for your time. Guess I must have been lucky, catching you in like this. What do you do anyway?"

He blinked; his eyes came up wary. "Investments. The market, real estate, wherever the action is. I look for trends, and if things are right, I jump in. You know."

Yeah, I knew. Dean was a pilot fish. A cheap little imitation shark that hung around waiting to gobble up any stray scraps the big boys dropped. Southern California has more than its share. They lurk on the fringe of respectability. Like elite jackals, they circle the community, ready to dart in and snatch overlooked morsels of useful carrion. They live well, but never really work. The men play a lot of golf. The women favor tennis, though each is competent at most games. They're very good at games. They read the classifieds before anything else. The catch of the day could be anything. A lot of Navy personnel get thirty-day orders to ship out. Some panic—they're stuck with a house to unload. The pilot fish comes around and offers them some small fraction of their equity in cash. Often enough to make it pay, the serviceman accepts, to avoid getting caught in the squeeze of having to continue making the payments after he's left and is getting hit for housing somewhere else. Within a few months pilot fish sells the house for its full market value and lives very well for another six months or a year. They do it with boats and planes and cars, too. Stumble, wounded financially, and when you look up, there they'll be.

If you compared them to vultures, you'd be doing those big old ugly birds a disservice. Vultures have the common decency to wait until you're dead to gut you.

The serendipitous burglar's latest call had been only four blocks north. If I kept it short and sweet, I could still make Louis's midday offering. The house was a fine, stately colonial, though looking a bit lost in its setting. It wore that bleak, unfinished look. The lot was nothing but greasy, gray clay. It would take many tons of topsoil to nurture a lawn this high up the hill. Some of the neighbors had solved the problem by spreading colored rocks or bark chips, but the end result remained dismal at best.

The slightly chubby girl who answered the door could have been my younger sister, if I had one. Clad in jeans and a sweat shirt, she wore a film of perspiration on her lovely face. She clutched a paint brush in her right hand. The color of the paint matched the samples on her cheek and clothes.

"Hi, I'm Matt Doyle. I can see you're hard at it, but I only need a minute. You're Mrs. Shore?"

"Heidi Shore—that's me! Houses painted, barns raised—you name it and I can do it." She brushed aside an errant wisp of honey-colored hair, managing to add a streak of beige with her paint-stained fingers.

"Hello, Heidi. Just a couple of quick questions about the robbery a couple of days ago. Do you mind?"

"Not as long as you don't mind if I keep painting as we talk. Enter at your own risk. There's wet paint everywhere, so I advise you to just stand over there in the middle of the room."

The house was stark inside. The walls were gradually turning from chalk white to the fawn color Heidi was sporting.

So was the carpet, I noticed, where there was a narrow gap between plastic drop cloths.

"I'm glad to see you're not letting the break-in get to you. Mind telling me what he got?"

She stopped swabbing the wall long enough to snicker over her right shoulder. "What he got was a rude awakening. Can you imagine anyone dumb enough to break in here when it couldn't be more obvious it's nothing but an empty barn? Whoever he is, I think he's in the wrong line of work. All he got was an onyx chess set we had upstairs. We usually play a game before we go to bed. It forces you to relax."

"Was it a very valuable chess set?"

"It was a beauty, but you can buy them all day long in Tijuana for about thirty dollars. Depending on how long you want to dicker. My husband says he hopes the poor schlep plays because he'll never get enough for it to pay his gas getting up here. But I somehow doubt he plays, don't you? Oh, darn! I just can't make up my mind about this color. The more I paint, the more it looks pinkish to me. Am I going bonkers or does it sort of look pink to you too?"

"It's fine, Heidi—no pink. The color looks great on both you and the walls. Did the burglar come in through the patio doors?"

She frowned into a big glass mirror stowed out of the way in one corner. "Good God! I look like something left over from the late, late show. Yes, he did. There was just the manufacturer's lock. May as well have left it open I guess. Michael's picking up a deadbolt, whatever that is."

"I assume you were left a carnation just like the others?"

"Sure was! Kind of a romantic klutz, isn't he? I wondered if everyone got one. The newspapers never mentioned it. I kind of hoped it was special for me." She shook her head and laughed to show she was kidding and because her reflection in the mirror amused her enormously. It was the nicest sound I'd heard in a while.

"Michael didn't think we should even bother you guys, but I insisted because maybe he took plenty from somebody else, and what if the only clue was here? Did you find any, by the way?"

"Find any clues? I wouldn't know, Heidi. I'm not a policeman. I'm a private detective. Sorry if I gave you the impression I was official."

"All the same to me. But I'm afraid we wouldn't be able to pay you much of a fee to recover our chess set. Next time we go across the border for the jai alai games we'll pick up another one."

After dutifully admiring her skill and taste in colors, I thanked her and left. I was grateful I'd saved Heidi for last. She left me feeling good about my fellow man in general and all plump, pretty girls in particular. She was a triple threat. Painted all day, played chess at night, and looked adorable in sloppy clothes. I hoped Michael was one of the good ones, too.

CHAPTER 3

I barely made it under the wire, but it looked as if Louis was having another of his all-too-frequent off days. There wasn't much on the table for lunch, other than a tray of silly little watercress sandwiches with neatly trimmed crusts. I kidded him that didn't he know all the food value was in the crusts? He shyly informed me that he'd seen a picture in one of his cook books and that was the way the sandwiches had been shown. That's the way he does it—he looks at the pictures. Besides, he added defensively, the crusts would be showing up the next day as stuffing in a chicken. I winced. His chickens usually ended up about the consistency of that rubber chicken that keeps popping up on the "Tonight Show." But there was no use trying to kid around with Louis. He took everything you told him literally, like a small child. He'd have made a great goat if there was anyone around mean enough to want to pick on him. Fortunately there wasn't.

Win didn't make an appearance—not at all unusual. He made a point of attending the evening meal, even helping himself to a small portion of everything served. He ate very little, if any, of what he did take. I think he only did it to please

Louis. Whatever nutritional needs he had were taken in the form of foul-smelling drinks concocted by Randy in his basement lab. That, plus bi-weekly injections of God-knows-what. I'd once asked Randy what exactly he was feeding Win. I guess he told me. After five minutes of dissertation on electrolyte imbalances and terms like beta tocopherol, inositol, and phylloquinone, I held up my hands in surrender. I guess it was Randy's subtle way of telling me to butt out; if so, it worked.

Dirk ate his lunch in silence. There was always an animal air about him, but never more so than during meals. His attitude clearly stated: "Leave me alone—I'm eating." I swear I believe he counts the number of times he chews every bite, too.

That left Randy and me alone to amuse ourselves. The good Dr. Bruckner had been a very successful internist, just getting rolling in Washington during Win's final public office years. He progressed from Win's personal physician to friend and golfing buddy. (It was difficult to picture Win playing golf but Randy assured me he'd once carried an eight handicap easily.) Randy had hated private practice. His first love was pure research in gerontology. When Win figured he'd paid his dues to his fellow man and retired inside his fortress by the sea, he'd invited Randy to kick the traces and come along. Randy had, and the result was a steady stream of research papers flowing out to medical journals around the world.

I made up for the delicate little ersatz sandwiches by packing away the pickled beets that Louis knows I'm partial to and keeps on hand by the case.

"Why the change in Win the last couple of months, Randy?"

"What do you mean? What kind of change?" His eyes rolled up to peer at me over his thick, rimless glasses. Randy was a short sausage of a man who wore a perpetually startled look. Where Dirk was all hard planes and sharp edges, Randy was all soft curves. Win said he was an endomorph.

"More irritable, touchier. Can hardly stand having me in

the room sometimes. I was pounding out a letter the other day and he suddenly ordered me to stop. Said I was making as much noise as possible on purpose. Ended up in a shouting match—and there've been plenty more of those lately."

Randy hesitated, then nodded. "It's true; I've noticed it as well. Perhaps I should have warned you. He was having trouble with his hearing for a while. I . . . ah . . . managed to reverse the loss, but in the process I allowed him to become over-sensitized to sound. Getting the exact titration has proved somewhat tricky, but I'm pretty sure I've got it now. His hearing checks out normal at the moment, but for the last two months I've found it helpful to speak in slightly subdued tones around him. Stupid of me not to advise you, but you know how he is about disseminating information about his health."

I stared at him and shook my head. "That's incredible! You could put Bell Tone right out of business. Have you published a paper on this little bombshell yet?"

He grinned mysteriously with a negative movement of his perfectly round head. "No, Matt; I only publish on subjects that are already under intense investigation. The remainder of my work is centered around Win and is very nearly unique. By mutual agreement we've elected to hold off publicizing any of that portion of my work as long as he's . . . well, you know."

"I see what you mean. We don't want to make the Old Man chief monkey in the zoo. But in the meantime, can't you slip a mild tranquilizer into that goo you feed him?"

"I modify his nutrient formula daily, Matt, but drugs or any chemical agents—never. You'll just have to be patient with him. I see him daily, so does Dirk usually, but you're the one he really works beside. You spend the day together in the office. You're the one who communicates with him on a personal level. We envy you for that. Dirk or I would be honored if it were one of us."

"That's me all over—honored. I feel honored the same way the Christian picked to go play with the lions felt honored."

* * *

I settled in behind my desk and went through with the farce of reporting my morning's interviews. An exercise in futility, since there was absolutely no point to any of it, but there was nothing for it but to play out the charade.

Win surprised me by showing increasing signs of interest as I laid it all out for him, including dialogue and personal observations whenever I thought them pertinent. After I finished he sat staring into space for a full three minutes.

"You haven't given me your conclusions," he said at last.

It was crow-eating time. "I conclude that there's a very inept burglar stumbling around Del Mar and that I've wasted half a day when I could have been doing something important like typing letters. Pretty good concluding, huh?"

I plucked the top sheet from his Out tray. "I'll start with this one to the French Legion of Arms telling them thanks for the offer of the medal, but there's no more room on your chest for another one."

He favored me with a fond look of bemusement. "You actually believe it was pure happenstance that you selected this apparently random series of illogical break-ins as a goad to me, don't you?"

"What else? I admit it. I had to get out of the house. But you act as if I've brought you something interesting. Are you nuts, or is it me? The only thing even remotely interesting about the whole thing is the certain fact that Dean Falwell is out to stick it to his insurance company. That's about as interesting as flowers in May."

He shook his head, smiling. "You really are astonishing, Matt; absolutely astonishing. You have the instincts of a master procurator, yet remain blissfully ignorant of the fact." He chuckled, apparently vastly amused.

I just sat there wondering whether I was being had. I made a mental note to look up "procurator" in the dictionary later. "You want to let me in on the joke? Something in my report made your eyes light up. I know that look. I admit I missed it, so give."

"My prescience does not enable us to alter events, unfortunately. At this point, we can do nothing but wait. Of course, it's remotely possible I'm mistaken, but I think not. Within the next three days I anticipate a rather startling turn of events involving your so-called artless felon. We shall see."

There was no getting anything more out of him. A sudden urge to pound on someone drove me outside to log some time on the exercise mat with Dirk. Only problem was, Dirk did most of the pounding, as usual.

CHAPTER 4

I rolled out of bed the next morning at eight sharp, thanks to an internal alarm clock that seldom fails. A long look out the big window thrilled me as always. I hated to think that the day would come when I had to leave this room in this house. The leaden sea lay placid as a mountain lake until it was twenty yards from shore; even then it could barely muster six-inch lumps in lieu of breakers. There was a Santa Ana building, bringing the hot, dry desert winds in from the Mojave, driving the temperature up to around ninety. This would mean great fire danger in the back country. In recent years it had become popular among the sickies to torch remote areas of the county during a Santa Ana.

I seemed to remember there were only three places in the world where the right conditions existed to create these unique winds, which caused heat by compression. I tried coming up with the other two. Morocco finally came to me, but the last one stumped me. It would be something to toss at Win during the course of the day. He'd not only know, he had probably been there.

The brush, comb, and scrape ritual was accomplished on

autopilot. I half listened to the "Today" show, which is the main reason for a TV in my room. It helps prepare me for the day by reminding me that I'm only one animal in a very large herd.

I bounced down the stairs and out the front door. Dirk was waiting. Early morning wind sprints along the beach were a long-established drill. It's the only time Dirk ever gets really chatty. Sit him in a room full of people and he could pass for a mute. Run alongside him and he turns into a monologist. My theory is he only does it to show he's not even breathing hard.

Breakfast was our just reward when we got back to the house. There's the big silver urn full of Louis's homeground coffee to begin with. It's so fine, for all I know Juan Valdez holds back all the best beans from Folgers, and ships them to Louis direct. I don't know why, but it's one of the few things he does perfectly. Then there were choices to be made concerning juice, followed by the usual tray of hen fruit. Sometimes his eggs are dry as dust, and sometimes you feel like requesting a straw, but today they were decent. The toast, on the other hand, was a disaster. The problem is that Louis has a short attention span. Still, things could be a lot worse. As long as he kept coming up with coffee like this I could put up with a lot. And sometimes he gets fancy and goes for something like eggs Benedict after browsing through the pictures in one of his books. That's when things start getting rough; sometimes it means cottage cheese and yogurt three times a day. Or it means Dirk, Randy, and I run down to Anthony's Sea Grotto in downtown La Jolla.

There are two copies each of the *San Diego Union* and the *Los Angeles Times*, San Diego edition on the breakfast table. I did a double take at the sight of the headline on the *Union*. "Cat Burglar Strikes Again: Kills." The copy read:

> Tragedy struck at the luxurious home of businesswoman/philanthropist Martha Neal Herbert in Del Mar last night. Summoned by the victim's nearest neighbor, who had seen Mrs. Herbert arrive home and gone over for

a visit, police arrived to find Mrs. Herbert dead. Cause of death is thought to be a broken neck, to be confirmed by autopsy later today. Time of death is known to have been at approximately 10:00 P.M., within the few minutes the victim was seen arriving home and the time the body was discovered.

Police spokesmen surmise the house was broken into by the same thief who has committed several robberies in the immediate area over the past several weeks. It is believed that when the victim arrived home, she trapped the thief in the house. Police decline to reveal what evidence exists to identify the killer as the same burglar involved in the earlier crimes.

Mrs. Herbert was president of Neal Pharmaceutical Manufacturing Corporation, founded by her late husband, S. R. Neal. She was active in local. . . .

I sat at the table in a trance, blowing on a now cool cup of coffee. Win's reaction the day before when I summed up the comic career of the Del Mar cat burglar raced through my mind. Louis placed more food in front of me, but this time it went untouched. I repeatedly reviewed the details of my run to Del Mar, searching for some false note. Something had tipped Win off, but damned if I could spot it. It was maddening because clearly he'd seen it coming.

I shoved away from the table and marched into the office, clutching the *Union* in one hand and the *Times* in the other. Win was buried in a copy of Plutarch's *Lives*, one of the Morocco-bound volumes from his fifty-four book set of *Great Books*. He'd once commented that the University of Chicago must have selected the material more for its snob appeal than for its literary merit, but I've noticed he seemed to be getting a lot of mileage out of the set. By the time I crossed to my desk and toppled into my favorite chair on earth, he was facing me.

"Good morning, Matt. I see you are aware of the latest exploit of the man you referred to yesterday as nothing more than a comic bungler. 'Schlep,' I recall, was the exact term you used. I'm not all that well versed in Yiddish idiom, but I believe I've approximated the correct meaning."

"Close enough. What have you heard about the murder?"

"Merely a brief summary on the morning news. Along with the rather fuller accounts in both of those newspapers. Your experience exceeds mine when it comes to dealing with the police, so let me pose a question. Are they really such simpletons? Surely they cannot be so naive as to accept this ineptly staged fiasco at face value?"

"If you're referring to the husband's alibi, not to worry. I can assure you Mr. Harold Herbert must have spent a long and decidedly unpleasant night downtown. The assumption he's guilty of either murder or conspiracy to commit would be automatic. Now it's your turn: How could you have possibly known this was in the works yesterday?"

"I didn't necessarily anticipate murder, though it seemed most likely. I entertained little doubt there was to be a major crime. It was patently obvious that an overall logic existed, some ultimate plan sufficient to bear the ponderous weight of these elaborately staged break-ins. There was no other possible explanation for three otherwise illogical crimes. Thieves do not risk their freedom to enter an unfurnished house. They do not walk away with worthless articles to the exclusion of valuable ones easily converted to cash. They are remarkably adept at apprizement. The restricted means of access is also suggestive. It is a clear indication the target homes were selected solely on the basis of ease of entry. To this add the incredible white carnation. It is tantamount to a calling card reading: 'See? It's me again. I'm just a burglar, but something noteworthy is about to happen and I want to make absolutely certain you know it was me.' Preposterous! Next to a certainty, the obvious conclusion is the true one. When you eliminate the impossible, what you have left . . ."

"Spare me; even I've read Sherlock Holmes. It's as simple as that?"

"It has been said," he purred, "that genius is nothing more than the ability to see the obvious and recognize it for what it is."

"Down with false modesty. So now what?"

"We need to acquire a number of facts which the police have not seen fit to release. Have you managed to establish a rapport with anyone in a position to provide us with such information? If not, it will require a visit to the Herbert residence."

I tilted my chair back and looked smug. "Unnecessary on both counts."

Win regarded me with an expression equal parts peeved and perplexed. It was sheer balm. "Explanation?"

"Easy! I called on all three robbery victims yesterday. Within twelve hours the case erupts into a homicide. The cops are going to find that impossible to swallow. They know we don't chase nickel-snatchers; they will have to assume we had information telling us these weren't just routine heists. We can expect visitors any minute. I can't wait to see us explain how in the hell we happened to begin a murder investigation twelve hours before the murder took place. Fun, huh?"

CHAPTER 5

Win was halfway finished dictating a lengthy letter full of requested advice to one of the prime ministers of an OPEC country when Louis stuck his head in the office door.

"Hey, Matt. Cop at the door," he hissed. For all my kidding him about it, he still couldn't help acting like a man in church when it came to the office.

I resisted an urge to leer at Win and headed down the short hall toward the front door. It was no surprise to find Inspector Carl Dixon scowling on the wrong side of it.

"Can't you train that French shrimp of yours to quit slamming doors in people's faces? What's he afraid of? Think I'll steal the silver?" Dixon looked a little like a young Oliver Hardy. He was the antithesis of the archetype homicide inspector: too young, too fat, and too comedic-looking. There was a reason. Dixon had come up fast from an unusual source. He was a criminalist, supposedly one of the best. It explained a lot of things. It explained why he didn't look the physical type. He probably hadn't struck anyone in anger or otherwise since the third grade, if then. His world was that of the lab and police science. But he was a man of strong opinions, some of which concerned Win and me. If he ever did haul off and hit someone, I was the most likely candidate. He had nothing but contempt for guys like us who thought we could solve crimes through what he sneeringly referred to as "divination." I guess that included anyone who'd neglected to obtain at least a masters in the criminal sciences. He had a Ph.D., but the funny part was he spoke like a character out of an old Hammett or Chandler novel. I think he was overcompensating for something. Friends in the department tell me he sounded like an Oxford don until he switched to Homicide.

Dixon couldn't have been more than forty, with a chin for each decade, and he wore his straight black hair flat against his head as if it were painted there. If the dark blue suit he was wearing was the work of a custom tailor, the tailor should trade his sewing machine in on a shovel. The front was liberally coated with ash, the result of a three-or-four-pack-a-day habit. Dixon might not have been the physical type, but he had a palpable air of intensity surrounding him. He reminded me of a hyperactive child—the world's largest child.

I stepped aside so he could enter; it was either that or risk being trampled. He jammed a cigarette into the middle of his big, fat face and lit it, shielding the match between cupped hands as if he were standing in a gale. Failing to see anything remotely resembling an ashtray in the hall, he shoved open the door and flicked the match out.

"Doesn't anybody around here have any bad habits? Next time I drop by I'll bring you an ashtray. They cost a whole buck. I realize how hard up you people are here."

"Don't bother. Dirk took my butts away from me the day I arrived and told me if he ever caught me with one he'd do something exceptionally obscene with it."

"I believe you. He's weird, that one. Everybody here is weird but you. You, you're cute—very cute!" He emphasized the point by jabbing me in the chest with a cigar-sized index finger. He did it with considerable feeling; it was obviously a poor substitute for the punches he'd like to be able to deliver.

We both knew he wouldn't be doing it if not for his position of power. He liked power; it was the reason he'd forsaken the lab and opted for Homicide. You couldn't jab your big fat fingers into test tubes. Mostly what you do is appear in court and let the defense attorneys make a monkey out of you. The scam around headquarters was that Dixon hadn't liked that even a little bit.

"You'll turn my head," I said. "Does this mean we're engaged?"

"You'd better believe we are. All my instincts tell me to put a ring in your nose and take you downtown to celebrate. You know damn well why I'm here, so let's get it over with. I'm going in for a long chat with your boss. You're invited. It's been a long night, so we're going to keep it short and sweet. I'm going to remind you both there are laws against withholding evidence; then I'm going to listen carefully and make notes while the two of you tell me things."

He turned his back and started down the hall.

"Hold it! Not with that thing you're not." I nodded at his smoking cigarette. He gave me an ugly look, took a deep drag, then sent it chasing after the match. I made a point of checking to make sure it had cleared the porch, then closed the door, and followed him into the office.

Inside, Dixon flopped into his usual chair, repositioning it slightly so he'd be able to keep an eye on both of us. He exchanged no greetings with Win. It was a problem he'd never quite succeeded in solving. He gave no outward sign of the awe most of our rare visitors exhibited, yet he couldn't quite treat Win with the contempt he showed other private operators like me. He'd choke on calling him Mr. Secretary, and plain Mr. Winfield stuck in his craw as well, so he always got off to a shaky start.

"Like I told Doyle, I've been at it all night, and I don't feel up to the usual preliminaries. You've got two minutes to convince me I shouldn't haul your boy here in on charges."

"Charges, Inspector?" Win flashed a bemused smile at

the agitated policeman. "I was under the impression you were assigned to Homicide. Surely Matt hasn't killed anyone. Have you, Mr. Doyle?"

Dixon's feeble attempt to bulldoze Win had been his worst possible approach. He had an absolute knack for it.

"No, sir! Not in a long time."

"At least not that we know of," Dixon grumbled. "But I can bring charges for impersonating an officer of the law and withholding evidence. I can make it stick, and I will, so you can forget the sarcasm."

"Matthew, it would appear there has been a misunderstanding of some sort. Surely you wouldn't impersonate a policeman?"

"Certainly not, sir. Mrs. Shore did assume I was with the department, but the moment I realized it I corrected her. Dean Falwell thought I was working for his insurance company and there was no way I could convince him otherwise. He asked to see my license and I showed it to him. I'm not sure what Mrs. Long thought. She was watching a soap on TV the whole time I was there and not paying much attention. Why would I claim to be a policeman? All I want is to be loved."

Dixon's tired red eyes narrowed at me. "Oh, I'm gonna love you, all right. I'm gonna love you all the way downtown to a cell. Actually, you belong in a cage, but a cell will have to do. According to Mrs. Long, you told her you deliberately hadn't studied the police reports so you'd have no preconceived notions. She'll make a fine witness. Now tell me some more lies."

"I did mention reports, but I meant newspaper reports. I certainly never spoke of police reports, and I definitely never identified myself as an officer. People are often prone to make that assumption. It's a problem. If I detect it I correct it right away, as I did with Heidi Shore. Ask her about it. I really doubt I can be prosecuted for failing to realize Mrs. Long had made an unwarranted assumption."

Dixon scowled and reached for his pack. He had one halfway to his face before he caught himself. Faced now with the awkward task of replacing it in the pack, he angrily thrust the works back into his pocket.

"We'll just see, wise guy. This time I'll talk to her myself and then we'll see. But what I'd really like to know is what in the hell you were doing in Del Mar yesterday anyway. Remember, this is a murder investigation. All stops are out. A-number-one priority. Mrs. Herbert drew a lot of water in this town. Plenty of friends in high places. Care to tell me how it is you just happened to spend the day working on a case you wouldn't normally cross the street for? There's no way you could possibly have had a client—I just don't get it."

His eyes worked back and forth between Win and me as if he were watching a tennis match. Maybe he thought we might try passing notes.

"May I make a suggestion?" Win offered.

"Sure, I like suggestions. But it better be something I can take to the bank or I won't be leaving here alone."

"Very well. I propose we pool whatever resources we might have." Win lifted an imperious hand to squelch Dixon's roar of complaint. "Answer one or two little questions, with the firm understanding of absolute confidentiality on the part of each of us here present. That done, Mr. Doyle will be in a better position to ascertain whether or not he is indeed withholding anything that could even remotely be considered evidential. He will then reveal everything pertinent, excluding nothing. In addition, he will swear under oath to the complete veracity of his statement, which may be provided in writing if you so desire. This naturally applies to me as well, though any knowledge I might have would be merely hearsay, of course."

Dixon faced my boss warily. "One or two little questions, is it? Let's just see where it goes then. I'd meet the devil halfway to hell to get a handle on this one. Go ahead."

"I'll ignore the malapert comparison for the sake of expediency. First question: Did the killer leave behind the customary white carnation?"

"That's off limits. Why do you want to know? What difference does that make?"

"Inspector, please; if you cannot achieve cogency, at least strive for consistency. In the same breath you have stated it is too vital a secret to share and also of no import whatever. You really must humor me. I already know the answer to be affirmative; I merely seek confirmation. A nod of your head will suffice."

"Yes, damn it, but you two better give as good as you get." Dixon glared at each of us in turn, dividing the threat evenly.

"Thank you. Second question: How did the killer gain entry into the Herbert residence?"

"That you can have with my compliments. It'll be in the evening papers. He broke in the back door. I mean literally. Took out the whole bottom panel of a solid wood door. Left scuff marks that show he must have kicked it in."

"Again, thank you. Now, where exactly was the body discovered? Don't stir so impatiently; this will be my final query."

Dixon cocked his head, obviously unable to dope out a reason for the question. I should have cocked mine too. "What the hell—in for a penny, in for a pound. She was jammed right up against the front door. Inside, that is, with the door closed. M.E. tells me there isn't a mark on her except for one big bruise low and behind her right ear. It looks like he gave her one big pop and it broke her neck."

"Is there any possibility she was killed elsewhere and moved?"

"Forget that. When she caught it, everything went. Bowel, bladder—hell of a mess." Dixon sat forward on his seat impatiently. "It's my turn now. That's more questions than I answer for the mayor and the commissioner combined."

"The critical points have been covered," Win muttered, obviously preoccupied. "We must now honor our part of the bargain, Mr. Doyle. Under whatever oath you subscribe to, do you possess any knowledge or evidence of the remotest possible kind pertinent to this homicide investigation? The Inspector has earned our candor, so do not cavil."

I tried looking forthright, and I'm pretty sure I'd never caviled. "Nope! Sorry, wish I did. I called on those three yesterday like a bum looking for a handout. Business around here has been just awful, Inspector. Oh, here's one little tidbit. I'll give you long odds Dean Falwell stands to make a killing if he can con his insurance company out of seventy-five thousand. My guess is seventy-five bucks would be more like it. He's planning a nice overseas trip with the profit. Yesterday I considered it possible he'd be slick enough to set up the scam by staging the other two break-ins, but I can't figure him for a murderer. He'd lift a dead man's wallet if nobody was looking, but somebody else would have to do the dirty work."

Dixon's meaty face flushed. "I should have known better." His voice moved up a notch as he shot to his feet. "If you two clowns think you can get away with pumping me, then clamming up, you're nuts."

Zeroing in on me, he rasped, "To sit there and tell me all you were doing was dogging the trail of some lousy bum who could have gotten more and better loot from any curb on garbage day! You're about to lose that grin of yours permanently, Doyle. I'm gonna . . ."

"Inspector, please," interrupted Win. "Restrain yourself. You give us too much credit. You came here with unrealistic expectations. No doubt Mr. Doyle and I should consider it a compliment that you presumed our paltry efforts could have succeeded so much better than your own official inquiry."

"Compliment! Now that's funny. The only assumption I had when I came here was that you both lie like rugs. I wouldn't trust the pair of you any farther than I could heave a . . ."

"Enough!" Win hit him with a verbal blast that made my desk vibrate. "You forget yourself, sir. Must I remind you that when you were still a child my word was one of the few reliable constants in a world gone mad? More agreements and treaties were built around my probity than you will ever know. I appreciate the fact you're in a sleep-deprived state, tired and agitated, but *never* sit before me again and impugn my verisimilitude. I simply will not tolerate it. Not from you—not from anyone."

Win paused, daring Dixon to challenge his statement.

"You appear to be regaining control," he resumed in his normal tone. "It is indeed regrettable you've received so little as a result of our agreement, but we cannot give more than we have. Perhaps I might be able to balance the scales with one or two conjectures you may find helpful. Mind you, they will be nothing more than that—mere putations. Would you care to hear them?"

Dixon's voice nearly failed him. He was mad enough to chew nails, but he knew he couldn't afford to pass up a chance at a scrap. He'd found this office to be a pretty good spot for scraps in the past.

"Sure, I'm all for conjectures. Let's hear them."

"Very well. There are three principal points of interest, as indicated by the queries I put to you. Means of entry is provocative because it represents a marked deviation. Until last night our felon had only entered homes offering access even to a precocious child. Had he been willing to risk more, he'd have selected his objectives with greater care. In addition, he offends all logic by taking nothing of any real value, even when there's an abundance at hand. This observation remains consistent if we accept Mr. Doyle's premise concerning Mr. Falwell's duplicity. I so accept it.

"The second point has to do with the murderous assault visited upon the victim. No thief would ordinarily react to the return of the homeowner by positioning himself just inside the door, thus assuring a confrontation. Certainly not the timid soul we believed in yesterday. Why not merely retreat by the way he'd entered? Only one explanation suffices—he was there for the express purpose of murdering Mrs. Herbert.

"The final point which intrigues is the common denominator of the white carnation. Even if we discarded the two probabilities above, we are left with a puzzle. Assume he entered the Herbert home in spite of the difficulties merely to steal and was inadvertently trapped near the front door. He lashes out in a blind panic. His single blow proves fatal. We are now obliged to credit the fact that he blithely elects to leave behind his usual calling card at the murder scene. Totally unacceptable! Even given the above sequence of absurd events, not even the dullest of larcenists would do anything to increase his jeopardy when it comes to a capital offense. It would be entirely irrational."

Dixon glared at Win. "Thanks for the speech. Maybe you should have charged me admission. A nickel would be about right."

He waddled to the door, turned and braced himself against the frame. "You think I haven't already been down that trail a hundred times? Guy lays a phony trail with a few robberies, then hits his own place so he can bump off his wife. The murderer gets lost in the shuffle because we cops are too dumb to add. Hell, it's the first thing we thought of. It's one of the oldest gambits in the book; we call it the 'hide the tree in the forest' dodge. You're right about one thing: all the evidence supports it. But there is one minor problem."

"I'll bite," I told him. "What's the problem?"

"The trail only leads to one man. Right to Harold Herbert. And the son of a bitch has an airtight alibi."

"Actually I anticipated that," Win assured us both. "Given the tedious preparation, certainly one would expect him to concoct a suitable alibi. It is nothing but another indictment of the man; the innocent can rarely muster an alibi."

Dixon shook his head angrily. His hand was reaching for another smoke, but he didn't know it. "For a man who knows as many words as you do, you don't listen very well. His alibi's tight—that means he didn't do it. His wife died between ten and ten-five last evening. She drove in at ten sharp, and her girlfriend next door went over for a chat as soon as she put some shoes on and found her keys. She discovered the body at five after. Harold Harbert was chairing a staff meeting at the office from seven last evening until we called him with the news. Twenty of the top management people were in attendance. They all say he never left the building. They'd like very much to be able to say he did, some of them, but they simply can't.

"Now if you gentlemen of leisure will excuse me, I've had my fill of lies and lectures for the day. I'm going back downtown where the big kids are. We employ something called police procedure. Perhaps you've read about it?"

I trailed him all the way out just to make sure he didn't torch the place. He was so steamed he might've been able to swing it without even a match.

When I got back in the office, Win was looking black. "Blast that man! He once did his level best to prevent me from obtaining my private operator's license. Did you know that?"

"You mentioned it a few dozen times. Most cops resent us private types, but he sure holds the record. He'll never forgive you the fact that you don't know the difference between a numerator and a denominator in defining fingerprints, and you really blew it when you once referred to him as a criminologist instead of a criminalist. Apparently that's about as bad as calling an open heart surgeon a horse doctor. Of course, the fact that we've beaten him to the wire and let the press know about it hasn't helped either. Do you suppose he's actually that dumb, or is it just an act?"

"It would be a mistake to underestimate that man. He may not be the intellectual giant he thinks he is, but I'm prepared to wager he's more than proficient at police science and procedural matters. Nor is he without guile. But normal police procedures will fail this time, I think. And I confess it would please me enormously to succeed in solving this case, thus serving the Inspector another generous portion of humble pie. The gall of that man to have come into my home and quizzed me about my qualifications when I applied for an investigator's license. It's intolerable!"

"Yeah, imagine him doing his job like that. What crust! I'd ask what humble pie tastes like, but then you're not likely to know either."

Win laughed. I picked up the pad with the unfinished letter to his pal in OPEC.

"That epistle to my avaricious friend may wait. There are aspects of the Herbert case that now genuinely interest me. We must amass data, and for that we need a client. I suggest you pay a visit to Harold Herbert, or, failing that, another appropriate officer of the Neal Pharmaceutical Company. Point out that he above all others holds a vested interest in securing justice for the slayer of their corporate head. Arrange financial matters to satisfy your own considerable ego, but attempt to show restraint. To provide the opportunity to vanquish the Inspector I'd happily pay the client."

I dropped the yellow legal-sized pad and bolted out the door. It was beginning to look as if my feeble effort to jolt Win into working was going to pay a dividend after all.

CHAPTER 6

It was only a fifteen-minute drive northeast to Sorento Valley, where the sprawling, sand-colored buildings comprising Neal Drugs shimmered in the hot Santa Ana winds. The fortresslike structure covered a good six or seven acres in a scorched little valley between dun hillocks of sage and greasewood shrubs. Another five acres of paved parking surrounded it on two sides. The architect might have used a shallow cardboard box for inspiration. Apparently he'd never heard of windows.

The temperature plummeted twenty degrees as I entered the plant. Standard chrome and Naugahyde chairs and settees lined the reception area, separated by low matching tables littered with battered medical magazines. The walls were plastic pretending to be burlap. They ended far short of the ceiling and left an open gap along the floor. It was one of those fully functional interiors that could be rearranged easily. Very practical—also very depressing. Movable, replaceable walls for movable, replaceable people.

The receptionist was on the right, seated primly behind her desk, doing a good job of avoiding the anxious and hostile stares of the dozen or so people strewn around waiting. At first glance she might have been a candidate for the Mrs. Matt Doyle Sweepstakes, but first I'd have to have a closer look at her eyes and listen to her voice. And that was merely the first hurdle; there were plenty more after that.

The nameplate on her desk had one of those little yellow smiling faces stuck on it. "Good morning, Helen Baker. My name is Matt Doyle."

"Yes, Mr. Doyle, good morning. May I help you?"

It was difficult to tell about the eyes. They were surrounded by layers of guck. Who knows? She may have had lovely eyes if only she'd pick a fight with her Avon lady. The voice didn't make it either. The poor kid either had a bad case of emphysema or she thought she was Monroe reincarnated. I can't help it—I'm picky.

"You certainly may. I'm a detective. Afraid I'm going to have to ask Mr. Herbert to spare me a few more minutes. He's had a rough night, I know, but it's important. Tell him I'm here and that I promise to keep it short."

"Please take a seat, officer. I imagine he'll be able to see you for a moment." As soon as she took me for a cop, her smile went south and she stopped hyperventilating. Obviously the Prince Charming she was on the lookout for wasn't likely to be one of San Diego's Finest.

In less than five minutes a young man in a natty three-piece suit waltzed into the waiting area and bent over Helen. She pointed at me. He trotted over and introduced himself as Jay Meadows. He was my guide.

The seemingly endless stretches of sterile hallways made me appreciate the necessity for a guide. I encountered an astonishing variety of odors along the way. Some pleasant, others gross. Eventually we pulled up in front of a door labeled Senior Vice-President. Meadows ushered me in but didn't follow.

It was only a fair-sized room with a wall of gray metal file cabinets. Another wall featured shelves full of office supplies and a photocopier in the corner. Straight ahead was an unmarked door flanked by a desk. Behind the desk sat a homely, dumpy little woman named Helga Metz, if you believed the plate on her desk.

Helga was slightly bizarre-looking. The desk was cut away in the center and I could see she was wearing a black body stocking that started at her toes and ended up around her short neck. If she ever wanted to view the world from five feet up, she'd have to trade in her square-toed flats for heels. Her long woolen skirt would hit her at the ankles when she stood up; her matching heavy shirt had half sleeves. Gray-streaked hair, coarse as a pig's, was gathered back into a tight bun. Her facial features were overstated for the space available. The effect was almost a hideous caricature. She was also just a hair away from working sideshows as the mustached lady—pun intended. Age indeterminate, and who cared? Her eyes were gunmetal gray, disinterested, slightly protuberant.

Still watching me, she pressed a button on the intercom. Her voice was a low monotone as she announced, "Officer Doyle has arrived." Without waiting for a response, she nodded once toward the inner door on her left. I opened it and went in, meanwhile hastily revising my theory that executive secretaries were selected largely for their decorative value.

My first glimpse of Harold Herbert was disappointing. I'd already penciled him in for premeditated murder, and I've never been able to get over the notion that when I meet a cold-blooded killer and look him in the eyes, I ought to be able to tell. Harold was one of those middleaged jocks found at your local country club or the better lounges everywhere. Regular features, full complement of dark wavy hair, tanned, but jaded-looking. But then, after the night he'd just been through, it was unfair to judge. We were close in height, with him maybe an inch under my six feet. He carried the physique of an athlete not too far off his prime. It was a bit of a shock to realize he couldn't be much over forty, tops. The pictures of his wife in the paper had made her look every minute of her fifty-eight summers.

"You're not one of the officers I met last night or this morning, are you?" Herbert inquired politely enough as we shook hands. "Didn't think I recognized the name. As I said, I'm at the department's disposal until this horrible mess is cleared up, so let's get on with it." He flopped back into his chair wearily, closed his reddened eyes, and began massaging his temples.

I leaned forward over his desk. "I'm a hound from a different kennel, Mr. Herbert. Private."

His eyes popped open, and he made a grab for the license I held in my outstretched hand.

"I work for Carter Winfield. He has asked me to convey his condolences to you, and I'd like to add mine as well. It's possible we may be able to offer you more than condolences. He's got some ideas about your wife's murder that should interest you."

He shoved the license back at me as if it were crawling with bugs.

"Carter Winfield? I know who he is. Quite a bit before my time, of course. Strange a man like that would want to involve himself with . . . affairs like this."

"Why strange? It keeps him young. And we just solve crimes, we don't commit them, so it's perfectly respectable. One day he just couldn't bring himself to do one more crossword puzzle, so he became a detective. And for my money, he's the best in the business."

He nodded dubiously. "With all due respect toward Mr. Winfield, I have no intention of retaining the services of anyone beyond the proper authorities. Poor Martha just had the misfortune to be at the wrong place at the wrong time. It's one of those terrible things you read about that are supposed to happen to people you never heard of. Anyway, I'm certain the police are fully capable of conducting the investigation. It's their job, after all."

"I'd guess you probably got a fair sample last night of how they're doing their job. How'd you like it? There'll be a lot more like it to come. Why not have the corporation hire us to wrap this mess up? Even if we strike out, the public relations benefits will be worth the price of admission to both you and your company."

We all form impressions, and since walking in the door I'd discarded all my own reservations concerning Harold's guilt. I had no idea what Win thought, but, to me, the idea of offering to catch a killer for the killer himself struck me as fairly ludicrous, but I was just a hired hand who followed orders—usually.

Harold was getting restive. He was turning stuffy on me fast. "I see. I wasn't aware your talents included public relations. It's true, I did spend an unpleasant night, but I can accept the reasoning behind it. I'm told most crimes of this sort are solved by the simple expedient of looking to the beneficiary. The truth is I don't mind the police doing whatever they think necessary, but I think I do resent your barging in here with this cheap attempt at extortion. Either I hire you or I run the risk of everyone's presumption of my guilt—is that it?"

It was a loaded question, so I didn't answer. He sprang to his feet in a fury. "Get out!"

I had the distinct feeling the interview was over. "Maybe my timing is just bad. Why not give it some serious thought, discuss it with your entire executive board. I'm not suggesting you employ us personally, but have the company hire us. Don't you think everyone concerned with the welfare of this business deserves a chance to vote on it?"

"I do not! None of this is concerned with company business in any way. You're not about to make a sale here, so please leave—now!"

Harold leaned forward, clenched fists braced on top of his desk, manly jaw thrust out stubbornly. I couldn't have positioned him any better in a month of trying. The urge to plant one right on the button for that crack about extortion was nearly overpowering, so I spun around and got out of there.

Murderers shouldn't go around calling other people names. It offended my sense of propriety.

Outside, the little troll was still there, guarding the castle gate. As I passed her I said, "Helga, I think the beast is hungry. Better throw him some raw meat." Nothing doing. She remained impassive.

There was half an hour to spare before lunch when I returned home. It was more than enough to report my total lack of success to Win. He amazed me by showing no signs of disappointment. All he said was, "No matter, Matt. It never comes as a surprise when, in the end, difficult arrangements always fall to me. Please don't concern yourself."

The old fart had somehow set me up for a finesse. I restrained myself from appropriate comment and headed for lunch. On my way out I did promise him I'd try my best not to trip over the rug and hurt myself.

CHAPTER 7

*T*wo days drifted by without any sign I could see of his so-called arrangements. All attempts to broach the subject of the Herbert murder were pointedly ignored, which was typical. If there's anything my damn boss loves more than appearing mysterious and omniscient I must have missed it. At least we caught up on all the correspondence.

"We still haven't drafted that reply to the French, who want to send you another ribbon. I guess one copy should go to the premier and one to the committee—right? Go ahead, try to sound humble."

"Nonsense! How can one value a gesture from a people who've elected Jerry Lewis one of America's greatest film geniuses of the century and H.P. Lovecraft one of America's greatest writers? To accept would be to join the ranks of the mediocre, at best. Besides, we must save such make-work for later, Matt. We would only be interrupted by the imminent arrival of our client." You wouldn't think a guy who rated a decoration from the Premier of France would be capable of smirking like a demented teenager, but he was.

"Oh? Have we got one of those?"

"I have every reason to believe we are about to." He didn't seem disposed to volunteer any more information, and I wasn't about to give him the satisfaction of begging. Louis cracked the door reverently ten minutes later and announced a caller. He looked pretty presentable that morning except for the fact that he was barefoot. He liked the feel of the cool tile under his feet and nothing anybody said could change it. Not that it bothered any of the rest of us, but I sometimes wondered about the effect on callers.

"That would be Miss Neal." Butter wouldn't melt in his mouth. "Please be kind enough to show her in, Matt." If smug was snow, he'd be a blizzard.

I found our potential customer standing at the head of the hall, gazing out the window at the sea. From newspaper accounts I knew she was thirty-one, only child of the deceased by her first marriage, and lived in New York, where she was studying and pursuing a career as an artist. But what the papers had negligently failed to mention was that she was slender, long-legged, and lovely, in an imperious sort of way. Dark auburn hair quit at her nape, framing a face with too much character ever to be categorized as merely beautiful. Closer inspection verified my impression that she was wise enough not to gild the lily with a lot of goo from a bottle.

"Hello there, I'm Matt." It wasn't my usual greeting to a prospective client, but I found myself wanting to be on a first-name basis with her yesterday. I waited until she offered a pale hand, took it in my paw, and gently squeezed.

"My name is Susan Neal. I'm here to speak to Mr. Winfield." Her voice was rich and warm, pitched lower than expected. It was also businesslike. I wanted to hear more of it.

"Actually you're here to see me, too. I suppose he neglected to mention the fact that I do all the work around here. He mainly reads books, but it's true he makes a good figurehead. I don't mind, though; I never complain. I'm basically very shy."

It worked—she smiled. It wasn't a bit more spectacular

than the average tropic sunset or the vision of a perfect rainbow after three days of rain. I could see getting bored with it in about fifty or a hundred years.

"Yes, I can see that. Of course I imagined, because of his age, he would have to have people working for him. The truth is I'm a bit intimidated at the idea of meeting him. I've read so much about him in the history books that it's like meeting a national monument. I'm not certain how I'll react."

"Just relax, everybody feels the same way until they've been around him about fifteen seconds. They tell me he used to be quite a ladies' man. Just do your best not to let him sweep you off your feet and you'll be fine."

"He sounds fascinating. Lead on—I'll do my level best to keep from going all gushy and girlish."

I'd left the door to the office open. Suddenly we heard Win shouting: "Mr. Doyle, cease your badgering of that poor child and bring her in here." She and I exchanged conspiratorial winks and went in.

Win smiled handsomely at Susan. "Welcome, Miss Neal. I trust you'll forgive me for not using the current term, Ms. At my age it becomes difficult to alter lifelong habits."

"The words don't matter as much as the way you say them, Mr. Secretary."

"An admirable philosophy; I couldn't agree more. But, please, that title is long obsolete. But, as you see, the man is not." Win motioned me to pull a chair up closer to his desk and waited until Susan was seated. He never kept a chair near his desk for fear the wrong person might one day sit in it.

"You must forgive my associate. His competence as an investigator is extraordinary, but he fancies himself a wit. Now then, if you have no objections, I'd like to have Mr. Doyle take notes of our discussion. It will facilitate matters, should you decide to engage us to act in your behalf."

"By all means," Susan agreed. "I've been thinking about it ever since you called, and I'm sure I'll want you to go ahead. Otherwise I'm terribly afraid he'll get away with it."

Win and I traded looks. So the old bastard had gotten her number in New York and called her? That would normally have been my job, but no, he enjoyed keeping me off balance sometimes.

"He?" inquired Win. "You said that as if you were prepared to name the culprit."

"Oh, I can. My stepfather, Harold—the creep! And I can prove it, too."

"Then do so at once, Miss Neal."

Susan promptly probed the interior of her leather bag, removing a small bundle of letters. Selecting one apparently at random, she opened it and extracted a two-page hand-written note.

"Listen to this:

Honey, it's really becoming impossible with Harold. He's either unwilling or unable to stop these sordid little affairs of his. At least he used to have the good taste to be discreet, but a few weeks ago I found out he was carrying on with Jane Goodman—his secretary! I fixed him. I got rid of her and installed Helga Metz as his girl Friday. You remember—that poor ugly little thing I've had as my secretary forever? Helga reports directly to me now, but what's the use? Everyone in the plant is talking about it. I can read the pity, or the contempt, in their eyes. (It depends on whether or not I approved their last raise.) It's all too humiliating. Your father's own business, and I feel like I have to duck my head every time I walk into the building to avoid hitting my very large horns on the overhead.

To make matters worse, he still hasn't given up on that contemptible plan of his to sell our company to the conglomerate I told you about. He's been skulking around behind my back drumming up support for the idea. The sad part is, a lot of my people seem to be going along with the plan.

I honestly don't know how I ever let myself get into this ridiculous situation. If it weren't for my love for you and my deep commitment to the business, I swear I'd spare myself the grief and just find a tall building and jump. Please come home to me, Susan. I've given Harold notice to move out. If he doesn't, I'll have him forcibly removed. He's asked for a little time, one month at the most, and then I'll be free of him.

I need your support right now. If you don't want to move in here, maybe we could find you a nice place on the beach somewhere nearby. There must be some way you could continue your studies in a city this size. It would make such a huge difference to me if. . . ."

Susan's voice was getting increasingly unreliable. Suddenly she began sobbing quietly into a fistful of Kleenex. Win raised his eyebrows in a silent query. I shook my head no. It wasn't the time to offer a shoulder or sympathetic words. She'd either resent it or come completely unglued. Left alone, I was sure she'd quickly get hold of herself. It took a few minutes, but she did.

"I'm sorry; I guess that part about needing me did it. My mother was such a strong woman, I never realized how much she really did need me. Now I'll never forgive myself for writing back and telling her I couldn't possibly leave before my December break."

"You hardly need apologize for your grief, Miss Neal," Win told her soothingly. "Indeed, I share a measure of sorrow at your loss. Though I was denied the pleasure of knowing your mother, that tiny excerpt from one of her letters tells me she was worthy of my grief. If, however, you flog yourself with senseless guilt, stop it at once. It is a singularly nugatory act."

I came around from behind my desk and touched her shoulder lightly. "Can I get you anything? Coffee? Tea? Something stronger?"

She shook her head. "I'm fine now. You can see from the

letter, and there are four others pretty much the same, that my stepfather's guilty—can't you?"

Win answered with a question, a bad habit he has and one that drives him nuts when anyone does it to him. "What is the date of the letter you read from?"

"Mother never dated her personal letters, but let's see . . ." She picked up the envelope and examined it. "It's postmarked October third, just over three weeks ago. It's the most recent one; his month was about to run out, don't you see?"

"Certainly the evidence suggests it as a strong possibility," Win agreed. "Sufficient evidence to convict is our objective, however. I stand ready to commit my resources toward that goal. Please arrange the details, Mr. Doyle."

"That's his euphemism for 'See how much we can stick it to the client,'" I explained.

"If you can prove he did it, I'll gladly pay any reasonable fee. And expenses, of course, even if you fail."

"We couldn't possibly undertake the case on that basis," Win declared sharply.

"Why not?" demanded Susan. "You just got through saying you were ready to."

"Not as you stipulated. Your words: 'If you can prove he did it.' That's not acceptable. What if we were to prove someone else did it? I won't hire out my services for the explicit purpose of a vendetta against Harold Herbert, no matter how convinced you may be of his guilt. Nor will I agree to secure evidence to convict only if the killer is someone acceptable to you, and abort the investigation if it leads me down some path abhorrent to you. I will suffer no restrictions. Either engage me to seek the truth or pray that I withdraw."

"Yes, I can see that. No one's asking you to frame Harold or protect anyone else." Susan brushed aside all objections, as Win had known full well she would. He accepted working for someone, but first he had to leave no doubts as to who was boss.

"Susan," I broke in, "we'd better define 'any reasonable fee.' It would help if I knew something about your current financial situation."

She studied me briefly, managed a shaky smile, and said, "I suppose I should claim to be a pauper, but actually I'm embarrassingly solvent. My father left me a trust that pays sixty-eight hundred dollars a month. Part of that I've managed to save. I'm a real miser. Then there's the twenty-five thousand shares of Neal common I received when my parents went public with the company. I guess it's worth about—"

"Currently trading at thirty-eight and seven-eighths." Win threw it away casually, the impression being he could quote every one of the sixteen-hundred-odd stocks on the Big Board at any given moment. Susan was suitably impressed, as she was darned well meant to be. I knew better. Win never read the market section, and considered the entire thing a real sucker shoot. Almost as big a waste of innocent trees as the sports page, according to him.

"Okay, how does this sound? Give us a retainer of one thousand now in order to constitute a valid contract. Later we'll bill you for another nine grand unless we run up against a lot of unexpected expenses. They don't figure to amount to much as far as I can see. That's a total of ten thousand plus expenses."

She pulled out a blue plastic checkbook without hesitation, flipped it open, and began to write, using her purse for a base. "If you don't succeed, am I correct in understanding there will be no additional fee over and above this retainer?"

She was an artist, but some of her mother's business sense had rubbed off. "If we don't nail him—complete with evidence to convict—you'll get that thousand back. Less any expenses," I assured her. We exchanged check and receipt.

"The funds are the least of the demands we may be forced to make upon you," Win warned her. "You must stand prepared to arm us with the shield of your unreserved support. Without this claim to legitimacy we cannot enter battle."

"You have it."

"Good! Now that all is arranged . . ."

"Hold the phone!" I jumped up, palms forming a stop sign. "Everything is not arranged. Those letters are dynamite. They're certainly evidence, and our neck will be out miles if we fail to turn them over—fast! Dixon will crack his first smile in years the day he can get our licenses pulled. This would do it."

Win merely looked mildly annoyed. "I trust the law allows us the right to examine material provided by our clients. When I've had ample time to study the missives, I may or may not deem them evidential."

He soon stopped glaring at me and turned to Susan. "In view of your attitude toward Mr. Herbert, why is it you haven't already turned the letters over to the authorities?"

"I intended to while I was out here for the funeral. I wanted to make sure they got into the right hands, not just drop them in the mail to some clerk."

"Is it now your wish to leave them here with me?"

"Certainly, if that's what you'd like."

"I would, with the clear understanding we may in turn hand them over to the police, should I deem it appropriate."

"Fine. I leave it to your judgment."

"Very well. Let us begin in earnest. Instruct us concerning the life and times of Harold Herbert. Omit nothing, no matter how trivial. If hearsay, label it so, but this is not a court of law and I want to hear everything."

She dug right in, beginning six years back with stories told her by her mother. Harold Herbert had washed out after a very brief and unremarkable career in triple-A baseball, third baseman, and ended up in Hollywood, where he managed to secure an equity card as an actor. She thought the best he ever did was join the crowd in background scenes. Apparently the one thing he had going for him was some athletic ability. This not only snagged him a few non-speaking parts, it ultimately got him to Martha Neal. One day she'd accepted a friend's invitation to spend the day on his boat out of Newport Beach.

Harold was aboard as well because it was a big schooner that required a lot of muscle.

Martha had been a widow for nearly seven years by then. Susan said she never did understand what attracted her mother to him. That was naive; it wasn't hard to figure. By then Harold would have been a pro: good at all the right games, social graces polished to a high gloss, witty, charming, and ever so careful the moment he discovered the stakes. Ten weeks later Susan found out she had a stepfather she had yet to meet. When she then moved on to enumerating his peccadillos, Win lost interest and called a halt.

We broke for lunch, with Louis and Randy making a big fuss over her. Dirk was a no-show; he'd probably locked himself in his apartment over the garage when he heard there was a female on the premises. Win even managed to do a little more than push his food around the plate. (I'd noticed before that when we had a case he ate a little more and became much more animated. That's another one of the reasons I try to keep us working.)

After lunch I took Susan for a stroll along the beach. We debated hotly the relative merits of our respective oceans. She said the Pacific was a faded and sluggardly excuse for a sea. I took the position that the Atlantic was the ill-tempered brat of oceans and totally untrustworthy. We babbled all sorts of silly nonsense back and forth like children on an outing. By the time we tramped back to the house, we were both amazed to find we were holding hands.

The afternoon session encompassed everything from the house in Del Mar to Susan's life-style in New York. She squirmed and looked as if she might like to bolt once or twice, but she stuck to her bargain and answered even the most esoteric of Win's questions. She never realized some of the probes dealt with her own potential as a killer. It no longer surprised me. Matricide wasn't unheard of or they wouldn't have needed a word for it, and she wouldn't have been the first to hire us as a blind. I halfway expected him to want to know where I'd been Sunday night around ten.

By four o'clock she was empty, and I had nearly fifty pages of notes and a bad case of writer's cramp. She said goodbye to Win with genuine fondness.

"I told you so," I whispered as we strolled toward the front door.

"Told me what?"

"Told you he'd charm you right out of your socks."

"He really is something, isn't he? Does he always talk like that?"

"Yeah, I'm thinking of providing pocket dictionaries to all visitors. He claims the average person's vocabulary consists of only about two thousand words, which isn't enough to communicate beyond the level of the average pre-adolescent child. I keep telling him it doesn't improve communications much when nobody knows what he's talking about."

She laughed. Not a twitter—a fine, deep, unrestrained outburst. "I've read a lot about him—his accomplishments in government—but meeting him is an extraordinary experience. I do believe he's the brightest man I've ever known. His powers of concentration are incredible for a man his age. He made me tell him things I didn't even realize I knew. That doesn't make much sense, does it?"

"It does to me. I live here, remember? Does it to me all the time. Makes you feel sorry for all those heads of state who had to go one-on-one with him, doesn't it? They say when he was in office we actually had a foreign policy everyone around the world understood, and it functioned smoothly. Ah, well, so much for the good old days. Anyway, I'm glad you like him. Can I offer you a ride?"

"I've got a rental car, thanks. I'm staying at the Plaza. When would you think you might have something to report?"

"Don't call us; we'll call you. In fact, after you get through the ordeal of the services tomorrow, why don't we get together for dinner? By then we should have some idea of the tack we'll be taking and we can discuss it. If you feel up to it. I should think the day will be depressing enough without having to walk into a strange restaurant and eat alone."

She touched my arm lightly. "I have no idea how tomorrow will affect me but, please, do call, Matt. I imagine I'll be back at the hotel by four. You're right; eating alone in a restaurant is rather grim, but then I doubt food will count for much tomorrow."

I watched her walk away, feeling helpless and inarticulate. I'd wanted to put my arms around her and say something profound but I have no gift for it at times like these. What would've come out was something asinine like, "Keep your chin up, kid," so I said nothing and just watched her drive away.

CHAPTER 8

*T*he image of Martha Neal that emerged from the four brief letters Susan had left behind was one of loneliness and confusion, yet great inner strength. When I'd finished reading them all for the second time, Win declined my invitation to be drawn into a discussion of the case. He has this theory that the subconscious is better equipped to assess facts and dictate procedure if left in peace to do so. Maybe, but I have a feeling Plutarch lying there unfinished was a factor. It's one of the things about him that makes me crazy. When I'm on a case, my heart rate goes up and stays there until it's over. You might just as well tell a hound trailing a rabbit to take a break and contemplate the wonders of nature.

It wasn't until the following morning when I showed up at the office that I found out what his id had decided we should do.

"Good morning, boss. Finish your book?"

He surveyed me with tolerance. "I have, thank you. Plutarch's insight into human nature was a benchmark in recorded mortal history. All truly worthwhile books should be read at least twice. I was remiss to ignore Plutarch for so long; I shall certainly avail myself of his enduring genius again."

"I know what you mean. I feel the same way about Charlie Schulz."

"No doubt. Now that we've exchanged literary views, perhaps we may begin earning our fee. A surprisingly modest one, by the way. It hasn't escaped my attention that your attitude regarding fees varies in inverse proportion to the winsomeness of the client. I don't quibble—it's your department—I merely note the fact out of interest. Please call Miss Neal and inform her you will escort her to her mother's funeral today."

"Since we're not quibbling, I won't bother with the crack about fees. As for Susan, I'll call and see. Girls don't take too well to being told these days; they prefer being asked."

"Again, your department. But bear in mind we are not requesting an idle boon. If she should object, it will be necessary to remind her of the unqualified pledge of support she gave us in this very room yesterday."

"What am I supposed to accomplish? Stand around watching for guilty looks? Won't work—everybody feels guilty at a funeral."

"I daresay you're right. Far too often it was my maudlin duty to attend those barbaric rites while in office. No, your sole purpose is not to see but to be seen. We must establish your identity as Miss Neal's confidant. This afternoon's service provides a singularly unique opportunity. Every principal involved in this case will be thrown together. I want each of them to see you at her side."

"Every principal? You expect the burglar to show?"

"I trust you can restrain your insatiable wit during the course of the ceremony, Matt. And I do feel certain it may be stated as an absolute: The culprit we seek will be in attendance."

I leaned back and put my feet up, braced on a half-open drawer. Feet on the desk are out. "Then what?"

"Then you will enlist whatever skills you may command to

penetrate the protective shell of Neal Drugs. Your guise will be that of close associate to the sole heir of the deceased. Beyond that, you require no direction from me on how best to conduct yourself. People unburden themselves to you readily—I've no idea why. You have the ability to amass data much as a long-haired dog collects fleas: just by being in the area."

"You flatterer, you. I think you've been sneaking a peek at "Hee-Haw" again. But aren't you forgetting something? Harold and I have met. He's not about to sit still for me sniffing around the plant. He'll know exactly what I'm after."

"I forget nothing." He was miffed at the reference to a TV show he had once described as the most tasteless bit of buffoonery to ever deprive the public of valuable air time. "Harold Herbert will have no choice but to grant you access if our client requests, no, demands it. I suggest you pass yourself off as her legal or business adviser. Business adviser, I think; you haven't adequate cozenage to be a convincing attorney. Few men do, much to their credit. Mr. Herbert's knowledge of your true colors may well work to our advantage. As an example, if someone else suddenly shows knowledge of your true identity, it would be highly suggestive. It should help us discover who his intimates are. You may find alternative suspects worthy of our attention. A woman at the helm of such a vast enterprise surely had her full quantum of enemies. This matter of a proposed merger grates heavily upon my mind. Again, it would seem to indict Mr. Herbert, but, given the stakes involved, there may be others with equal motive. Bring me names. For all we know right now, the murder may have been an assassination voted and approved by committee. You smile, but believe me, a corporation is not unlike a political state, and many an assassination has come out of conferences of state."

"I'll do my best, boss, but it's going to look damn funny for me to be wandering around pretending to be a business adviser while grilling everybody in sight about the murder."

"With sufficient effort," he purred, "you might achieve some slight subtlety. You won't find the situation as cumbersome as you imagine. All companies the size of Neal thrive on intrigue. Gossip abounds—it's their veritable staff of life. A result of the crushing sameness of the work, I imagine. The subject of their president and co-founder's murder surely monopolizes all their thoughts right now. The real trick would be to get them to talk about anything else."

I looked up the number of the Plaza Hotel, dialed, and asked for Susan. She answered quickly and gratefully accepted my offer to accompany her. We arranged to meet an hour early so I could brief her on the approach. With any luck, she'd hand me a club I could hold over Harold's head.

I arrived downtown sporting my most subdued charcoal-gray suit and a tie borrowed from Randy that was definitely funereal. The lobby of the Plaza held enough antiques and paintings to furnish a small museum. I headed for the nearest bank of elevators, but got ambushed by a Prussian general. He tactfully suggested I have the desk call ahead to inform their guest of my existence. The desk clerk made the call and a fraction of a nod to the general bought me a quiet ride in a plush elevator piloted by an old man in a red suit with black trim at lapel and cuffs. He reminded me of the monkey who used to panhandle all along the Loop in Chicago years ago. Their outfits were identical, except the monkey's trim had been real velvet, and his suit had been a better fit.

Susan's room turned out to be a suite. Garbed in a rather severe-looking tweed suit, she pressed my forearm lightly in greeting.

"How about some lunch first?"

"No," she replied hastily, "I'm not up to lunch today. Just tell me what I have to do."

I gave her the gist of it, omitting the part about assassination by committee. She didn't need to hear that. Win had been just spouting when he'd said it.

"I don't know, Matt—I don't think I could bring myself to ask any favors of that man."

"Harold? What favors? I should think you'd jump at the chance to hold his feet to the fire."

She took a deep breath and assumed a look of stubborn determination. "Of course I'll do whatever you say. That's a nice way of putting it—if only we could use real fire."

"If we can nail him, it'll be real enough. How does the idea of my being your business consultant hold up under scrutiny?"

"Pretty well, come to think of it. We could claim I'm concerned about the future of the company without a Neal left to run it. I'm trying to decide whether or not to dispose of my huge block of shares, weighing the considerable tax bite against the possibility of a decline. That sort of thing. I hadn't actually thought much about it yet, but it's just what I should really be doing."

"Good! Then all I have to do is look like I know the difference between a gross profit and a debenture. Which, by the way, I don't. Since your dad founded the company, and your mother ran it after his death, everyone concerned ought to accept the premise of your taking a personal interest. It should fly."

It began with nothing more than a slight quiver of her lower lip and spread. The next thing I knew she was bawling her heart out. I pulled her around and let her rain on my right shoulder. I held her tightly, fully aware she was one very nice armful of girl. Eventually the storm passed.

"I guess what you just said struck a nerve—about my being the last of the Neals. I don't even have the excuse that I'm crying for Mom—I'm not! I'm just crying for selfish me, because I've never felt so alone before. Hell, I've never *been* so alone before." Her voice was muffled by my shoulder and sounded oddly childlike.

"If you feel alone, Susan, all I can say is, you're not paying attention. There's damn near two hundred pounds of me right here, and I'm enjoying every minute of it. Cry all you want—don't worry about the suit. Everything's drip-dry these days."

I held on, inhaling the tantalizing aroma of girl with the slightest trace of soap, or maybe shampoo. This, I suddenly realized, was going to be one hell of a contender in the Mrs. Matt Doyle Sweepstakes.

When it was time to leave, she was able to manage a smile and tell me she'd come to terms with her mother's death in her own head, and what was to come was just stupid tradition. Between that and the fact that it took her only five minutes to repair the damage, she endeared herself to me all the more.

We drove north on Highway 5 toward Del Mar with the windows half down, the pleasant, dry desert air from the Mojave washing over us like velvet. I had a sudden inspiration.

"Susan, how's this for an idea? Let's forget about the expert business adviser crap. I'll be your fiancé instead. I flew out here with you because we're madly in love and inseparable. That way we can bill and coo all over the place and still remain in character."

At least it brought her out of her funk. "Are you serious?" She favored me with a look of skepticism.

"Sure I am. It's just as good. In fact, it's a whole lot better because I won't have to worry about getting mousetrapped by the first guy who challenges my business background. And it's a more sympathetic role because I'll almost be family. People are bound to be more open. The best part is it makes it more acceptable to show an interest in your mother and what kind of person she was. Except for the fact that it severely limits my ability to meet girls, it's perfect!"

"Just as I thought—you aren't serious."

"Huh? Watch my lips. What did I just say?"

"I meant that part about billing and cooing."

"Don't be silly. Where do you think my mind's been, to come up with a sneaky scheme like this? The receptionist at the plant thinks I'm a cop, but I can cover—explain it was just a ruse to get to Harold."

In the end we both agreed the approach would be both safer and more flexible. Not to mention more fun. After that I quit trying to distract her and just let her tumble down into her private well of silent grief.

The church where the services were to be held was more like a set for a well-financed science fiction film. Call it twenty-first-century high renaissance modern. Tall, narrow stained-glass windows under a soaring roofline that looked like either a rocket launch or a ski jump, depending which end you considered first. Inside, we were ushered into a small room peopled with nervous, miserable faces. Most were making valiant attempts to sustain small talk, without any notable success. Every eye fastened on us immediately, including Harold's. He quickly broke away and advanced toward us, sporting an icy glare.

Before he could open his mouth, Susan stated in a loud voice, "Harold, I'd like you to meet my fiancé, Matt Doyle." Then added, *sotto voce*, "I will explain later." Her voice deadly calm, she enunciated each word as if she were addressing a naughty child. It was a fine performance, and I was justly proud of her.

Harold alternated between looking angry and confused. A small sea of people engulfed us. Susan seemed to know most of them, and I could see they were genuinely fond of her, not just going through the motions. I smiled as much as I thought circumstances permitted, trying to look like a good catch. It was a role I'd never expected to have to play; one for which I suspected I had little talent.

In a blessedly short time we were summoned into the church proper. There was a feeling of vast space under the soaring overhead. As we neared the front we were confronted by a ten-foot-high floral display at the foot of the gleaming coffin. It was a replica of the triangular-shaped logo of the Neal Pharmaceutical Manufacturing Corporation, Susan informed me later, utilizing four colors of flowers. It might have been left over from a sales convention. I felt her stiffen, as appalled as I was at the rank commercialism.

The service dragged on interminably. A self-righteous sounding minister said a lot of fine things about Martha, and possibly some of them were even true. He dwelled heavily upon her charitable works. He made a lot of sweeping statements about the hereafter and God's thoughts and plans, none of which he could possibly know anything about. Someone from the company got up to extol her virtues as a friend and leader. He had to pause several times, and he sounded as if he really meant it.

The curtain act was almost beyond belief. A very large woman looking like a fugitive from a Wagnerian opera came out in a full white gown that swept the stage and began a singsong recital, swaying to her own cadence. She began every stanza with the code words: "Don't say she's gone, dear friends; don't say she's gone." It was rough on Susan. Her left hand threatened to make it all the way through the sleeve of my jacket. It made me doubly glad she wore her nails short.

As soon as the big blond Brünnhilde finished, it was over. All I could think about was the classic line about the opera never being over until the fat lady sings. The pews behind us had nearly all filled, making for an impressive turnout.

Next we were urged to rush out to our cars like Grand Prix drivers and take part in a Kamikaze chase down the freeway behind a motorcycle cop who thought he was Evel Knevel. The turn at the gravesite was tough. Susan trembled and some tears tracked down her face, but it was soon over.

I headed back toward the car in a direct line, but she pulled me up short with a look of horror on her face. My course led us right over the top of some of the older residents of the cemetery. I nearly pointed out they weren't likely to mind, but with her mother barely five minutes underground it would have been tacky even for me.

Some had a few kind words as we walked to the car along

the winding gravel road. Susan politely declined attendance at a gathering of some of the corporate officers who were supposedly closest to her mother. There were several other warm offers of food and companionship, all of which she passed on with genuine gratitude. Harold was waiting beside my car, his face a stiff, angry mask. He opened his mouth, but I waved him silent until I'd opened the door for Susan, then came back around to face him.

"Climb in," I advised him. "We can chat while we're rolling. Unless you want to create an amusing little scene right here."

He slid into the back and slammed the door. I got under way.

"Susan, dear," he demanded sternly, "will you please tell me what you are doing in the company of this . . . troublemaker. And to introduce him as your fiancé! Don't you know he's using you? He even tried to shake me down. At least I had the good sense to throw him out on his ear."

I glanced at Susan. She looked used up. "You talk to him, Matt. Just tell him what you expect from him. He'll either do it or he'll be sorrier than he can possibly imagine." After that, she slumped down in her seat and stared fixedly at the passing scenery. She'd somehow managed to make it sound as if her stepfather weren't even in the car. The result was far more demeaning than shouting at him would have been.

"You see how it is, Harold. I'm asking very little from you, just the right to do my job. I'll be showing up at the plant tomorrow as Susan's intended. I'm going to nose around a bit, talk to a few people, nothing disruptive. You'll provide me with whatever clearances I'll need. Reason: I'm out to protect your stepdaughter's interests. She's concerned about future stability and growth. We're deciding whether to hang on to her twenty-five thousand shares of stock and continue collecting dividends, or sell and make Uncle Sam happy. That's it."

I'd adjusted the rearview mirror in order to watch him. It bothered me more than a little to allow a killer to occupy the high ground behind me. Yet all he did was lick his lips and frown. When he did speak, his words tumbled out petulantly.

"Susan, you'd be extremely foolish to sell right now. Why, I've got plans for the company that will . . ."

"Skip the dumb act, Harold." Our eyes met in the mirror. "You know damn well what I'm after, and it has nothing to do with projected earnings."

He glared at my reflection. "You're an adult, Susan; do as you wish, of course. But I will not abide this cheap chisler wandering around my plant stirring everybody up. Things are very touchy just now as it is. You have no idea . . ."

She spun around like a cat, kneeling on the front seat, her lovely face contorted in absolute fury. For an instant I thought she was going to go for him, and so did he. I saw him wedge himself as far back into the opposite corner as he could.

"*Your* Plant! How dare you refer to the business my parents created and devoted their lives to as 'your plant'? You may have manipulated my mother, but you'll never get to Square One with me."

"Susan, please, I'm sorry . . ."

"Shut up and pay attention, damn it! I'm only going to say this once, and I really don't think you're all that bright. I'm perfectly satisfied with my life in New York. Dabbing paint on canvas makes me absurdly happy, but now I make you a promise. You fight me on this and I'll spend the rest of my life sitting in my mother's office peddling those stupid pills. And I'll do it just so I can make sure you end up right back where you belong."

He didn't look dangerous or even angry. He looked like someone who'd just been sucker-punched in the gut.

"Susan," he pleaded in a ragged voice, "there's no reason to act like this. You don't know the first thing about running your parents' company. Just let me—"

"I don't know the first thing about it? That's rich, coming from a third-rate, washed-up ballplayer who didn't know where his next meal was coming from until he hustled my poor misguided mother. Let me give you some food for thought. How many of the top brass in the company would side with you if we were to battle it out? Most of them have known me all my life. That's *my* name on all those labels, you idiot! You think the last of the Neals couldn't pull that chair out from under you? Somehow I doubt they're all that fond of you, Harold. Too bad the office girls don't get to vote.

"Now let's talk power. How many shares of stock do you either own or control? My parents retained a huge block of common when they went public eighteen years ago. Who do you think is going to end up with it? It wouldn't be much of a fight. If I were you—*God* forbid—I'd smile, speak only when spoken to, and do exactly as I was told."

It was a bravura performance. She'd managed to convert a lot of anger and frustration and pain into useful words. I was glad, because I knew it would help her mend. If she hadn't scored a knockout, it was at the very least a T.K.O.

The conference seemed about over, so I circled back. As I pulled up to the rear of Harold's car, I turned to look over my shoulder and survey the carnage. He sat slumped in the seat, apparently fascinated with his folded hands. Maybe he was praying. His dark blue Brooks Brothers suit suddenly looked as if it were meant for a considerably younger man.

"I'd say the lady summed it up pretty well, wouldn't you, Harold? Look for me in the morning, bright-eyed and bushy-tailed. If you decide not to invite me to lunch, I'll understand."

The best he could muster was a slight nod. He fumbled a bit before managing the door latch, then climbed slowly out, standing there looking bewildered.

As we drove off I reached over and patted her knee. "You do good work, Tiger. You'll sleep like a baby tonight—you just off-loaded a ton of crap you've been lugging around for days."

The crystal-clear light and air that comes with a Santa Ana made the passing landscape too vivid, like a poster that had been airbrushed. But she wasn't in a mood to appreciate it; she lay curled against the door with her head on the window frame, her eyes closed.

"Get me back to the hotel, Matt. I feel sick and dirty. I want to take a long, scalding shower. I'm afraid it's no on dinner tonight. Tonight is for being alone. Maybe I'll tune in the most insipid program I can find on TV and just detach. It's more than a little frightening to realize I'm capable of hating another human being so much. All those things I said? I didn't know it until I heard myself saying them, but I meant every word. If I'd had a gun I really believe I might have shot him."

"Next time check with me. I've got one, and I think I might have let you borrow it. But cheer up—a gun would have been a kindness. You know, once you work up a head of steam, you're bad. To tell the truth, I'm already having second thoughts about our engagement."

The girl had dug deep and depleted what was left of her reserves of nervous energy. She couldn't muster enough for a suitable retort. I elected not to even try talking her out of her dismal plans for the evening. She needed time alone to let the well refill. Besides, we had all the time in the world.

CHAPTER 9

I hit the deck running the morning following the funeral, arriving at the plant at seven-twenty. Though I was champing at the bit, the door was locked, so all I could do was sit in my car, listen to the news on KNX, and champ. Within ten minutes a small group began stacking up outside the door. Someone eventually deigned to unlock it from the inside, and the crowd poured in. I trailed the herd, which led me to a spotless but austerely plain cafeteria. Four white-uniformed women gathered around one of the Formica tables and began a serious assault on some coffee and Danish. I drew a cup myself as protective coloration, and strolled over and asked permission to join them.

"You bet, doll," replied the one with the frosted hair, leering at me over her cup of steaming brew.

"Down, girl," cautioned the sharp-eyed Chicano beside her. Examining me with suspicion, she stated, "Didn't I see you at the services yesterday? Right up front with Mr. Herbert?"

She'd made Mr. Herbert sound like a gutter word. "Yes,

you did, but not with Harold. I was with Martha's daughter, Susan—we're engaged to be married. My name's Matt Doyle."

"That poor dear—how's she taking it?" inquired Frosted Hair, desperate to change her image.

"As well as might be expected. She asked me to come out here on a little errand. It's a bit out of my line, and I'm not just sure how to go about it." I gave them my best little-boy-lost look, hoping some of them were mothers.

"What's that?"

"Well, Susan's concerned, or maybe I should say confused, about just where her duty lies regarding this place. My guess is her parents instilled a pretty heavy sense of responsibility into her where this company is concerned. She still tends to think of it as a family enterprise, even though it's become such a huge operation. Right now, she's uncertain about whether to return back East and pick up where she left off or stick around here and put her shoulder to the wheel. You know—the last of the Neals and all that."

The four exchanged hesitant yet eager glances.

"Like mother, like daughter," murmured the chubby one on my immediate left. "I certainly meant that as a compliment, Mr. Doyle," she added hastily.

"Matt, please, and it sounded like one to me."

"What exactly do you want from us?" asked Sharp-Eyes, still under the control of some native caution.

"Any input would be a help at this stage. I never got the chance to even meet Mrs. Neal—Mrs. Herbert, I mean. We were scheduled to spend Christmas out here and now this awful thing. How did the employees feel about her? A woman heading up an organization this size is unusual, even today. Was she really in charge, or was she a figurehead with the magic name? That's a sample of the sort of thing I need to find out in order to help Susan reach a decision."

"Figurehead!" squawked the scrawny one with the chicken neck on my right. "She sure wasn't no figurehead. More like the cornerstone, I'd say. And I'll tell you how folks around here felt about old Martha, all right. If it wasn't for her, a hell of a lot of us wouldn't have put up with that . . ."

"Maude!" Sharp-Eyes cut her off. Without taking her eyes from mine, she told them, "I saw him talking to Mr. Herbert yesterday. They drove off in the same car together." She made it sound like an indictment.

"Do you think I care?" Maude was off and running. "Maybe you want to stick around with Mr. Macho runnin' things? Probably figures to replace us all anyway. With twenty-year-olds with big . . ."

"That's enough!" hissed Sharp-Eyes. She gave me a challenging look. "You've got your answer. Mrs. Herbert will be badly missed, but none of us is qualified to talk about the effect it might have on the business. We all work in packaging—don't you think you should be talking to management?"

I grinned at them all. "Isn't that a little like asking a politician in office whether he doesn't think someone younger and brighter ought to run against him? It's your angle I want. Harold's already given us his advice, that's what Susan and I were talking about with him in the car yesterday. He told her to go home and collect her dividends and not to bother the big kids. I'll be perfectly honest with you ladies: Susan doesn't hold her stepfather in very high regard."

It was an open invitation they couldn't resist, with the notable exception of Sharp-Eyes. Each did her best to top the others' tales of Harold's incompetence and lechery. When there was finally a break in the conversation, Sharp-Eyes fixed me with a glare and demanded suddenly, "You're a policeman, aren't you?"

I nearly spilled my coffee. "Lord, no, do I sound like one?"

"You do to me. Too bad, I was hoping you were."

"Why is that?"

"Never mind. If you're not, it doesn't matter. Let's just say most of us don't believe in coincidence."

A loud, harsh buzzer sounded. An echoing screech of

chairs scraping over the gleaming tile floor marked the quick exodus of everyone in the room. I thanked my breakfast companions as they hurried off to begin their workday. Pondering what they'd told me, I wandered over and deposited my still-full cup of coffee in a service bin. It was a little discouraging to realize my disguise hadn't even held up with a worker from the assembly line. Good luck with the department heads I was on my way to see.

I was barely fifty yards from the cafeteria when a uniformed guard gave me the eye. "May I help you?" he inquired. His tone suggested it was highly unlikely.

"Nope, just making the rounds. Got some people to see. If I get lost I'll just ask directions."

"It don't work that way. Until you get clearance, you don't go no place."

"What makes you think I don't have clearance?"

"Easy. If you belonged in here, you'd have a visitor's pass stuck to your jacket. Let's go."

We backtracked all the way to a tiny office just inside the reception area. The door stood open. Inside, a snaggle-toothed old dear reeking of lavender peered up at me darkly.

"The general here says I need a badge or something. Call Harold Herbert. Tell him it's Matt Doyle. Make it quick—I think the general has an itchy trigger finger."

I got a dirty look in stereo, but she picked up the phone and punched three digits. I wasn't betting my last nickel on it—Harold had had time to recoup—but apparently he came through because she hung up, shoved an open ledger at me, and told me to sign in. I did, ignoring the column for company affiliation. She duplicated my name on a white label, including the number 5, which corresponded to my entry number in the book. I dutifully peeled the tag from its backing and patted it onto my lapel.

"Am I official now?"

"Just make sure you stop here on the way out," she ordered. "And that doesn't authorize you to enter any door marked RESTRICTED."

"Yes, sir!" I nearly saluted, but it occurred to me I was there to make friends, not alienate people. It's just that I've always had trouble digesting tin horns and little Napoleons.

The brightly lighted halls were teeming with people, most clad in long white lab coats. The men wore ties underneath, which struck me as silly-looking. I wandered more or less aimlessly until I spotted a door marked VICE-PRESIDENT, SALES. It seemed a likely place to start.

The effervescent secretary within greeted me with a big smile. You always get the biggest smiles in sales. "Hi! The boss in?"

"Hello. Yes, Mr. Burns is in. May I tell him who's here?"

I pointed to my name tag. "Just tell him it's old Number Five."

She squinted and leaned closer. "I just hate to wear my glasses in the office," she confessed. "I'll see if he's available, Mr. Doyle."

She disappeared into the inner office, returning almost immediately. The door stayed open. "Please go right in. Mr. Burns will see you now."

He was standing beside his desk waiting for me. I'm not used to looking up at people, but, unless I wanted to eyeball his neck, I had no choice. Burns was an easy six and a half feet, whip-thin, brown hair shot with gray, and an unruly mustache. His long bony fingers engulfed mine.

"Don Burns, Mr. Doyle. Nice to meet you. Grab yourself a chair and tell me what I can do for you."

I caught a glimpse of cowboy boots before he put the desk between us, and the drawl was classic Texan, right out of central casting.

"You can start by making it Matt. It's not going to be easy, Mr. Burns, but I'll give it my best shot."

"Don," he corrected me.

"Fine—Don. Susan Neal is my fiancée. I'm here on her

behalf. You may not be aware of it, but this company means a great deal to her. I'm talking family pride and commitment, not dollars. She's sitting on a big decision. There are two options: Sell out her stock, go back to New York and try to forget about it, or follow what she considers family tradition. Meaning pitch in here and help run this operation. She's asked my opinion. There's no way I can give her an informed reply until I understand the situation here."

"What situation's that?" Don's face was a wooden mask; he concentrated on the pencil he was rolling back and forth between his fingers.

"There's no time to be coy, so let me cite an example. What kind of chief executive is Harold Herbert going to make? I frankly don't find what little I know of his background to be very encouraging. Susan is concerned because she personally thinks he may be implicated in her mother's death."

"Does Harold know you're here?"

"He's the one who authorized this visitor's pass. With prejudice, at Susan's demand. If you'd like to give him a call, I won't take offense. And if you're thinking I might be a stalking horse for Harold, you've never been more wrong in your life."

My instincts told me to open up a little with Don. I couldn't see him as one of Harold's cohorts; the two men were worlds apart in every way. Don looked like the guy in the Marlboro ads, twenty years later.

I could see him struggling with his uncertainty. Finally he shrugged. "What the hell, Matt—I'll give you a straight answer to a straight question. I don't rightly give a shit whether you report this to Harold or not. I got me over two hundred acres of some of the finest grove land in southwest Texas. Trees comin' up on three years old. Be producing in another two, three years, so maybe you'll end up helping me make a decision, too."

"I'm not reporting anything to Harold. Except for Susan, everything you say to me is strictly confidential."

"Ain't nothing confidential about it; he knows exactly how

I feel." It amused me to notice the accent grow thicker the moment he found out it wasn't company business. "I expect the idiot will sell the store here directly, so that makes it all academic as hell anyhow. It is my honest-to-God opinion Harold Herbert couldn't run a hot dog stand alone, and he's got the morals of a dirty yella junkyard dog. Old Martha wasn't much for screwin' up, but she sure fumbled the ball when she took up with that one. I could have strangled her myself when she come draggin' that dirtball back home.

"So you tell Susan ole Donny Burns would be purely delighted to see her take a hand here. You tell her, if she can find a way to swing it, I'm for her."

"Thanks, I will. What did you mean about Harold selling the store?"

"Trans-United, one of those big multinational conglomerates that snap up successful little companies like this the way I eat popcorn. They're purely set on acquiring Neal Labs. It saves them fifteen, maybe twenty years of paying their dues to break into the pharmaceutical racket. It would take at least four or five years and maybe ten million dollars to get aspirin approved by the FDA today. Harold has been panting over the idea ever since they made their first approach way back last year. Martha wouldn't even discuss it, but he's jerked Trans-United around with promises and kept the door open, so now I reckon he'll make the deal."

"He can't just do that on his own. He'd have to sell the program to a lot of folks."

"Don't underestimate the guy, Matt. I called him an idiot just now, but he's a great con. He's invested a lot of time and effort selling the idea that a merger would be a blessing. Makes me sick seeing all the chowderheads willing to swap their souls for a few more company benefits. The damn fools don't realize that within a year after Trans-United takes over, most of us will be out on the street."

I debated taking the next step. He'd set it up and seemed to have a pretty good momentum going, so I elected to go for it.

"You said something, Don—it's got me thinking. You said Martha absolutely opposed the idea of the merger, and Harold wanted it so badly he could taste it. Suddenly she's dead and he gets his way. Could there be a connection? Tell me if I'm out of line, but it seems to me things have worked out amazingly well for Harold. And it even looks as if he knew it would. Otherwise, why was he keeping a lock on the deal? Why work so hard to promote the sale when he knew there wasn't a chance in hell she'd change her mind?"

Don rolled his pencil even more furiously. "If you quote me on this I'll deny it. There is such a thing as slander. But it has occurred to me. And there's not a doubt in my mind he'd do it, as long as he was absolutely sure his ass was covered. Still, there's a problem. They say she was killed at ten Sunday night. I was sitting across the table from the son of a bitch from seven on that night. He was still sitting there at ten-forty when the police called."

"It can't be more than an eight-minute drive to his house from here. Are you positive he didn't take an extra-long bathroom run? Half an hour?—even twenty minutes if everything clicked just right."

Don shook his head slowly, regretfully, it seemed to me. "No, I've thought about it a lot. We all made a quick head run or two, what with all the coffee we were pouring down, but the only time Harold was out of the room more than a couple of minutes was when he and Helga left for half an hour so he could dictate a bid we'd finally agreed on. They worked in his office; she was with him the entire time."

I hadn't expected the break to come so soon. It was a struggle to keep from betraying my mounting excitement. "Helga, huh? How solid is that? Maybe he'd done the bid earlier. Nothing unusual about a secretary covering for her boss."

"The Horrible Hun? Not a chance. She hates the sight of Harold. All her loyalties were to Martha. She was Martha's secretary for a good ten years, but when she found out Harold was boffing the sweet young thing he had, Martha sent him

Helga as a replacement. We all chuckled over that for a solid week.

"Besides, the bid was settled on just before they left to prepare it. Ten minutes earlier, no one could have predicted the details of it. It was a big Army contract, and the deadline was the next day—Monday. That's why the unusual Sunday-night session."

I'd spotted a hole and I didn't appreciate his plugging it. It made me spiteful. "How did you feel about Martha?"

He smiled, a distant look on his face. "Old Martha and me, we fought like alley cats all the time. She'd call me 'that dumb West Texas saddle bum' and I'd come right back with 'old biddy' or worse. We both thrived on it. I loved that gal, son—it's your loss you never got to know her. If I ever found out Harold had anything to do with killing her, I'd skin him and stake him out over one of those big red ant hills behind the plant."

"Suppose he used an accomplice—who would it be?"

"Nobody in this outfit. Someone from his past. Hear him tell it, he had some pretty freaky friends during his salad days. Likes to tell some mighty weird stories after bending his elbow often enough."

Don's pert secretary stuck her head in, looking properly apologetic. "Sorry, Mr. Burns, but you've got that ten o'clock appointment over at the training center coming up fast."

"Thanks, Betty, I'll get on my horse and ride." Still, he remained seated, looking thoughtful.

"Spill it," I prodded him. "I know that look. Don't stop to analyze it."

He eyed me with a frown. "It was when Betty mentioned the training center. There's a young fella down there named Nick Barber. Martha kicked him the hell out of management, and he's working there temporarily. Guy's mad as a hornet and mean as a snake. And he's been pretty tight with Harold lately, too."

Don stood up and stretched. "You had the two-bit tour yet?"

"Nope, you were my first stop."

He covered the distance to the outside door in half a dozen quick strides. "Betty, honey, would you holler at Bob Springer and tell him to get on over and give Matt here the works?"

"Right away, sir."

He paused at the door just long enough to say, "You tell that pretty little filly of yours what I said, hear? I think it's one hell of a fine idea, her coming in here. Anything I can do to help, I will." Then he was gone.

When Betty was off the phone, I told her, "I think I like your boss. He's one of the good ones, isn't he?"

She beamed as if I'd complimented her. "He really is. You know, he was top salesman in the company before they brought him into the home office. Everybody's always asking him how he did it, what his secret was. He keeps telling them he never had any secrets, but I know better. His secret is he's the finest man I know."

Talk about falling in love with the boss, this kid had it bad. "That's some sales gimmick, but I don't think it'll ever catch on," I told her.

Bob Springer bounded in, and Betty introduced us. He had an oddly simian look: features a little too close together, torso of a six-footer perched on top of a pair of stubby bowlegs. He told me he was an instructor-trainee, just recently brought in from the field. He didn't waste any time trying to figure out where I fitted into the pecking order.

"You coming here to work?"

"You might say I'm taking a shortcut, Bob—I'm marrying my way in. Susan Neal and I are engaged, and I'm here to find out what makes this place tick."

"Congratulations! Mr. Burns wants you to have the works, and I guess you're entitled, so let's go."

I got the works. Dozens of isolated chambers, each with a

different pulse, disgorging colorful pills and capsules relentlessly. We had to slip on paper surgical masks before entering one room. Inside, nine women scurried about in a blizzard of fine, white dust. A bizarre stainless steel machine stamped out an endless river of pills. It dumped them into a hopper, carried them off on a belt, fed them into funneled measuring cups that rhythmically opened at the bottom to deposit the pills into small brown glass bottles. The source of the dust was a stamping machine at the far end. The faces and clothes of the women were uniformly white. They each wore caps, masks, full body coats, and disposable paper boots.

Bob plucked a tablet from the flowing river and offered it to me.

"What is it?"

"Antacid—try it. Best-tasting on the market."

I obliged with reluctance. It was amazingly creamy, almost like an after-dinner mint. Outside, we brushed off the chemical snow.

"Why were those three girls rushing up and down the conveyor belt?"

"All they do is pick out the broken pills. Never been able to automate that little trick. Too bad."

I shuddered, horrified at the thought of spending five days a week sealed up in a room with the machine-gun chatter of the stamping machine and chemical dust. The heavy stench of peppermint had been enough to gag a goat. I suddenly remembered Win's remark about gossip being the only relief from the crushing sameness of factory work.

We carried on through rooms that were supposedly sterile, where antibiotics were prepared and packaged. Then came labs full of thick, slate-topped tables and glassware of every conceivable shape. As we left one of the rooms at the far end of a hall, I could hear dogs barking.

"Guard dogs?" It might be something I'd need to know.

Bob hesitated. "Okay, follow me. This is interesting, but just remember—you asked."

He led the way through a door marked RESTRICTED. Inside, the entire left-hand wall was lined with three levels of wire cages. Dogs of every description went mad at the sight of us. The din was unbelievable. I detected something odd about a handsome German shepherd nearby. Edging closer, I could see an apparatus projecting from the crown of his head. There were two circular, coil-like objects with what could only be plugs on the ends, obviously meant to accept cables from monitoring devices on nearby benches. The dull metal cap stood out from the surrounding fur like an evil malignancy. The pitiable beast's eyes were wide with frenzy. The desperate sound of his bark was heartrending. The light was dim, but, before I had sense enough to look away, I realized many of the others had similar plates in their skulls.

Outside, I braced myself against the wall, denying a wave of nausea.

"That was probably stupid of me—I'm sorry," Bob apologized.

"Not your fault. My idea. But I wasn't prepared for anything like that. It's hideous! Like walking into a Bosch painting. Is that sort of thing really necessary?"

"I don't much like it either, but how else do we test the new compounds? We use rats, which doesn't seem to offend anyone for some reason, but some sort of higher life form is also needed. We buy a lot of rabbits from Australia. Used to get a lot of frogs and monkeys from Africa, but the cost went out of sight years ago. People bring us all the dogs we can use at twenty-five bucks a head, so we use dogs.

"It helps if you can rationalize the fact that they'd mostly be gassed at the pound anyhow. If the results are good, and safe enough all along the way, we end up using volunteers from certain state and federal prisons. Not here—the drugs are administered at the jails. The prisoners do it because it looks good on their records when they get in front of a parole board. Would you believe we catch more flak about the dogs than we do the people?"

"Why not? The poor mutts didn't volunteer. And the people don't end up with steel gizmos embedded in their skulls."

"True. As long as we're in the back of the building, we may as well have a look at the money pots."

"Want to run that by me again?"

"That's what we call them—money pots. You'll see."

Bob led the way through a pair of substantial steel doors. He stooped to wedge one open with a handy rock. The bright sun seared my eyes momentarily. Then I saw the three forty-foot structures that looked a lot like the old water towers that once existed alongside railroad tracks all across the country.

"I give up—what are they?"

"That's where we make heparin. It's an anticoagulant given to cardiac patients to thin their blood. Also used for thrombophlebitis and a few other things. Probably our biggest profit spread. All we have to do is pick up the lungs of any domestic animal—hogs are the best—from the local slaughterhouses and dump them up there in those housings. The lungs are used because they aren't any good for anything else, so we get them for practically nothing. As they age, the heparin is expressed. It's a totally natural substance. We all have to have it, or our blood would clot right in the vascular system. There's a little more to the process than that, but not much. You wouldn't believe what we charge for a few cc's of the stuff."

"You make it sound as if this is a pretty profitable business."

"I won't kid you, Matt. Back in the late fifties a Senate investigating committee looked into the pharmaceutical industry. At the end they summed it up by calling us the last of the robber barons. They never knew the half of it." Bob chuckled.

"Wasn't anything done after the committee published its findings?"

"Yes, in 1963 they changed the rules at the FDA so that we had not only to prove a new drug was safe but that it did what it was supposed to do. But for the most part, all such investigations blow it. They invariably argue the unfairness of a drug costing a fraction of a cent to manufacture being sold for, say, fifty cents. So the industry responds, sure, you could no doubt manufacture a cure for cancer with the sweepings off the Senate floor, but only after a couple of billion dollars is spent in research.

"We're a sacred cow, Matt. We've got the same thing going for us as religion—fear. Next to God, the thing people fear most is pain, illness, and death."

"But that's a valid point—about having to spend a fortune to develop a new drug, isn't it?"

"Not for most companies it isn't. Most of the money we blow is used to figure out different shapes and colors to make the same old products more marketable. The closest a lot of drug companies come to research is to figure out different combinations of the ingredients they have already gotten accepted by the FDA. And they buy or swap old formulas from each other. It saves millions of dollars and many years of delay and doubt, wondering if the government will ever let you market something new.

"The part about spending millions is certainly true, but not on research. The big money goes into sales. Figure it out yourself. It costs us on average maybe fifty dollars every time one of our salesmen calls on a doctor—two hundred and some salesmen making an average of eight calls a day. And that's only outside expenses."

"You're kidding! That adds up to over eighty thousand dollars a day just for your field force."

"Sell, sell, sell! How about some lunch?"

I was surprised not to find any long lines at the cafeteria until Bob explained that the lunch breaks were staggered so that production never halted during the workday. We sidled down the stainless rails past the rows of food. I selected the least offensive-looking fare—a bowl of chowder and a green salad.

Settled at a corner table, I pressed Bob for more information. "Tell me more about this racket. It's beginning to sound like a license to steal." Though it had nothing to do with the case, I found myself both repelled and fascinated by his obvious pride in being "one of the last of the robber barons." It was like listening to a pirate bragging about his booty.

He didn't require much encouragement. "It certainly can be that if it's done right. Here's an example: We make a pill to lower blood pressure, right? Now get this. We sell it under our trade name for twenty cents each to wholesalers. We sell the same product to large accounts on direct bid—the VA, foreign countries, the military services. Only they don't require a trade-name product; all they want is a generic equivalent. So the same pill from the same machine is shipped to them minus our logo on the pill. We sell tons of it that way at maybe eight to ten cents each."

I paused with a spoon of watery chowder halfway to my mouth. "In other words, you drop the price and sell it at a loss to prevent the competition from having the business."

"Hell, no! We make a good profit on the stuff we sell on bid. The point is, imagine the profit we make on the ones we sell at twenty cents apiece. The principle holds true for most of our drugs, and we're no different from the majority of the other companies."

"I don't get it. Why don't the doctors prescribe generic drugs and save their patients a bundle?"

"I doubt it'll ever become common practice. See, the doctors are hand in glove with us. Why do you think we've got all those salesmen out there? As a public service? We convince the docs the generics aren't as consistent or as effective. Lots of them dispense their own drugs, and those who don't often have an interest in a pharmacy. Ever wonder why they want to phone in the prescriptions for you? So they get their cut, that's why. Even the straightest of them get bound to us in any one of dozens of different ways. Maybe we helped pay his way through medical school; all the drug companies spend a bundle on scholarships for med students. And there's nothing a doc loves more than to conduct a so-called clinical study and get his name in the journals. Who do you think underwrites all those studies and does the technical research? They just about all do backflips to support the 'ethical' drug companies."

"I'm glad to hear we're ethical. I was beginning to have my doubts."

"Sorry to disappoint you—'ethical' refers to companies like Neal that don't engage in direct advertising to the consumer. The doctors hate that; it circumvents them. That antacid I gave you earlier is far superior to any on a grocer's shelves and any you see advertised on TV. We could run an ad campaign and eventually make a hell of an inroad into that over-the-counter market. But we'd be cutting our own throat with the doctors if we did. We never will.

"I'm telling you, Matt, we have literally dozens of ways of keeping the medicos on a leash. Tickets to a ball game. Box seats all season if your script count is high enough. And of course we give away more drugs than we sell."

"You can't be serious!"

"Like hell I'm not. What do you think I've been doing out in the field all these years? The rep's job is to dump as many samples as he possibly can—in the right place. We know exactly how much is sold and how much is given away, because we have to run them off in separate batches. The drugs we give away are supposed to have 'sample' or 'not for sale' clearly stamped on them. The reason for that is, a lot of the cheap bastards would sell the stuff we give them free. Even then, some doctors and pharmacists pay a kid to sand the 'sample' off the pill and sell them anyway."

"Sounds like a lot of work for very little return. Is it legal?"

"Hell, no! It alters the composition of the drug as well as the dosage, for Christ's sake. And the return isn't bad if you consider plenty of pills sell for over half a buck. A kid could do well over a hundred an hour, easy. Pay him minimum and you net fifty bucks an hour pure profit."

Bob seemed content to continue his oddly proud recital, but by this time I'd had enough. I gave up on the thin chowder and wilted salad and glanced at my watch as ostentatiously as possible. Jumping to my feet, I told him, "Oops, sorry, Bob, but it's nearly one-thirty. Thanks a million for the liberal education. I really appreciate it."

He looked stricken. "But there's lots more to see. Wait until you see the training center."

"Have to be another time. I'll tell Don Burns what a super job you did." That seemed to cheer him up. I beat it to the door and ran right into Harold.

He eyed me as if I were something he'd found swimming in his soup. "Having a good time, Mr. Doyle?"

"Fine, thanks. Sorry I can't join you for lunch—I've already eaten." I winked at him and left.

It occurred to me that since I knew where he was for the moment, it might be a good time to have a closer look at his part of the castle. With a few side trips, I managed to retrace my steps of a few days earlier and pulled up outside Harold's office. I opened the door and walked in to find Helga, Martha's plant, still in position.

"Hi, Helga. Mr. Herbert in?"

"No," she admitted grudgingly.

"How about you and me having a talk then?"

She treated me to a look suitable for curdling milk. "I'm busy."

I tried a new approach. "You were Mrs. Herbert's secretary, weren't you, Helga?"

"No."

"'No,' you weren't her secretary, or 'no,' you don't want to talk to me?"

"Yes."

I gave up. When it came to communicating, she was

maybe half a notch up from a brick wall. "Okay, Helga, but just remember—you're my dream girl."

I was now zero for two against the troll. Down the hall I came across a door labeled VICE-PRESIDENT, PRODUCTION. I went in and found the room empty. Opening the door to the inner sanctum, I surprised a man in the act of pouring a healthy portion of Seven High Bourbon.

"Who in the hell are you?" he demanded. A good forty pounds overweight, his ruddy face looked like a map of a rural county, with the secondary roads marked in purple. A pitted, tuberous nose nearly mated with his upper lip. Picture W. C. Fields and you'd be close.

"Matt Doyle, sir. Didn't mean to startle you, but I guess your secretary's at lunch and I'd really like to talk to you."

His expression was one of speculation, not concern. "So you're Doyle, eh? Sit, boy! Care for some of this? It's the only real miracle drug in the whole fucking place." He hoisted the quart bottle so I could read the label conveniently.

"Thanks, I'll pass for now. May I ask your name?"

"How come you're so all-fired hot to see me and you don't even know my name? Pete Durning. Reason I don't have one of those asinine little signs on my desk, everybody who should know me around here already does, and to hell with the rest. I helped Scotty, Scott Neal, Susan's father, start this cockeyed business nearly thirty years ago. Now I'm just hanging around to catch the last act. It's all over but the shouting, and I'm a little surprised to find I really don't give a good goddamn." He gravely lifted the dark, amber-filled glass in mock salute and took a long pull.

"How is it you know about me, Pete?"

"I doubt there's a soul around here by now who doesn't. The Pentagon could learn something, studying the powder room wireless we've got here. Got to be the most efficient communications system in the world."

I chuckled. "What's the morning line on me?"

Pete regarded me through pale, watery eyes. "The word is you're a second generation Harold Herbert."

It was ridiculous, but I couldn't stop it. I felt the heat rise in my face. "In that case your highly-touted powder room wireless may be efficient, but I wouldn't give a plugged nickel for its accuracy. Anybody says that to my face gets a long nap and a fat lip."

Pete figured to be one of the good old boys—Oklahoma, by the accent—no longer in vogue within the corporate circles. The Petes had once ruled supreme. Henry Ford was one; so was Edison. Short on formal education, long on ingenuity and loyal as a hound, they functioned best under adversity. Plenty of the *Fortune* 500 companies were solvent today because men like Pete had dug in their heels, stuck out the bad times, and held everything together with spit and bailing wire. But they didn't look good in three-piece suits, didn't like BMWs, drank straight liquor instead of drinking wine coolers and using nose candy, and had an embarrassing tendency to say what they really thought. It made the new wave of subtle manipulators nervous.

He nodded, ending his lengthy examination of me. "Look like you might could do a passable job at that, boy. Got a look about you. If I ever did have a talent, it was the ability to size folks up. I'd have to guess you're a man with some mean to him. Not like most of the young ones around here, all soft and round so nothin' sticks to 'em."

He wagged his head back and forth, laughing inwardly. "Pay me no nevermind. I just realized I'm starting to sound like my dear old grandpappy."

He was just what I needed—a living biography of the company and everyone in it. And he was in a contemplative mood. We were going to become buddies if it killed me.

"Does that offer of a drink still stand?"

Like most boozers, he was gratified at not having to drink alone. He fished a fairly clean tumbler from a drawer and filled it half full. I rinsed my lips with the oily liquid and smacked them in phony approval.

"Nice! Thanks, Pete. I'll bet you've seen it all, haven't you. But what happens next? Susan's concerned, so I am too."

"That gal of yours, she was the sweetest kid. Only a couple of years old when her daddy and me started all this. Used to pester me all the time to sit down so she could play 'horsey' on my foot. We didn't get much chance to sit in those days. Wasn't here—this monstrosity came along much later.

"Anyway, to answer your question, what happens now is we all tread water for a while till that donkey's behind up the hall flushes the rest of my life down the toilet. Not that it really matters. First Scotty, now Martha—there isn't much point left to it anymore. The fun's long gone. The team from Trans-United will arrive, shake their forty-dollar hairdos in disgust, and rush out to file lots of negative little reports. After that will come the efficient ones with the cold eyes. I'll be the first to go. God, how I hate the new breed with a calculator in one hand and a stop watch in the other. They hate me, too; I'm just an old rogue elephant. Too tough and too smart—a threat! So the first thing all the young bulls do is gang up to drive me away. It's human nature, I guess. Like I said—no complaints. My retirement account was fully funded years ago. Cheers." He raised his glass and tossed back a swig.

"What would you say if I told you it doesn't have to be that way? What if Susan decided to stake her claim here, stepped in to run the company, and put a stop to this merger?"

His rheumy eyes cleared, coming into sharp focus instantly. "Don't make any promises you can't keep, boy. That would be Christmas, New Year's, and every other damn holiday I ever heard of all rolled into one."

"No promises, Pete, but she is considering it. It'll make a difference, knowing where you stand."

He stared into space for half a minute, then shrugged his beefy shoulders. "I'm afraid she'd never pull it off. Too many of the young crowd around here favor the idea of the merger.

Silly twits think it'll give them more room to grow. Harold's had almost a year to peddle the idea."

"He still has to sell it to the stockholders."

"Don't know much about it, do you, boy? No problem there. Neal stock would convert to Trans-United at a very favorable ratio, they'll see to that. Stockholders will eat it up with a spoon."

"Susan's got a fair-sized block of shares already, and a huge chunk due from her mother's estate. She can make a fight of it, don't think she can't."

Pete cocked his head and grinned at me. "I should have known that little gal wouldn't have much quit in her. You tell her for me that I've got a fair chunk, too. She can count it in her corner for sure. And there are some old-timers left around here I can herd into line. I guess I've got enough starch left in me for one more good tussle. You better believe I have!" His seamed, old face was suddenly animated.

"I'll tell her. There's something else I'd like to run by you. Susan's preoccupied with her mother's murder right now, as you might well imagine. She thinks her stepfather may have had something to do with it. What are your thoughts?" I sat back and played with my drink and held my breath.

Pete inhaled clear down to his toes. "If he did, no one can prove it by me. If you're asking my opinion, no, definitely not."

"I'm not impressed with his alibi of the meeting here Sunday evening, Pete, if that's what you're going by. He was out of the room for about half an hour, remember?"

"Wasn't even thinking about that. Harold's nothing but a coward—he wouldn't have it in him. Give you an example: He picked the wrong man to bad-mouth on the phone once, something about a shipment shortage. Fella came out here looking for Harold with blood in his eye. The big baby ran into his private office and locked the door. Didn't show his face until an hour after the guards escorted the guy off the grounds. I laughed so hard I got my hernia to acting up again."

"That doesn't mean he couldn't commit a cowardly act of violence against a woman."

"I've learned to trust my instincts, boy—they're pretty reliable. Harold personally, no, but that's not to say he'd lose much sleep over hiring it done. If it was me, I'd take that up with the Nolte brothers."

"Nolte brothers?"

"Local pair of hoods. Harold likes to gamble now and then. More now than then, from what I hear."

"He bets the nags?"

"No, too much class and too public for our boy Harold. He apparently considers himself something of a poker buff, which is damned unfortunate, because he hasn't any of the qualities of a good player. I know, because I just happen to be one hell of a player myself. The Noltes accommodate his fantasy, and the word is he's dropped quite a bundle lately. It's at least some true because he got so desperate a couple of weeks ago he even hit me for a fair chunk of a loan. Maybe you can guess how far that got him." Pete savored the memory as he sipped his dwindling supply of bourbon.

"Humor me for a minute, Pete. That half hour he was out of the conference room roughly corresponds to the time of the murder. You knew that."

"I know, but he never left the building."

"That's only as good as Helga's word. Question is: How good is that?"

He chuckled. "That queer little duck? She's so straight you could use her for a ruler. If she needed a paper clip at home, she'd go out and buy some. She'd have walked through fire for Martha. I bet it must have broken both their hearts when Martha sent her over to bird dog Harold; Helga'd been her secretary ever since Scotty died. And you just know every move Harold made from then on went right back to his wife. If you're looking for me to back up your theory that Helga covered for Harold while he went out and murdered his wife, you couldn't be further off base if you took a rocket to the moon.

Helga loved her and hated him—doubt she'd give Harold a drink of water if he was dying of thirst. We kid the Horrible Hun, but the fact is she's one of the most valued and respected employees in the place. She all but ran this outfit several times when Martha took sick. Poor thing's loyal as a dog and about as good lookin'."

"Story of my life; there goes another perfectly fine theory down in flames. Say you're right, then. It wasn't Harold. And just for the sake of argument, say the Nolte brothers had nothing to do with it. Who's left? Others must have hated Martha enough to make the list."

He didn't hesitate a moment. "Nick Barber's the only name on the list as far as I know. Might have been one other, but that was four years ago, and he's long since got over his mad."

"Tell me about that last one."

"Sorry I mentioned it—shouldn't have. If you must know, Donny Burns was trying to romance Martha hot and heavy back then. In fact, that's why she took so much time away—to make up her mind. Donny felt sure she'd give him the nod when she came back. Him and me and Scotty and Martha were all like family. Donny went pretty crazy when she waltzed back in here with that lounge lizard on her arm. Put Harold right on in as second in command, too. We all resented it, but Donny got purely mean about it. You'd think it'd be Harold's pelt he wanted, but no, he blamed Martha. Threatened to do lots of insane things, including break her neck.

"Now before you get all het up, boy, understand it was just drunk talk. Donny's as fine a man as ever walked the earth. He got himself some shrink who must have done him a lot of good, because it was no time at all before Donny was back to his old self and able to sit across a conference table from her without clenching his fists and turning beet-red. They went right back to their old relationship of cussin' each other and thoroughly enjoying it. Don't waste your time on that line of country."

"All right, then tell me about this Nick Barber."

"Hard driver. Tough and determined, you know the type. Reads all the books about how you got to walk over everybody else to get to the top. Started as a salesman down in Phoenix. Made district manager in record time. Drove his men hard and kept going up like a rocket until three months ago. Came in as a regional manager, one of only four in the company. This brought him into Martha's path for the first time, and the sparks began to fly. I was at their first meeting, and it was the worst case of bad chemistry I've ever seen or heard of. She demoted him right back down into the field. Not back to district manager, mind you—all the way back to Square One—rookie salesman. And he'd been out of the field for over ten years.

"I hear his wife took it hard, left him. Word is, she was mad at him for blowing everything they'd worked for all those years. Refused to hang around in limbo, waiting to find out what godforsaken territory he'll finally get. While he's waiting for a spot to come open he's working in the training center. I understand he hates it. Probably true, because there's a big push on right now to get more women into the field and the current class is nearly half females. Martha may have had that in mind when she put him there; she could be a vindictive bitch when she wanted. You've got to understand, Nick is one of the world's great chauvinistic porkers. It must be hell for him. He's also suffering from a bad case of hoof-and-mouth disease, which is why he's there in the first place. He's been heard making noises about getting even for what she did to him. Pretty dumb, though, if he was serious. And no way is he dumb. Wouldn't want to say what he's capable of, but he is a mean one. You'll see that in him right off."

"Was Nick Barber at your meeting Sunday?"

"Would've been if he'd known when to shut his mouth. Only meetings he's got rank for now are held in the cafeteria. They're called coffee breaks."

I put down the glass of bourbon, still one-third full, and

stood up. "Thanks for all of it, Pete. I'll be letting you know soon what Susan decides. Your support may swing the vote."

"She used to call me Unca Peety, not long after she first learned to talk. You tell her Unca Peety is still here whenever she needs him."

I left and hurried down the long hall, searching for a clue to the whereabouts of the training center. A door marked ADMINISTRATION looked promising. I found Bob Springer inside. His eyes lit up.

"You decide to finish the tour, Matt?"

"Not now, Bob, I really need to talk to Nick Barber right away. Point me toward the training center."

"Nick? I'm afraid he's gone for the rest of the day. Dental appointment or something like that."

"Thanks. See you later, then." I'd run out of fresh ideas, so I elected to head back to the office and report. Win had said he wanted facts—"data," as he called it. I'd give him facts. My work would soon be over for the day—his was about to begin.

CHAPTER 10

*I*t took me nearly two hours to deliver the details to Win. He often stopped me to ask clarifying questions, sometimes even insisting on getting tones and facial expressions exactly. I dream of delivering a report without a single interruption. I know it's only a dream. At times like this it became painfully obvious how maddening it was for Win not to be able to go out into the field and observe and experience things firsthand. But he couldn't—we'd tried it once or twice. The trouble is, you can't observe something when your very presence creates change. Win was unique. One pundit had referred to him as a "national treasure." The result was he couldn't enter a room without becoming the center of attention. Fine for a movie star, but a distinct disadvantage for a detective.

"Unless you've got a better idea, I'll get back out there in the morning for a long hard look at this Nick Barber."

"Do so." He sounded distracted. "This gambling aspect nettles. It bears investigation, but I'm at a loss how to proceed."

"Leave it to me. Your trouble is, you're only used to dealing with presidents and kings. You've neglected the true aristocracy of our time. Barber in the morning, and the Brothers Nolte after that. Should work out fine. I doubt they're early risers."

"It is understood you are to take no unnecessary risks. Dirk will accompany you on the latter call."

"Don't need him. What do you make of all this so far? I think Harold's alibi stretches the laws of coincidence beyond the breaking point. I'm not buying it."

"I'm inclined to agree. I once had a secretary who'd happily have sworn I was on Mars if I'd asked it. But I doubt he'd rely on Helga's steadfastness as an accomplice when she loathes him and was an intimate of the victim. If Mr. Herbert is culpable, it would appear he is once removed from the crime itself."

"Maybe. Now, I'm headed for a shower. What do I tell our client when I see her tonight?"

"Use your own discretion. Nothing need be withheld, with the exception of your Mr. Springer's appalling account of the ethics of the pharmaceutical industry. It should hearten her to know there are those in high places who would support her claim to stewardship of the company."

At the door I stopped to ask a question that had surfaced in my mind several times during the day. "By the way, what was Dixon's reaction when you told him about the letters? I was half-expecting Dixon to show up at the plant and drag Harold back downtown for another serious round of grilling."

Without batting an eye, he replied, "I have retained the letters thus far."

My jaw dropped. "Are you nuts? I told you the score with those things. We've been sitting on them for two days now. Dixon'll crucify me."

"You are fully aware of my antipathy for that man. But if you feel such a strong sense of civic duty concerning those letters, see that he gets them." He reached into a drawer and tossed me the bundle.

"Yeah, swell, I'll do that right now. It'll save them the trouble of coming all this way to arrest me."

I still took time for a long shower. It seemed prudent, given the crowded jail conditions I kept reading about. By the time I pulled into the parking lot of the old Spanish hacienda-style building at Market and Pacific Coast Highway, I'd come up with a way of staying clear.

Trotting across the street to a pay phone, I rang the Plaza. "Susan? Me, your fiancé—remember? Are we on for dinner tonight?"

"We'd better be. I'm famished. I think I got all the ugly-uglies out of my system last night. Please come soon—I truly am starving."

"Okay, just one thing. Unless you want to see me behind bars in the next five minutes, I need your help. Win, the ignoramus, didn't bother to turn over your mother's letters to the police. I'm doing it now. I have to. Not only is it the law, but they might very well be a substantial portion of the evidence needed to convict Harold. Now, you're just an ignorant private citizen—no offense. The letters belong to you, so there's a huge difference between your holding onto them until now and my doing it. Legally, I'm an officer of the court, and I'm supposed to know better."

"Tell me what to do. It's not that I mind the idea of your going to jail so much—you've probably got it coming—it's just that I can't face eating alone in my room again."

"Cute! Here's what we do. It's nearly five. Say I left there, your suite at the Plaza, around four-forty-five. You just showed me the letters for the first time, and I couldn't wait to rush over here and deliver them to the proper authorities. Got it?"

"Sure, you left here with the letters fifteen minutes ago. Drop them off and hurry back—I miss you already."

"On my way."

I hurried back across the street and entered the arch leading into a central court. The red tiles on the edge of the roof were uneven, and the stucco was badly cracked here and there. Still, the place had a lot more charm than any other police station I'd ever seen. I followed the covered walkway around to Homicide Division and went in.

Three guys were hunched over their terminals. One glanced up at me and nodded toward the rear. I couldn't remember his name, so I just waved. The Inspector sat in his shirt-sleeves in an untidy, little office. A Styrofoam cup of coffee leaked slowly onto his battered desk. I didn't like the wolfish grin on his pudgy face.

"My, my, if it isn't Mr. Matthew Doyle in person. Such an honor. What brings you down to the slums?"

"My civic duty, Inspector. You may find these interesting reading." I handed over the thin bundle of five letters.

He removed the top one, opened it, scanned it quickly, then looked up at me. I had yet to be invited to sit. "I suppose there's a story goes with these?" His smirk was entirely inappropriate to the situation. He should have been shouting wild accusations at me by now. I was beginning to worry.

"Not much of one. The letters belong to the addressee, Susan Neal. As it happens, she's retained our services to look into her mother's murder. Brought those letters with her from New York and just showed them to me a few minutes ago. It occurred to me they might constitute motive, perhaps even evidence, so here they are. Just like it says in the book. No charge, and I do not accept gratuities. But I would like photocopies if you would be so kind." I thought the request for copies was a nice touch.

Dixon leaned back in his chair until it groaned in protest. He was grinning broadly—a rare and unnerving sight. "That's exemplary. I'd like a record of this to show future generations what a fine citizen you were. How would it be if I bring in a machine and have you say it again, just for the record?"

Now I knew there was something seriously wrong. I had no idea how it had gone wrong, but I could feel a ton of bricks poised somewhere overhead, about to fall on me. Worse yet, I had no idea which way to jump.

"I'm really in kind of a hurry. Ms. Neal is waiting for me."

"Kind of a hurry, are you, Doyle? I'm sorry as hell to hear that, because you're just going to have to adjust your busy little schedule. You're under arrest. *Sit down!*"

"It's too late to be polite—you should have invited me to sit when I first arrived. What's the charge?"

"Withholding evidence in a homicide. A capital murder case, Doyle. It'll cost you a couple of years, hot shot. And you can forget you ever owned a license." He was enjoying this, he really was. What he didn't say, but I knew he was thinking, was: This is for the Bowen case. That was an old murder case that Dixon had once declared closed and had then gone to the Grand Jury with the wrong man. Win had been so incensed at what he considered Dixon's blindness that when we solved the case we took it to the District Attorney, thus leaving Dixon alone out in left field looking like an absolute ass. The papers had had a field day. I'd actually felt sorry for him at the time. Now I felt sorry for me.

"What withholding? I just handed you the evidence. Assuming it turns out to be evidence."

"Dumb, Doyle. I've been expecting you. Your boss called twenty minutes ago. Told me he was fully responsible for the decision to sit on these letters since Tuesday. *Two goddamn days!* You pocketed them for two days, and then had the brass balls to walk in here like a Boy Scout looking to earn a merit badge. I told you your cute little tricks would trip you up someday. This, my friend, is the day."

"If I'm arrested, I'm entitled to a phone call. I'd like to make it now." I was shaking, trying hard to control my seething anger. The fact that Win had meant well wasn't much consolation at the moment. As a team, it would seem we needed a few more practice sessions.

"Sure, wise guy—use mine. Later I can have it bronzed. I think I'll put it in my den, right under your old license, which I'm going to mount on my wall like some guys put up stuffed heads."

He strutted out, laughing obscenely. He said something I couldn't catch to the other three, and they all looked at me and joined in the laughter. It was definitely going to be a long night.

I used my allotted call to alert Susan to the situation. At least she could stay clear, in case Dixon attempted to include her in his vendetta. I wouldn't have put it past him. She promised to relay the good news to Win. I was tempted to give her a truly nasty message for him, but I bit my tongue.

Dixon returned as soon as I hung up the phone. "Hope your lawyer was in."

"Actually, I used the call to break a dinner engagement with a lady. That should please you."

"Oh, my, yes; I'm very pleased," he assured me smugly. "The lady would be too, if she knew you as well as I do. Let's go."

"I hate to get technical, but aren't you supposed to read me some facts about my rights off a card or something?"

"Don't shit me, Doyle; you've probably got the Miranda tattooed on your chest. Read it to yourself."

He led the way outside to his official car. It was no way to conduct a dangerous felon, but he may have had snipers posted. A bored-looking patrolman opened the door for us, and we climbed in the back together like chums. It killed me to see his face; he was so obviously savoring every second.

We made the six-block run over to the city jail, where I spent the next forty-five minutes remaining stoic about being folded, spindled, and mutilated. When my initiation was over, I was nattily attired in threadbare green cotton trousers and shirt instead of the plum tropical worsted I'd come in with. The green cotton outfit did nothing for me. It wasn't me. I was led into a small room, lavishly furnished with three metal folding chairs. Dixon straddled one; there was a tape recorder set up on another. I folded myself into the third and awaited developments.

"You know the drill, Doyle. We can both get our sleep tonight or we can spend the night playing games. It's up to you entirely. Some people say I'm not at my best if I don't get my full eight hours, so how about we turn on the machine and get it over with?" His pie-plate face was split by an obscene grin. He reminded me of one of the kids from the old *Our Gang* one-reelers but I couldn't remember his name. It was the one the other kids were always playing tricks on because he was too fat to run.

I crossed my legs and smiled gaily. "Sure, we're pals, aren't we? Turn the little sucker on."

He gave me a suspicious look, hit the "record" switch, and spoke into the hand mike, giving it names, date, and time. His first question was, "Do you admit you received five letters from Susan Neal Tuesday, November fourth, two days ago?"

"I haven't the faintest idea."

"Don't come on cute now, Doyle—I'm warning you. Answer the question."

"Sorry, I can't remember a thing. Maybe I fell down on the way in here. I think these pants are to blame. Just look at the way they hang down over my shoes."

Dixon jabbed the "stop" switch savagely. "You're in no position to be funny. You got any idea how much trouble you're in? This only makes it worse."

"Who are you?" I inquired innocently. "More to the point, who am I?"

"Without the tape running then, damn you! In your own words: When and where did you first see those five letters?"

"I don't remember any letters. Are you sure it was us? Maybe it was two other guys."

He only lasted about half an hour. The last I saw of him, he was stalking out, muttering something about riding the DA's office to make damn sure I got two years, minimum.

Someone else soon took his place. He was a thin, pale

guy of indeterminate age with a faraway look in his eyes. He didn't seem the least bit interested in the proceedings. He fed me the identical questions endlessly, reading from a sheet of paper, his voice flat, and never listening to my answers. He wasn't much fun. After nearly three hours he left, too.

I knew the quiet time of lulling me into a false sense of security was over. Sure enough, within minutes—enter the tiger. This one was rapier-thin, quick-moving, and very, very intense. He didn't ask me questions—he lashed me with them as if they were whips. The cadence never varied. One question after each puff of an endless cigarette. His angle was catching me off guard by springing a totally unexpected question sandwiched in between the now familiar ones. I had to concentrate to stay ahead of this guy. He tried some cute tricks, including questions about the likely sexual habits of five men living together. The density of smoke in the tiny room became brutal. The worst mistake I made all night was to ask if I could be seated in the "no smoking" section next time. From then on all his exhaust was directed right in my face. I soon developed a splitting headache. Fortunately he got into a coughing jag and had to call it quits after a couple of hours. If the guy's lungs had held out another half hour I'd have gladly confessed to anything, including the Lindbergh kidnapping.

No one came to take his place. Forty minutes passed before a guard showed up and herded me toward a cell. I was ready. Neither of the two bunks was occupied, so I dropped into the nearest one and lay there, trying to rub away the throbbing pain in my head. The smell was thick enough to slice with a knife. The keen aroma of disinfectant couldn't begin to overpower the stench of years' accumulation of sour urine and stink of naked fear. I fell into fitful sleep, awakened frequently by the sounds of people coming and going past my cell. I vaguely remember switching bunks at some point to get some relief from the light in the corridor. It didn't help.

I gave up trying after a passing guard reluctantly admitted the time was nearly 7:00 A.M. My headache had receded to nothing worse than a dull throb. Later, breakfast was served, about which the less said the better. Since no one had offered to feed me the night before, my usual standards were somewhat flexible anyway. The rest of the morning didn't last much more than a week. Finally a guard pulled up and unlocked the door to my cage.

"Don't leave nothin'. You ain't comin' back. I think your Shylock's here to spring you."

What the hell did I have to leave behind? "'Don't leave nothing' is a double negative, my good man. Technically it means I should leave something behind."

"Suit yourself."

My clothes were restored to me—they'd lost track of my dignity—and I was asked to sign a statement to the effect that all my possessions had been returned intact. After signing, I was given a sealed manila envelope supposedly containing everything they'd stripped me of on the way in. It did, but I still maintain the system is back asswards.

One last locked door was opened and I was free to endanger society once again. Waiting on the other side was a tall, lanky fellow, pale, with straight straw-colored hair and restless eyes.

"You Doyle?" he asked me.

"Used to be. Now I'm just another ex-con. A cipher among men. Nothing more than a blister on the butt of the world."

"Yes, I was warned about your . . . sense of humor; I'm glad to see it's intact. I'm Hoffman Price, legal type. Let's get out of here. It doesn't smell too pleasant."

"You take me, you take the smell, I'm afraid."

We hoofed it for about a block until we arrived at his car.

"Can I give you a lift home?" he offered.

"Thanks, my car's at the station on Market. I'll walk there. It feels good. What was the tab on me?"

"Bond was twenty thousand. Two thousand and change to post it. Started at fifty, but I was able to get the judge to give consideration on the basis of your employer. Still more than was warranted, but so it goes."

"What about the charges? Can that fat ape Dixon make them stick?"

Hoffman scratched his head, frowning. "I really don't see how. Somebody jumped the gun on this. They've got an awfully steep legal hill to climb in order to convict. First they have to prove the letters are evidential. To do that, they're going to have to solve the Herbert murder, and, I think, integrate the letters into the prosecution's case. Then, there's the fact that you did turn them over—belatedly. That's when we'd open the whole can of worms of the privileged relationship existing between a licensed private detective and his client. It's very muddy water, and it's never been properly defined by the courts. We'll know more about how hard the DA is going to push it when your preliminary comes up in ten days."

"And my license?"

"Pulled—temporarily. Both yours and Mr. Winfield's. But that's nothing more than simple harassment. I'll be able to get them reinstated the minute the charges are dismissed."

I loved the way he brushed aside the fact of my unemployment and pending prosecution. He was certainly intrepid in the face of my peril.

"I hadn't considered that. So Win's in the same box?"

Hoffman nodded happily. "He certainly is. It's an interesting situation. Can't very well drag him into court though, can they? I relish a case like this—it has so many truly unique aspects."

"Remember how much fun it was when you send us your bill. I'm in one hell of a spot and you're having orgasms of ecstasy. What do you say I go out and plug somebody—that should really cheer you up."

He drove off laughing. My theories about lawyers remained intact. They must get innoculated for feelings and they're all a little weird.

I set a brisk pace back to my car, feeling a bit more

human with every step. The engine was running before I noticed the paper under my wiper blade. It was a parking citation for leaving my car overnight in a one-hour zone. Four lousy bucks was all it would cost, but it said something about Dixon. I added petty to my list of his attributes. Then, in order to be fair, I had to add paranoia to a list of my own. It was entirely likely that the ticket had resulted from a routine sweep of the lot.

The world appeared flamboyant as I motored north on 5. Everything was as overdone as a Disney animated movie. Just seventeen hours in that gray environment of jail had affected me more than I cared to admit. It made me wonder how I'd handle seventeen months. If a certain inspector of Homicide could swing it, I'd soon be finding out.

I drove the short stretch between the freeway and the house slowly, fighting to contain the banked rage that was still threatening to flare over Win's untimely phone call. For a guy who was frequently referred to as a genius, he sure knew how to pull a boner with the best of them.

As I walked into the office, I was impressed with how great everything continued to look to me. Win closed his ever-present book, regarding me in silence for a moment. Then he quietly asked, "Which of us was the bigger fool, do you think, Matt?"

It was a valid question. "How about we just call it a draw? It's like the warden told Cool-Hand Luke: 'What we have here is a failure to communicate.'" I realized I'd just gotten a glimpse of the great negotiator he'd been. With that one simple question he'd doused the fires in my gut.

"Needless to say, in future we must strive for improved coordination of effort. Never improvise such an impulsive act again without conferring. Whatever possessed you . . ."

He should have quit while he was ahead. "Leave it lay, Win. I'm giving you sound advice—drop it! If we start discussing improvising impulsive acts, I'm bound to have a few thoughts of my own." I could feel my face warming.

"I see that you are not entirely yourself. Quite understandable. Very well; state it that culpability is to be divided equally."

His face registered dismay as I approached my desk. "What in heaven's name is that loathsome odor?"

"It is I. Or is it me? Sorry I offend. If they put another jail bond issue on the ballot, I think we ought to vote for it."

"I can scarcely even speculate upon your ordeal, Matt. But are the penal facilities so overcrowded that you were forced to spend the night in a urinal?"

I took the hint and backed up a few steps. "I see you've managed to nail down the essence. Actually, I had a private room, but the result's about the same. I understand it's customary among the inner circle to use the walls; probably some sort of editorial comment. See you later—after several showers and doubles at lunch."

After a marathon shower I called Susan. We made a date to dine that evening, assuming I could make it all that way without being incarcerated. Then I established a house record by consuming three of Louis's Black Bulls, which pleased him enormously. A Black Bull's a super sandwich he must have seen a picture of and duplicated successfully, for once. It featured dark rye bread wrapped around some ground steak and smothered in two or more melted cheeses and sauerkraut. It tickled me to see him so pleased. You'd think his kitchen was the Manhattan Project and he was Dr. Teller.

Back at my desk, I waited out the inevitable final paragraph before he could put down the book. Once, I'd kidded Win about reading so many novels instead of sticking to nonfiction. I said I thought there must be plenty of "real" books around, so why waste all that time on a story some clown just dreamed up? He replied that people who never read novels were emotionally stunted, too limited in their perceptions. He claimed that novels allowed one to experience many lives, many viewpoints, thus gaining understanding and a greater depth of emotion. Too many of us have only a single narrow standard to bring to bear, he explained, but fiction readers had many. He insisted he could see things from the eyes of anyone from a suburban housewife to an African pygmy because he'd walked around in so many heads reading well-written novels. He even had a theory that if some way could be found to get everybody reading good fiction, it would solve most of the world's problems in no time. He was half-convinced, he'd told me, the only reason Russia and the United States hadn't yet gone to war was because too many of us had read Tolstoy and Dostoyevsky and too many of them had read Hemingway and Steinbeck.

That's the sort of thing I get when I make the mistake of opening my mouth around the office.

Win finally looked up. "Are you equal to resuming your work?"

"As equal as I ever was. But have you forgotten our licenses have been suspended?"

"That's of little consequence. Our sword over Harold Herbert remains intact. Today is Friday. I'd like you to interrogate Nick Barber before he's lost to us over the weekend."

"Dixon will think it's of considerable consequence if he gets wind of it. If he finds I'm still functioning as an investigator he'll land on me with both feet."

"Nonsense, you merely humor the wishes of your betrothed by learning something of the business that is hers by familial patrimony."

"Write it down for me. That's what I'll tell him as he's slipping on the cuffs. 'Familial patrimony,' I'll scream. It might confuse him—last night she was a client, today a fiancée. I'll admit I'd love to have a look at this Barber, though. If it turns out Harold isn't our man, Nick sounds like the perfect understudy. What the hell—I'm off."

Halfway to the door I stopped. "Something I'd like to

know. Who's paying the two grand plus legal fees spent getting me out?"

His lush eyebrows lifted in surprise. "The client, of course. Any such ancillary expenditures will be itemized and added to Miss Neal's statement under the general heading of expenses."

"Except we only got a grand up front. Want me to hit her up for another chunk tonight? We're having last night's dinner tonight."

"Certainly not! If you failed to anticipate expenses adequately, we may scarcely hold her to account. We will honor the agreement to collect the balance due when the case is satisfactorily concluded."

I shrugged, closing the door behind me. I loved the way he talked as if the job would be finished in a day, maybe two at the most. So far, by my count, we had lost our means of livelihood and were in the hole more than a thousand bucks. Worse, I thought Harold had committed the murder somehow and was going to get away with it. This wasn't a case; it was more like a bad dream.

CHAPTER 11

I'd kept my visitor's pass in case Harold had changed the rules and Snaggle-Tooth wouldn't let me in again. I parked the car at the far end of the lot, then walked to the back of the building where the trio of hogs' lungs was efficiently converting throw-away viscera into dollar-a-drop heparin. I stuck the badge back on and kicked the door. A young man in a soiled white coat opened the door and peered out hesitantly.

"Thanks," I told him, as I pulled it wide and brushed on by. "Just stepped out to check the heparin vats. I put a rock down to hold the door open, but I guess the wind got it."

A few minutes of brisk walking got me to the training center without encountering any familiar faces. There was a woman doing some filing in the office with the door open. I asked her where I could find Nick Barber.

"You want to see Nick Barber?" Her tone clearly implied disbelief that anyone would voluntarily want to do so.

When I confirmed it, she pointed across the hall. "In there somewhere. There's classes going on, so I don't know if he can see you, but that's where he's at."

Automatically noting that her legs were far superior to her

grammar, I crossed into a room about the size of a basketball court. Half a hundred men and women were scattered around, some staring raptly into audiovisual monitors, and others studying colorful promotional literature. I asked the nearest one to point me toward Nick Barber. He scanned the room quickly. "That's the Nazi over there in the gray suit."

Approaching Nick, I had to agree with the accuracy of the brief, one-word description. "Nazi" fit him. His light hair was worn in a crew cut; his eyes were the blue of a winter sea. Chiseled features over a bull neck reinforced the image of a slightly overaged poster boy for the Brown Shirts. He was intent on the scene before him. A man and a young woman sat facing each other across a desk. I assumed the man was a doctor because he was wearing a stethoscope around his neck. The girl was offering him a brochure and pitching the blazes out of some drug. The whole scene was being reproduced off to one side on an in-studio monitor.

"Nick Barber? Can you break away for a minute? I need to talk to you."

The cold eyes washed over me, and he held up two fingers. They formed no obscene gesture I was aware of, so I took it to mean a couple of minutes. He'd returned his full attention to the sales simulation. Having nothing better to do, I watched too. Apparently the idea was for the doctor to throw stumbling blocks in the way of the salesperson to see how well she handled them. The trainee's hands were shaking, and she had a film of sweat on her, but she was definitely game. Finally the pitch ended and the two shook hands.

Nick walked over to the woman. "You blew it every way I know, and some I never even thought of, Paula. He handed you half a dozen openings on a silver platter—lead-ins, code words—you remember we talked about them? You failed to pick up on any of them. You left that physician without a single convincing argument to cause him to alter his prescribing habits, or to even give your product a try. Haul your dumb butt into the film library and study tape number thirty-three until I get back. Then we'll review the film just taken of your pitch, dissecting it line by line. Frankly, I think it's a waste of my time, but we'll do it anyway."

I couldn't help thinking, Lucky you, Paula. It was a toss-up whether she was going to make it to some private place in time before the crying began.

Nick looked around and found me. Beckoning, he led the way to a small conference room. Inside was a long, narrow table surrounded by a dozen chairs. He hooked out a chair with his foot at the far end and sat, glaring at me mutely.

"My name is Matt Doyle. I'm making some inquiries for my fiancée, Susan Neal. Frankly, I'd like to know how you'd feel about her taking over. There's some talk you don't much care for women executives." I wanted to rattle his cage and see how he reacted. Selecting a chair midway down the table from him, I sat too. He looked very fit, so I figured it was close enough.

Our eyes probed each other. His eyes were as fixed and soulless as those of a large, poisonous snake. "Doyle, you're a lying son of a bitch." Still his eyes didn't flicker; his voice was devoid of anger or any other inflection. It was a simple stated fact, of little or no interest to the speaker.

"What kind are you, Nick?"

"What kind?"

"Of a son of a bitch. Are you a murdering son of a bitch? It's no secret you owned a very big hate for Martha Herbert. Then suddenly she's turned up dead. Makes me wonder what kind you are, Nick."

Now I'd gotten his interest. In fact, it was quite a sight to watch his neck swell and his face go all splotchy and dark. "If you've got a badge, creep, produce it fast, or I'm going to redecorate the walls with you."

He rose slowly to his feet, fists clenched. You always hoped at times like these they'd go a little crazy and make mistakes, but I could see that wasn't the way it was going to be. Nick was going to be the methodical type. He'd been there before. We were about the same height and weight. He carried more of his around his middle, but I knew he'd be strong as a bull.

I followed his lead and got up. "It's interesting to find you're the type that begins punching people when you're upset, Nick. I wonder, does that include helpless, middle-aged women? Martha Herbert upset you pretty badly, didn't she? Where were you last Sunday night, Nick? You weren't here at the meeting because she'd kicked your ass all the way back to the bottom of the ladder. A single punch killed her, Nick. You like hitting people, don't you?"

His face was an ugly mask of hate, but he maintained control. Slowly, with relish, he moved along the table toward me. A step and a half away, he lunged and launched a left at my face. I snagged it easily enough with my forearm, but it was merely a decoy. The real plan was to bounce me off the ceiling with a sizzling right coming all the way up from his shoelaces. Had I been fractionally slower, it would have worked beautifully. As it was, he had to settle for grazing my cheek as I spun sideways and jerked my head away.

That made it my turn. Before he could regroup, I took full advantage of his momentary lack of balance. Grabbing his lapels, I pulled him in to me hard and launched myself backward. I braced him with my knees as he fell on top of me. The instant my back hit the floor I extended my legs with all the force I could muster, while continuing my backward momentum. The results were extremely gratifying. Nick performed a first-class cartwheel, ending up beyond me, flat on his back. By the time he stopped bouncing, I was kneeling over the remains. For a finale I hammered him just under the sternum with the heel of my fist.

Nick lay there with his eyes wide, fully conscious, but utterly paralyzed. The only signs of life were his fingers twitching spasmodically and his dilated pupils following my every move.

"You're a lot of fun, Nick. I'll bet that sucker punch of

yours has worked for you in half the bars in Phoenix. We'll be talking again soon." I patted his face lightly a few times, looking deep into his eyes. I wanted him to remember this helpless feeling and the humiliation. It would save a lot of time when we next met.

I ambled out of the conference room, closing the door behind me. As I crossed the training center, I smiled and nodded happily at people. Provoking him into a fight had served some small service. I'd gotten a crash course on Nick's violence quotient—it was very high. And, just as an added bonus, I felt great.

On my way back down the hall I ran into the hard-drinking Pete Durning, lumbering toward me, splay-footed.

"Matt!" He glanced furtively up and down the corridor. "You sure don't fool around, do you, boy?"

"Hi, Pete. Sure wish I knew what the hell you're talking about."

He went dumb while three people passed, then went on in his guttural whisper, good for listening at twenty yards, easy. "What I am talking about is Harold's arrest. And don't waste time playing dumb with me—I figure it was your doing."

I shook my head reflectively. "You're giving me a news flash, Pete. Honest! But I doubt you really mean they arrested him. They've just taken him in for another round of questioning, I imagine. It's overdue." The letters would suggest a lot of new questions, but no way did they amount to beans as far as solid evidence went. They *couldn't* have arrested Harold—if they had, then evidence had surfaced somewhere else. And if they had him, it meant they had me, too, for hanging onto those damn letters.

"If you say so," Pete said, obviously unconvinced. "They dragged him out of here half an hour ago. Arrested for murder, according to what Helga said when I passed her in the hall. Yesterday I told you I didn't think he had it in him, but I've been wrong before. I mean, they wouldn't have arrested him unless they had some pretty convincing proof, would they?"

"You never know, Pete. I know a guy got arrested just last night for no good reason. Thanks for the bulletin. I've got to run."

"Yeah, me too. Looks like I'm in charge around here, God help me."

I was out the door and home in half the time it had taken me going the other way. Maybe it was my rapid breathing, but something tipped Win. He waited expectantly from the moment I entered the office.

"Dixon arrested Harold less than an hour ago."

"That is absurd! On what grounds?" It was almost amusing to realize, Win was outraged that the police would have the audacity to arrest one of his own suspects.

"No details available yet. Wait—I'll try a phone call." I snatched my phone and hit the private number of one Gloria Stern, Public Relations Assistant for the SDPD. She was a boating nut, too; we belonged to the same sailing club.

"Gloria? It's me, Captain Bligh. This number I called is a direct private line—right?"

"It is. Why?"

"Top security call. Do the skipper you love a favor. Run down the hall and have a chat with the girls on the switchboard. Inspector Dixon arrested a guy named Harold Herbert exactly one hour ago. Find out what the formal charges are, if any, and call me right back."

"Are you nuts? I won't spy for you here. What are you trying to do to me?"

"Nothing, really. It's hardly a state secret when you people arrest someone, is it? I'd call Dixon, except I'm mad at him today. Hell, honey, it'll be in the morning papers."

There was a long fifteen-second silence on the line. "I'll see if anyone knows about it," she told me stiffly, "but I don't like this, Matt."

"Bless you, my child. You're hereby promoted from deckhand right up to chief petty officer." I hung up and grinned at Win.

"How's that, boss? I've got a pipeline right into the heart of the enemy camp."

"Fortuitous. I laud your ingenuity, if not your moral standards. Did you find an opportunity to interview Mr. Barber?"

"Therein lies a tale. Until the moment I heard about Harold, I was ready to switch my bet to Nick. I'll give it to you verbatim. See what you make of it."

The replay took only two minutes. There hadn't been much dialogue, and the brawl had been short and very sweet.

Win surprised me by looking concerned. Sometimes I forget how much he abhors violence. "You're certain he's quite all right? Should you have left him alone like that?"

"He's in a lot better shape than I'd have been if his haymaker had connected. Which it damn near did. All I did was stun the nexus of nerves in his solar plexus. Under the circumstances I did him a favor. By now he's back on his feet without a mark on him. No doubt making the lives of his trainees pure hell."

Win was quiet for a while. "Your Mr. Barber would appear to be a direct and rather sanguinary sort. You believe him capable of murder? I ask for an opinion based on your best judgment. Fortunately, not many people are, you know."

"No doubt in my mind. Remember, he blamed all his troubles on Martha Herbert, and he's got a barrel of troubles. No more wife. Has to go back to pounding a beat God knows where. If it's not Harold, I definitely want to get a bet down on Nick—on the nose."

"Has it occurred to you that an indictment of either does not necessarily exclude the other? Didn't you find his conduct toward you suggestive?"

"You call it suggestive—I call it mayhem."

"Don't you recall I told you it might prove providential that Mr. Herbert knew your true colors? I stated if someone shared that knowledge, it would indicate a privileged relationship. It would appear one does indeed exist between Mr.

Herbert and Mr. Barber. It's the only cogent explanation of his behavior today."

"That's a point. I hadn't thought about it, but I guess the last thing he'd do is tee off on the guy he really believed was marrying the girl who might be his future boss. Maybe he is tight with Harold. How's this sound: Harold has to kill his wife because he's about to get the boot and there's a fortune at stake with this merger deal lurking in the wings. But he hasn't got the guts to do it himself; everybody agrees on that. He knows Nick has a big hate on for his wife. For his part, Nick is painfully aware his career is permanently stalled as long as Martha sits on the throne. Harold and Nick come to terms. It's a natural! They both get what they want. No doubt Nick is promised a top spot. Each knows they can trust the other because both have a loaded gun held at the other's head. And I don't think Nick would mind doing the scut work a bit. My guess is he'd enjoy that part of the deal just fine. It's a tight fit all around; I dare you to find a seam."

"It serves well enough as a working hypothesis," Win agreed. "But it does nothing to account for Mr. Herbert's arrest." He still sounded like a kid who found someone playing with his toys.

The phone rang right on cue.

"It's me," Gloria said. She was either nervous or out of breath, I couldn't tell which. "I tried to get the information you wanted, but someone must have gotten their wires crossed. You had it all wrong."

"That's why I called you—so you could set me straight."

"Harold Herbert hasn't been arrested. Inspector Dixon did go out to question him and he did bring him in. I don't know the details, but apparently he wasn't being cooperative, and it led to some kind of confrontation. From what I've been told, it could turn into quite a siege for Mr. Herbert. He's not here; they took him over to the jail, and the dispatcher told me the inspector plans to be there for a long time. He left orders not to be disturbed."

I wondered if they'd bring in the skinny guy to blow smoke up Harold's nose. "Too bad—Dixon's already disturbed. You're a lifesaver, Gloria. Next time we go out on the bounding main, I supply the picnic."

"It had better be a beaut. Seriously, Matt, don't ever ask me to do this sort of thing again. It's unfair."

"Relax, you didn't break any laws by telling me someone wasn't arrested. I had to ask this once. One of these days I'll tell you all about it. Later, my sweet—thanks."

I looked over at Win, held my hands out and shrugged. "Pete gave me some bad dope. Harold's just been pulled in for a good long grilling. Dixon was apparently willing to do it there, but Harold either got stubborn or gave some bad answers. The inspector probably hit him with some trick questions, based on information from those letters, and Harold wasn't quick enough to see it coming and duck. He's over on C Street, apparently for an overnighter. That's all there is to it; our theory is still intact."

Win beamed. "Then we may proceed as planned. How soon can you locate these nefarious Nolte brothers? We certainly cannot afford to discount the possibility they may play more than minor roles in this affair. At the very least, they may provide us with additional grounds for Mr. Herbert's candidacy as a suspect. It is also true that criminals are not unlike any other businessmen; they usually know what the competition is doing."

I reached for the phone again. Three calls later I had it nailed down, but I didn't much like the way my evening was shaping up. "Here's the scoop. Starting with a guy I know who's a poker buff, I got the numbers for a couple of card rooms on El Cajon Boulevard. The first was a dud, but with the help of my pal's name, I hit on the second one. Carl and Paul Nolte lease a box down at Agua Caliente. Word is they're definitely going to be there tonight for the dog races. Tomorrow they're off to Las Vegas for a busman's holiday—I'd bet a business conference—length of stay unknown."

"Then it must be tonight. I'm aware that you have plans. I'm sorry, but you see how it is."

"I knew it was coming. Of course you realize this makes it two nights in a row I've stood up the client?"

"We may only pray she's suitably impressed with our extraordinary devotion to her cause," he responded dryly. "You will have Dirk drive you; he's to accompany you at all times. I am adamant on this, so don't bother belaboring the point."

"Fine with me. Friday night in Tijuana should be a real learning experience for Dirk. Any suggestions for the script when I have my little chat with the underworld's answer to the Bobbsey Twins?"

"Not possible; circumstances and attitudes will dictate. You are equally adept at deception, cajolery, and intimidation. Allow the brothers to choose which they prefer. You understand what we want from them?"

"Sure! I start by confirming Harold's lousy record as a poker player, find how deep he's buried, and how hard they've been leaning on him to collect. Then, for a big finish, I'll ask them whether by any chance they were kind enough to suggest a hit man to help Harold pay off his debts by eliminating his wife. The reason I intend to save that for last is I'm afraid there's a chance it may offend."

"I daresay it might. Be careful. I dislike dispatching you on errands like this, but there's no alternative in this case. Report back on your return, regardless of the hour."

I hunted Dirk up in the garage, wiping imaginary dust off the gleaming finish of the black Continental Win refers to as the "house car." Anybody can use it—as long as Dirk's behind the wheel.

"Go put on your glad rags, pal. We're going out on the town."

He stopped rubbing and eyed me with grave reservations. "One of your jokes?"

"Nope, serious—boss's orders. You're going to drive me to Tijuana and stick to me like glue. We're going to the racetrack and chum it up with a pair of hoods. Some fun, huh?"

Dirk's closely spaced, black eyes widened in horror. "Take this car down there? The way those people drive?"

Someone who didn't know better might have taken the look of dread in his eyes as fear. I knew a damn sight better. He'd have taken on the Third Army if Win asked it. Looking at his fine, aquiline features and compact build, you might think he wouldn't be much of a physical threat, either. You might also take a wolverine to be cute, cuddly, and harmless.

"Stop worrying about the damn car and start worrying about me. There are cars stacked up all the way back to Detroit, for Christ's sake. But look at me—I'm unique."

I rushed upstairs to change into something appropriate, meaning one of my suits specially cut to allow for my S & W .38 over my right hip. It occurred to me as I was clipping it over my belt that my concealed weapon permit was undoubtedly defunct now, too. Then I had to laugh, realizing it wasn't worth a damn in Mexico anyway. It was when I got Susan on the line to cancel last night's dinner tonight that I ran into a buzz saw.

"Matt, you are pure poison to a girl's ego. If you can't stand the sight of me, why don't you just have the guts to say so?"

"Stop fishing for compliments. Haven't you noticed the hangdog look I get whenever I'm around you? I'd give up my subscription to *Playboy* to see you tonight."

"You're not puerile enough or inhibited enough to subscribe to *Playboy*. And you are seeing me tonight. I'm going with you."

"You certainly are not. I'm working—for you, as a matter of fact. Besides, Dirk is coming and he wouldn't approve."

"What's his problem? Male chauvinist or gay?"

"Neither, he read in one of those health magazines that

girls have a bad effect on stamina or something. He avoids them for the same reasons he doesn't drink or smoke."

"You can tell Dirk I'm all for stamina. I don't drink or smoke either, and how much damage can I do to his constitution riding in the backseat with your arms around me?"

"Sounds like fun, but I really can't. This doesn't shape up to be much of a pleasure trip. There's an outside chance it could even get nasty. In any event, Win would skin me alive. Sorry, my pet."

"Though you just mentioned it, I'll remind you that I'm the client you're doing all this chasing around for. I'm sick of the inside of this hotel, and I insist you take me with you tonight. You owe me some kind of report—no arguments! What time should I be waiting outside?"

"Look, try to understand. There's no party tonight. Dirk and I are going to Tijuana to talk to a couple of hoods who have ties to your stepfather. Taking you is out of the question."

"That's perfect! I've been dying to go there. I promise I won't get underfoot, Matt. You can lock me in the trunk when you go to see them if you want to. But at least let me ride along and get a look at the place. As your employer, in a way, surely I have some rights, too!"

She ended on a familiar peremptory note. I knew, in spite of all the banter, she was deadly serious. "Forty minutes give you time enough?"

"Fine. All I have to do is swap my heels for some walking shoes. Bye."

I hung up and left the house, deliberately bypassing the office. Later would be too soon to inform Win of the new recruit. Dirk had the Continental purring. I slid in beside him. He'd opted for a dark suit and turtleneck. He never wore a tie. Claimed it was stupid to walk around with a noose around your neck, begging for some obliging soul to use it to strangle you. While this may sound as if he has a somewhat negative opinion of his fellow man, I must point out in his defense, there are reasons.

As we traveled south toward downtown San Diego in silence, I had plenty of time to think. Dirk drove, as he did everything, with total concentration. I was remembering a time when I'd first arrived from Chicago more than three years earlier. Part of it was Dirk's strange, quiet ways, and part of it was that Win had had him run me through a conditioning program that pushed me way beyond my limits. I hadn't liked him very much; in fact I considered him a real spook. One day, sore as a boil and mad as hell from being tossed around by him on the exercise mat all day, I'd confronted Win in the office.

"I've had about all I can take from that sadistic son of a bitch. I've spent most of every day with him for nearly a month, and I'm not even sure he knows my name. He damn sure doesn't care. What the hell's his problem, anyway?"

"It's true, Dirk is extremely reticent concerning personal relationships," Win freely admitted. "Perhaps the time has come to give you some background. What would you say his ancestry was?"

"Who cares? Creole, I guess. How can a guy who spends most of his time outdoors stay so pale he looks like a year or two indoors wouldn't make any difference?"

"He's Cajun. The two are often confused, even by those who should know better. Remind me to lend you a book on contemporary anthropology.

"When Dirk was seven years old, his father murdered his mother by drowning her in the shallow swamp that bordered their rude home in the bayou country southeast of Baton Rouge. Unknown to the father, his small child witnessed the violent death of the one person on earth he loved.

"The genesis of this black deed was his father's lust for a girl of sixteen. Apparently she was not privy to the crime. They were subsequently married, or at least began cohabiting. The child kept his own counsel—which is uncanny when you think of it—and continued dwelling in his father's house. Needless to say, the relationship was preordained to be one of mutual hatred.

"Dirk was attending school in the nearby village, learning what little they may have had to offer, but he devoted most of his time and energies to thoughts of vengeance. These thoughts were soon transmitted into action. The obsessed child virtually lived as an animal in the woods, running, tracking game, fishing. This wild existence served both to lessen the boy's dependence on the father even for the food he ate, and provide an outlet for his fierce anger. Indeed, if he had not developed these primitive skills early on, he might not have survived. When he was finally forced to return to that cursed house at night, more often than not it was to receive a beating in lieu of supper.

"Guilt no doubt gnawed at the father's already flawed nature and he sought the surcrease of excessive drink. Thus passed the years; the boy, with no one to object, soon abandoned all pretense of attending school. The new young wife apparently did little to ameliorate the situation. Possibly she was relieved not to have the boy underfoot. Dirk's frail child's body responded to the self-imposed regimen. The primitive diet from woods and stream, coupled with ceaseless conditioning, continued unchallenged and unabated.

"Then one night, barely thirteen, the boy was told by his father in a drunken rage that he was about to get the beating of his life for some imagined infraction. Though not yet fully grown, Dirk was hard as a hickory tree, quick and supple as the game he hunted with his bare hands. The dam of reason finally broke. The boy told his hated father that he knew him for a murderer and he would never again submit to his discipline. No doubt infuriated, and threatened as well, his father determined the boy would die that night. If not for his budding prowess, fueled by six years of seething torment and hatred, no doubt Dirk would have.

"The two fought like animals. The woman sensed the finality of the struggle and fled into the night. Whether afraid for husband, stepson, or her own life, I do not know.

"Dirk's feline agility alone saved him a score of times as his father struck blow after savage blow with a fireplace poker. Though somewhat dissipated, his father was still a large and powerful man, universally feared and avoided by most of his peers. Dirk's characteristics were more those of his mother, and, in his drunken madness, his father cursed him by her name, as if his mind had snapped and he thought it was she he sought to kill again.

"Countless blows were landed by fist and foot, both combatants heedless of the terrible punishment they were sustaining. With the passing of time, the man's strength began to ebb, yielding inevitably to the boy's incredible endurance. The father's opportunity had passed. Dirk at last rendered his hated sire unconscious, trussed him and carried him down to the punt tied to their dock—the selfsame boat that had ferried his mother to her grave six years before.

"Imagine the terror of the father, regaining consciousness, which he did, lying bound in the stern of the foul boat, watching his son rowing inexorably toward the exact spot both knew too well. Realizing his fate, he made the woods and swamps resound with his cries, but there were only creatures of the night, and one who did not care to hear.

"When Dirk reached the unholy spot, he unshackled the crude cement block from the bow and fastened the anchor to his father's belt. The boy remained impassive to whatever entreaties, threats, or promises were offered. Then without hesitation, he dropped the rough anchor overboard and rolled his father over the gunnel after it.

"Naturally the boy never returned home. He pointed the bow north until he ran out of navigable water.

"Time passed, and he managed to slip into the army. His unique qualities led to assignment with the Green Berets and duty in Laos and Cambodia. Strangely enough, it was the awarding of a distinguished service medal with attendant publicity that led to his capture and conviction for patricide. He has chosen not to speak—even to me—of the seven years he served in prison.

"I was made aware of his case—it doesn't matter how—and was instrumental in securing his parole. I trust this abbreviated biography will serve to temper your judgments concerning Mr. Bomande. In his own unique way he is quite extraordinary, as indeed we all are here. There was a time when I hoped he could fulfill your role, but it wasn't possible. His physical gifts you are all too aware of, but he has no instinct for phenomena, which is as close as I can come to describing the gift you possess and the reason you are here. Worse, he can scarcely tolerate being indoors for anything beyond brief periods. As for getting him ever to function as a social animal, I'd be a fool to try. The man is a blunt instrument, but within his limitations there is no one better equipped to oversee your training. His loyalty is one absolute in a world of uncertainty, and that loyalty extends to everyone in this house, including you. He is a man of qualities you will come to cherish in time, as I do now."

Win had been right, as usual. From then on I had learned to accept Dirk's silent ways. And now I valued his friendship only slightly less than I did my right arm. I could think of at least two instances where he'd undoubtedly saved my life. I kidded him without mercy; though he seldom responded in kind, I think perhaps he needed it and loved it. And thanks entirely to him, I was in such disgustingly superb condition that I could probably make the Olympics team in any number of events. If I lived in someplace like Tierra del Fuego, that is.

We were nearing the off-ramp leading to the downtown area so it was time to break the news about Susan. He didn't say a word, just glanced over at me with a sort of sick look on his face. She was waiting under the Plaza canopy when we pulled up, looking very festive in white slacks and a red oriental-fashioned jacket with lots of gold brocade.

She didn't know the Continental, so she was still looking up the street expectantly. I jumped out and circled the car. "Ah, so; rovery Chinee rady want ride?" I inquired. She spun around, laughing, and threw her arms around me. I returned the favor. After we got untangled, I introduced her to Dirk.

"It's nice to meet you, Dirk. I hope you don't mind my tagging along tonight." She stuck out a hand and Dirk, after staring at it for a moment, caught on and clasped it very gently.

"Customer's always right," he mumbled ungraciously.

I opened the rear door and we scooted in. Susan remained in the center, which made it cozy. She slumped down a little to make certain Dirk couldn't see her in the mirror, put her hand to her mouth and stifled a giggle. She pointed at him and shook her head in amusement. I reached around behind and pulled her close.

"Ow! What in the world is that?" She pulled away, turning sideways in the seat. Patting my side, her eyes went wide when she realized the anomaly she'd felt was a gun.

"Just something the well-dressed detective wears out on the town. Don't worry. I seldom have occasion to use it, but experience has taught me if I leave it behind, that will be the time I'll wish I had it." I slipped in front of her, switching sides. "There—no strange lumps on this side. Forget it's there—that's what I do."

"Are you expecting that kind of trouble tonight?" She sounded more intrigued than worried.

"Of course not. We're merely paying an unexpected visit to two of San Diego's leading citizens. Dirk's anticipating some trouble, though. He's terrified a Tijuana taxi's going to make a bank shot off his car."

As we drifted south toward the International Border, I filled her in on most of what I'd picked up the last two days. She listened carefully but didn't come up with any questions after I'd finished. It was obvious she wanted to consider this a date, and wanted to encourage as little shop talk as possible.

Dirk pulled up to a Mex-Insur office just a few yards from the border and went in. We sat and laughed like demented children, watching him inside through the plate glass window. Dirk and the guy behind the counter were alternating shaking heads at each other.

"What's taking him so long?" Susan gasped, tears beginning to form.

"He's probably insisting they raise their coverage. He's so sure we're going to get it he's like a Las Vegas gambler who wants the house to waive the table limit."

If he noticed our flushed faces and shortness of breath when he returned, Dirk ignored it except for one brief glance of exasperation. Which we richly deserved. Then, bracing himself like a tank commander going into battle, he drove the short distance to the gates.

The United States guard posts were unmanned. Fifty yards farther on, Mexican border guards lounged, chatting amiably. As Dirk slowed to a stop, one of them put out a hand, waving him through without ever taking his eyes off his pal.

"Strict, aren't they?" laughed Susan.

"The problem isn't getting in. Strict comes later, when we head back out."

After half a dozen blocks we crossed an old bridge and found ourselves crawling along the main street, Avenida de la Revolución. Traffic was jammed bumper to bumper. Taxis of unlikely hues jockeyed for position, showing complete disdain for any threat short of a head-on collision. This attitude was reflected in the condition of their bodywork. Quite a few were "hors de combat," being pushed toward narrow side streets by laughing men. Apparently the only part they considered essential and kept in good working order was their horns. Throngs of people wandered aimlessly, crisscrossing the street at will. Some, obviously tourists, even used the designated crosswalks. Garish lights rebounded harshly off the facade of open shops, with their endless tiers of plaster saints, guitars, serapes, and velvet paintings. Very young children ran up to wipe our spotless windshield with filthy rags at every stop, thrusting out tiny hands before we moved on. Incredibly explicit signs and posters marked the multitude of nightclubs, and determined barkers patrolled before them, all but forcibly shoving the passersby inside. On each corner gaudily dressed women dispassionately accosted every man who passed, including some with female companions.

"It's unbelievable!" Susan exclaimed. "Why don't the Mexican authorities do something? It's disgusting."

"Either you're forgetting," I began, "or else no one ever told you that this isn't primarily a Mexican town. This is all for the benefit of the tourists. We're the consumers who created this place. We come here by the millions and we're buying what they're selling. Apparently they're providing just what we want. The average Mexican is extraordinarily moral, and this disgusts Mexicans far more than it probably does you. They look upon us with contempt, but it's called survival. Not an easy trick in Mexico these days. It never has been.

"The clincher is, up until World War II this was just a nice sleepy little village. Some admiral took a notion to clean up San Diego; the downtown district then was a real snake pit. So the Navy gave all the clip joints on Broadway their marching orders and was able to make it stick because the city was almost totally dependent on the Navy in those days. The sleazes relocated here, across the border. So you see, this is a U.S. institution, and we're in no position to cast any stones on the Mexicans."

"Sorry, I stand corrected. You really like these people, don't you, Matt?"

"Yeah, I guess I do. The ones I've met have a quiet dignity I admire. They're a gentle people with a fine sense of humor. And guts to spare. Yes, I like them a lot."

Dirk was able to make better time once we left the mayhem of the business district behind. Ten minutes later we were parked outside the big oval structure that was Caliente Racetrack.

"Susan, I want you to stay in the car with all the doors locked—understand? Dirk and I shouldn't be gone more than about twenty minutes."

"Can't I just go in and see a couple of races? I've never even seen a dog race. Do they really chase a rabbit?"

"Not a real rabbit, no, but they use a real skin to make the scent authentic. It leads the dogs around the track on a rail. Dirk and I have to go up to the top where the private boxes are; it could get a bit tricky. Behave and we'll do whatever you want after I've conducted my—your—business."

We waited until she'd locked all the doors. She made an ugly face at us and sat in a mock pout with her arms folded. (At least I hoped it was a mock pout.)

Inside, the stands were more than half empty, but only because the smaller bettors preferred to mill around nervously down on the grounds, and next to the fence along the track. The third race was just finishing. The rising crescendo of the mob's voice died to an uncanny silence the instant the greyhounds crossed the finish line. I nudged Dirk's arm and pointed to the top of a long flight of filthy concrete steps.

The climb lifted us above the dinginess of the bleachers. Dozens of comfortable stalls overlooked the course. Up there it looked a lot cleaner and smelled a lot better. Opposite the booths a long, plush bar stretched along the back wall. White-coated runners scurried back and forth between boxes and betting windows, sometimes pausing at the bar to bring sustenance. The entire roof section was closed off from the stairs by a locked turnstile featuring a sign reading: "Stadium Club. Private." The grave Mexican guarding the gate watched our approach impassively. I beckoned him closer. "Señors Nolte, *por favor*," I said as I pressed a ten-spot in his hand.

The bill disappeared into his pocket with a practiced, fluid motion. A flood of soft musical Spanish washed over me. All I could do was shake my head, repeat my request, and admit, "No habla Español."

He sighted down his patrician nose at me, gratified at

having called my bluff. His point made, he condescended to address us in English. "You are the invited guests of the Señors Nolte?"

"We're business associates, but we've never met. If you would be kind enough to point them out?"

I could tell before he'd opened his mouth that we'd lost our momentum. "I'm sorry, the club rules do not allow this. You must go back down. This section is not open to the public, *si?*"

The bum could have at least returned the ten. My blue eyes assaulted his black ones as we exchanged increasingly rancorous dialogue for the next few minutes. My hand went to the railing; I was considering vaulting it to see what happened when I heard an unexpected but familiar voice.

"Hey, Matt, over here!"

I jerked my head around and spotted her waving impishly from a booth center front. Susan was standing sandwiched between two men, both of whom were observing me with great amusement. Then she sidled out of the box and walked quickly toward us, pouring out a torrent of Spanish that made our snotty guard gasp. He quickly released the turnstile and stepped aside to allow us in.

"How the hell did you get up here?" I demanded.

"The Club elevator." She waved her hand toward the one at the far end of the bar. "Carl says you're probably the only two to climb those stairs in weeks. Nobody ever uses them. Come along and meet Carl and Paul. They're really very charming. I doubt you'll have to shoot them."

"How the hell did you manage to get tight with them already?"

She gave me a sweet smile, the kind an adult would give a backward child. "I rode up on the elevator, asked the *regente*—that's the manager—for an introduction, and we were having the nicest chat by the time you two appeared like lost waifs at the top of all those stairs."

Dirk made sure I got a good shot of the smirk on his face.

"What was all that lingo back there? I thought you'd never been to Mexico before."

"Not until tonight, but I've got some Puerto Rican friends in New York who got me in the habit of listening to one of their radio stations while I'm painting. The music is better to work to and the bonus is I've picked up quite a bit of the language. My two best friends back in New York left me no choice; they absolutely refuse to speak English when we go out together. I told the guard the Noltes didn't like him humiliating important people who'd done them the honor of a visit." She led our little parade to the booth and formally introduced us to the evening's quarry.

Carl and Paul were nearly alike, and pleasant-enough-looking at first glance. Carl was a bit taller and clearly the elder by maybe five years. Paul's face was fuller and his hairline was in retreat. Both were dark-featured and either one could have had a good shot at modeling men's wear. We shook hands and exchanged totally insincere pleasantries.

"As I was saying"—Susan resumed a conversation she'd apparently been having—"if my stepfather owes you any money, I'll make it good on a one-time basis—never again. Of course, I'd have to see the signed notes. How much is the poor sap into you for?"

The two brothers exchanged glances. Carl looked down at the tote board. "It's nearly time for the fourth race, Miss Neal," he told her in a silky voice. "May I place a bet for you?"

"No, thank you, but I would like to get an answer to my question."

"Carl has to bet every race," chided Paul. "Don't you, Carl? He's evolved the most boring system of all time. Tell them about it."

"It may be boring," Carl protested, "but it's also foolproof. I'm sure no one wants to hear it."

"I would," I volunteered. "I can't imagine any safe system for betting the dogs. Horses, maybe, but never dogs."

Carl held up his right hand and a runner promptly appeared. He handed him thirty-two dollars. "One to win," he said, and the runner took off. Carl smiled and spread his hands. "That's it—the sum total of my system. I bet the one dog in every race. And I cannot possibly lose."

"I don't get it," I told him. "After all, there are eight other dogs in the race and the post positions are drawn by lot, so you're going to be backing a lot of second-rate long shots."

"True, Mr. Doyle, but I don't have to win any specific percentage of races. The dog with the first post position has the inside track, therefore he runs a slightly shorter course than any of the other dogs. The bad part is, he stands a better chance of being squeezed off at the rail, too, but it's a fact the one dog wins more often than any other over a period of time. Just now you saw me bet thirty-two dollars. If I lose this race, and I undoubtedly will, I'll double my bet in the next. I'll continue to double after every loss until I win. Ultimately I have to win. When I do, I'll recoup all losses and the profit I would have made if I'd won lesser bets all along the way. Simple! And guaranteed."

"Yes," agreed Paul. "Guaranteed to bore anyone to death. You have the soul of an accountant."

"I am an accountant," Carl reminded his brother, smiling thinly.

"The system should work," I said, "provided you're always able to float the next bet. With the price progressing geometrically, you wouldn't have to lose too many races before you lay out some real money."

"The one dog is seldom out of the money for long, but you're right. It would be disastrous to try it without the money to back a long dry spell. In that respect, it's no different from any other conservative business venture.

"Let me just give you an example of how right you are, Mr. Doyle," Carl continued. "I've already lost five races. Doubling down after each, I'm now having to bet thirty-two dollars, after starting with the standard two-dollar bet. If I lost, say, nineteen races, I'd be forced to lay out five hundred and twelve thousand, two hundred and eighty-eight dollars to cover my twentieth bet. It's like the old trick question they give you in accountant's school to teach you the impact of geometrical progression: How much would you have if you saved a nickel one day, and doubled the amount each day for thirty days? Most people guess between a few hundred and a couple of thousand dollars. The correct answer is twenty-six million, eight hundred and forty-three thousand five hundred and thirty-seven dollars and sixty cents.

"For bettors with limited capital, the system works as well betting place or show instead of win. Naturally, the rewards are reduced, but the risk of a long dry spell is all but eliminated entirely."

For a minute we all stood in silent awe. I didn't want to be impressed by the man, but I couldn't help it. "Wouldn't your system work as well with any other post position?" I wondered out loud, attempting to conceal my amazement and to regain the initiative.

"It would, to a slightly lesser degree," Carl replied. "The next most profitable number to ride would be the nine."

"Wait a minute," Susan protested. "That doesn't make sense. The nine dog runs the longest race."

"I think I get the idea," I told her. "The outside spot would be the next best because he's got all the room in the world to run. He's the least vulnerable to getting bumped off stride at the beginning of the race. That happens a lot, and the dogs involved seldom recover and finish well."

Carl smiled thinly. "Precisely, Mr. Doyle. I can see you're something of a fan yourself."

"Not really, but I've been here twenty minutes and I've got eyes. It doesn't exactly require a Rhodes scholar to dope out the gen on a bunch of dogs chasing their tails." It helped make up for the gaffe at the turnstile. Besides, I thought it was time to stir the pot. All that bon homme with two well-groomed lice was beginning to make me ill.

Suddenly the PA system boomed. "And there they go!" We all became intent on the sleek animals flying around the track below. Carl's number-one dog was a small brindle bitch, and she set the early pace. Then, fifty yards short of the wire, she lost stride and fell back to finish fifth.

Susan had been cheering on the brindle; now she turned to Carl with a disappointed look on her face. "I was positive you'd win. Why did the dog just stop trying like that? It was almost as if it were on a leash and someone pulled on it."

Carl tossed the worthless ticket over the railing in what looked like a gesture of contempt for the plebians below. "That's exactly what happened. There are plenty of ways of keeping a dog on a leash during a race. My guess is her trainer gave her a nice big drink of water half an hour or less before the race. That's one of the easiest and most common ways. Another is merely to exercise her excessively the day of the race, or even the day before."

"But why would her owner want her to lose?"

Carl shrugged. "She's been placing pretty consistently lately. That makes her odds too short; the owner can't make any money. The purses are very small, the money must be made wagering. Tonight she went into the race at five to four, no way to make a dime. A few poor finishes and she'll be back to running at eight or nine to one. It's customary." He gave an eloquent gesture of lifting his shoulders with his hands held out in acceptance of the facts of life. It was an old man's gesture.

Paul and Carl made a good team. They'd exchanged no signals, had barely looked at one another, but somehow a position had been adopted. They'd brushed aside Susan's persistent questioning, my gibes, given a treatise on racing as a stall, and now the proper response had been formulated.

"Miss Neal," Paul said politely, "you will understand, I'm sure, if you find us reluctant to discuss business details that are very personal. If your stepfather doesn't wish to confide in you, we certainly must respect that."

"Not if you want to ever get paid," she snapped.

"If Mr. Herbert is in debt to us, and I don't say he is, we are not concerned. We never let anyone get in over his head. That's one of our strictest rules."

Susan leaned into Paul, stabbing his chest with her finger. "Well, this time you broke your precious rule . . ."

"Susan," I broke in, "you brought me along to handle things, remember." I pulled out my wallet and displayed my now defunct license. I deliberately fumbled putting it back, exposing my revolver for a good long look. "I work for Carter Winfield. Ring any bells?"

"We've heard of him," Paul admitted.

"Good! Susan doesn't think the police are going to nail her mother's killer, so we're on the payroll. First, you'd better face the fact that Harold has all the future prospects of a Kamikazi pilot. Susan's inheriting everything, including his shoe trees. His wife had already tossed him out of her life and her will, and, in case you haven't heard, he's in jail right now on suspicion of murder. Even if he beats the rap, Susan's certainly going to bounce him from the firm. Now tell me again how unconcerned you are about getting paid."

Until then I'd been concentrating equally on the two brothers, but suddenly I realized Paul was Chairman of the Board. Carl had glanced sideways at his younger brother twice. It was a natural mistake, to assume the elder brother was the boss; no doubt it had worked to their advantage many times. Paul's onyx eyes appaised me coldly. I could almost hear the machinery clicking behind them, culling data from the brain files, considering, rejecting, narrowing the potential risks, always seeking a safe path to the reward.

"It doesn't follow, Mr. Doyle. Why would Miss Neal rush to pay her stepfather's gambling debts if she thinks he may have killed her mother?"

"There are valid reasons—valid to her, not to me. She feels the obligation was contracted by a family member, and reflects upon the family. Paying you is her way of kissing him off, you might say. It makes her feel she's been more than fair with the guy, but he doesn't get a dime, see? Since she's due to end up with all the marbles, she can afford to indulge. And there's another reason: it's going to have to buy us some answers. Now how much more do you intend to kick and scream before you agree to accept the lady's money?"

I turned to Susan. "I've said it a hundred times, now I'm going to say it again. A gambling debt is not a legal debt, and you're nuts to even think of spending the money. Unless these birds materially help our investigation, which I sincerely doubt, let's just say we made an honest effort and let it go at that. I'm ready to leave any time."

"Wait!" Paul said. His silky voice had gone hard on me. "You've made your point, Doyle. Herbert's into us for seventy-five thousand. We cut him off about three months ago; since then he's been heavy on promises but light on cash. We assumed after what went down last Sunday we'd be seeing our money soon."

"You'll have to produce signed notes. Don't try to take advantage of the lady."

"There's only one note. He signed a new one each time he hit us for more. We'd give him the old one back. The man should find other interests: golf, tennis, anything but stud poker. He thinks he's basically lucky—poker players who believe that go broke in a hurry."

"Did he have a chance to get lucky? Any chance at all?"

Paul's mask of impassivity slipped another notch. I caught a glimpse of a small furry animal, vicious and mean-looking, peering out at me. It was gone in an instant, the mask back in place.

"That was uncalled for," he told me evenly. "Carl and I set things up for select people who get their kicks from a high-stakes game of poker. We insure a safe, quiet atmosphere, free of phonies and clip artists. We don't play—ever! We have no association with any of the players outside of the game. Herbert's regular group included a local surgeon, a real estate broker, and, believe it or not, a municipal court judge. All are top people in the community, same players every time. We take ours off the top. Five per cent of the buy-in. Once we tried to get him to switch; there was an opening with another set. Lower stakes, maybe a little less savvy around the table. He just got mad and refused. Said he liked his bunch. Truth was, like most losers, it had become personal; he had to get even with the same guys who beat him. Letting it get personal is as disastrous as thinking you're lucky."

I faced Susan. "It's still up to you. Seventy-five grand is a lot of going-away present for a guy you can't even bear the sight of."

She hesitated, not sure of where I was trying to lead her. She decided to play it safe. What a gal! "I leave it up to you, Matt. Handle it. If you tell me it's legitimate, I'll pay it."

"Legitimate doesn't exactly apply. Paul, it looks like you're going to get lucky, but not until I extract some value received. You'll remember I mentioned that as part of the deal. How hard did you two push? You've been waiting a long time for your money."

"I see where you're headed, but you're wrong. It's been weeks since we broke anybody's knees over a late payment. We kept in touch, sure, asked how things were shaping up. We don't get involved with bums, so we don't sweat it. Every time I'd turn around I'd see his wife in the paper, giving a bundle to some charity or other. Why should we worry? I did suggest he tell her we were a tax-free charitable institution and maybe she'd pay us." His feeble attempt at a laugh stopped at his teeth.

"What would he say? How did he propose to come up with that kind of money?"

"He just kept telling us he was going to see a real bundle soon. A commission, he called it, for putting together some kind of a deal."

"You're really putting him on the hot spot, Paul. The deal

you're referring to wasn't possible while his wife lived. You make it all but certain he knew what was coming. Which means either he did it or had it done. What do you think?"

"How the hell would I know?" he snarled. The party was about over anyway, so I figured I might as well gig them good.

"You'd know if you two helped out. Maybe all you had to do was provide Harold with a phone number or a post office box. In your circle they're called problem solvers, and who'd know better where to find them? I think it's a definite possibility." I could sense Dirk's presence on my left, which let me know he was taking sole responsibility for Carl.

Paul's eyes traveled down to where he knew my gun was, reminding himself of its existence. If I hadn't made a point of showing it to him, he'd have been all over me like a blanket. "You're way off base, Doyle—you may have such ties, but we don't. You're lucky I don't—but then, I figure we're both local boys, and someday soon I may bump into you when you've left your artillery home. It could be quite a bump."

"Sorry I've bruised your delicate feelings, but I still like the idea. Harold's problem, your problem—one simple solution. But what if he suckered you? Now you'd know. It's one of the reasons I thought maybe you'd be upset with him and grateful enough to Susan to blink or nod your head if I'm right."

No winks or nods, just icy malignant stares. I tried once more. "Harold would be the one to go down; nobody here gives a damn who the mechanic was. I'm not a cop—nothing leaves this box. What'll it cost you?"

Paul stood silent, rigid as a board, glaring in angry frustration. He was in a fix; not only was I armed, but he had visions of seventy-five thousand dollars fading into the sunset. I was tempted to hang on a while longer, just to enjoy the expression on his face.

"Let's go, children," I told Susan and Dirk. We headed for the elevator. Inside, we faced front; I could see the Noltes still planted like two cigar store Indians, glaring at me.

On the way down in the stale lift, Susan asked, "Am I really going to have to pay them all that money?"

"Don't be a goose. You never were, but even if it were a straight offer, they know it's off because they didn't talk. I think we had them at least half convinced there for a while, so they must have a good reason for remaining mute. And we did help them out financially."

"We did?"

"We distracted Carl from betting the fifth and sixth races. His one dog didn't come in either race. That's a hundred and ninety-two bucks we saved him."

"He sure didn't look very grateful," Dirk observed.

Back in the car, I accused Susan of disobeying a direct order from a superior officer. Dirk and I considered suitable punishment at length, not neglecting the serious fact that the infraction took place on foreign soil under wartime conditions.

"Some superior officers, you two." She sniffed. "If I'd stayed in the car, you'd still be up there on the wrong side of the fence arguing with a peon."

"Nonsense," I informed her stiffly. "We had the situation well in hand."

"That's right," Dirk agreed. "I was about to suggest you shoot him. I think you might have taken me up on it."

I stared in amazement. Then I understood and had to grin. Dirk was as pleased as I was with the way Susan had handled herself. She had gotten to him. Dirk was normally good for about one crack a year, usually as funny as an abscessed tooth.

When we hit the glut of downtown traffic, Susan suddenly shouted, "Pull over and park, Dirk. I've just got to go into one of these clubs and see what it's like."

"You're not serious?" We both groaned.

"Yes, I am—really! It's probably the only chance I'll ever get. Please, guys? Just for laughs?"

I held up my arms in surrender. "Pull this tug into a

berth, Dirk. Make it fast—she's got a hammerlock on me and I'm afraid my arm'll go."

With great reluctance, he nosed into one of the too-narrow diagonal slots along the right-hand curb. Susan leaped out and darted into the nearest shop. Dirk showed no inclination to move, so I went up and leaned on his door.

"Oh, no, you don't, pal. I said the order of the day is to stick to me like glue, remember? Lock it up and let's try to keep up with Tinker Bell."

"I'm going to stay right here. Look at the size of these parking spaces. Somebody is bound to pull alongside us and ding the car with their door."

"Then it's better you be somewhere else and don't see it. You'd probably kill them and end up rotting in a Mexican jail. Come on!"

We found her staring in horror at a solid wall of paintings done on what appeared to be velvet.

"Have you two ever seen anything more gross? I was hoping to see some examples of the bold, imaginative work some of the best Mexican artists are famous for. This stuff is . . . ghastly."

The subject matter at hand ranged from madonnas to bulls, with a heavy accent on unlikely-looking nudes featuring breasts somewhat larger than their heads. All were done in the same media, apparently phosphorescent paint. They had all the subtlety of a neon beer sign.

"What did you expect—original Diego Riveras? This is for the folks from North Dakota. You'll find every shop offers the same wares. Each of these original beauties is duplicated in a hundred shops up and down this street. The artists soon get so they can turn out a painting in half an hour. They usually do the same one, or two, or three, over and over again for years."

Susan shuddered and ran out onto the crowded sidewalk. She spotted a dive labeled "The Green Fox." With childlike delight, she raced to the entrance and waited impatiently for us to catch up.

"I don't think you really want to go in there," I protested. "If you want me to buy you a drink, there's a nice bar at the Fronton where the jai alai games are held. We could walk it from here."

"No! I've never been in a place like this before. It'll be a new experience for me. Please?"

"Falling out of an airplane would be new, too. Okay, you asked for it. I don't know what your expectations are, but stand by for major revisions."

I led the way, followed by an eager Susan and a grim-faced Dirk. Inside, they were doing a fine job of conserving energy. Lighting was at a premium, but from the little I could see it was just as well. I found a table with my thigh and fumbled around for chairs. At the far end of the low room there was a long bar. On top of the bar a tired-looking woman of indeterminate age shuffled back and forth listlessly to tinny sounds from a portable radio. Her unadorned body was thick-waisted, flaccid, and totally uninspiring. Her act did, however, feature a pair of four-inch heels painted with Day-Glo.

Only two other tables were occupied, but half a dozen men sat at the bar. No one seemed interested in the floor show except one kid whose burr head identified him as a probable marine recruit from Pendleton. He hunched over the bar, chin cupped in hands, looking up at her dreamily, swiveling his head with her as she patrolled the runway.

"She's not very attractive for that sort of work, is she?" whispered Susan.

"Not very. If you're thinking of trying to beat her out of the job, I think you've got a pretty fair chance."

"Thanks a lot! I'm afraid I don't see what's so exciting."

"Who ever told you it was? That's the trouble with you girls. You think guys have a ball at these places, don't you? Well, for one, I'm happy to have this opportunity to set you straight. Now you know—our lives are unspeakably dreary and dull. Some of us even get so depressed we overreact and get married."

"Ha! You wouldn't think Miss Universe was good enough to shine your shoes."

"Not true. Just bring her around, I dare you. She can start with my shoes, and then we'll see."

"You're a real sport. Just tell me—do you guys find this sort of thing sexy at all?"

"Sexless, not sexy. I doubt anyone here does, with the obvious exception of that young gyrene at the right end of the bar. He's so drunk and lonely she's beginning to look good to him."

A squat Indio woman came up to the table silently.

"Tres cervezas, por favor," I told her.

When she'd gone, Susan complained, "I don't like beer."

"I wasn't about to suggest you drink it, but you certainly aren't going to drink anything else here."

The woman on the bar had disappeared, replaced by a young girl with an attractive face, who looked no more than fifteen in the dim light. She was slightly chubby, which gave her a comic appearance when she began making a concerted effort to marry her movements to the shrill music. The waitress brought the beer and demanded four-fifty. I paid it, fully aware the Mexican customers at the bar were paying less than half that.

A curtain parted in the back of the room and a woman entered. Standing hipshot, she slowly surveyed the clientele. When she spotted us, she froze. Her hair was piled high atop her head, and she wore a shimmery silver dress off the shoulders. At the distance the effect was that of a 1940 torch singer stepping out onstage to do her number. Slowly, deliberately, she undulated toward us. The illusion shattered and vanished as she drew closer; she became instead a middle-aged woman in a stained and shabby dress. Her face, though coarsely featured, was by no means ugly. She hooked a chair from a nearby table, placed the chair next to Dirk's, sat, and gave him a monkey grin.

"Why ees sooch a nice-looking hombre alone, eh? Mus' be Rosa's locky night, eh? Ju' tell Rosa jour name, eh?"

Susan gripped my hand and fought mightily to contain the spasms of laughter resulting from the look of misery on Dirk's face. Her efforts proved futile, as did mine, but Rosa ignored us completely. She had eyes only for Dirk, and even our laughter couldn't deter the old pro from her appointed rounds.

Giving us both an evil glare, Dirk turned to face his unlikely-looking admirer and attempted to thwart us. No one was more amazed than I at what followed.

"My name is Percival, charming lady. I'm a Knight of the Realm and a Peer of the Blood. Never mind those two; they are low-born and suffer from weak minds."

That really did it. Susan lost all control, and I wasn't far behind. It was a side of my pal I'd never seen before.

"Perceeveel?" Rosa repeated carefully. "Percee! Percee, ju come with Rosa and she weel make ju, ver' 'appy." She grabbed his left wrist and pulled tentatively.

"Alas, no, dear Rosa," Dirk told her sadly. "I've long since tired of life's pleasures. Now I devote myself exclusively to taking care of the mentally handicapped." He indicated the two of us with a wave of his one free hand.

Rosa stubbornly maintained her hold. "Ju' come upstairs, eh? Eef Rosa does no please ju', ju' weel no pay, eh?"

By this time I was pounding on the table, gasping for air. Susan seemed to be bordering on hysteria.

Dirk gave me a pleading look, but I couldn't stop laughing long enough to help myself, much less him. "Forgive me, Rosa," Dirk said, standing, "but it's time for me to escort these feeble-minded ones back to the home." She did her level best to restrain him, but he wrenched his arm gently free and bolted out the door.

Susan and I formed a mutual brace in order to make it to our feet, racked with laughter, tears streaming down our faces.

Holding on tightly, we staggered for the door. As we reached it, Rosa called out to me. "Señor," she said loudly, "ju' tell Percee Rosa weel wait here for heem, eh?" Then she fell to laughing as hard as we were, together with most of the patrons in the bar. Apparently, we'd been the comedy relief act in the floor show.

We made it through the door, but had to stop and lean against the front of the club. Puffing and gasping for air, we tacked uncertainly toward the car. We got some dirty looks from the tourists, who no doubt thought we were drunk as lords.

The minute she got in, Susan threw her arms around Dirk's neck from behind, hugged him affectionately, and assured him he'd missed a great career in the classic theater. He surprised me again by obviously loving it. When she told him Rosa's departing message, it got us started all over again. Dirk turned out to have quite an impressive belly laugh. If this kept up, she'd have him baying at the moon.

There was a half-hour's delay waiting to reenter the States. By then we were starved, so we stopped at a place I'd heard good things about. The Butcher Shop was not far over the border in Chula Vista, and it was no disappointment. The steaks were Texas-sized and arrived as ordered, an event worthy of note when you order them as rare as I do. The owner must have had some kind of Amazon fetish. The hostess, barmaids, and waitresses were all pushing six feet. Susan said it made her feel like a Munchkin.

Back in the car, we drifted north peacefully. Paradoxically, it had been a night of sheer magic for all three of us. I didn't want it to end. Nothing was said, but tactile messages were being exchanged in the backseat. Susan's face glowed whenever a passing light hit it.

"Stay on the freeway, Dirk. Head for the barn." Dirk just kept driving.

Susan tilted her face closer to mine and whispered, "Am I being abducted?"

"It's a thought. Actually, I figure it's only ten-thirty and I did stand you up last night, so I really owe you two dates. I can't stand being in debt. Let's pick up my car and I'll show you a spot I think you'll like. It's got a fine view of the ocean."

She chuckled. "Good God, the man wants to take me to watch the submarine races. I haven't had that line pulled on me since I was sixteen."

"You're long overdue then."

We all piled out in front of the garages at home. Susan promptly marched right up to Dirk. "That was truly the most fun I think I've ever had, Dirk. Thank you for a marvelous evening." She quickly stood on her toes and bussed him a good one on the cheek. He mumbled something I couldn't catch, then hurried away to open the garage door and put the car to bed.

I fired up my less conspicuous Chevy Caprice and she skipped impishly over and slid in. "He's really terribly handsome in a mysterious sort of way," she told me dreamily. "I like your friend. He looks like he should be a bullfighter."

"I'd hate to be the bull. You really shouldn't have done that, you know. The poor guy will be up all night, worried about his health."

"You don't seem too concerned."

"I've had all my shots," I told her, slipping the shift back into park and reaching over to pull her in to me. We kissed long and languorously. Later I remembered how to operate the gear shift and we got under way.

After a ten-minute drive I pulled up against the guard rail at Torrey Pines State Park and we got comfortable, both becoming quickly mesmerized by the soothing regularity of the incoming breakers. The tide was near its peak; the creamy lace reached two-thirds of the way up the beach. We watched the black hills completing their five-thousand-mile journey and, in the final seconds, turn white as they stumbled and fell. The sound of low thunder and sibilant hissing rolled over us. The air was pure balm.

We exchanged five-minute biographies, but we were more interested in who we were now than in who we'd been before we met. "I like your spot, Matt," she whispered. "I think maybe you were right about the Pacific being a very fine ocean."

"Honey, they don't call this America's Finest City for nothing. There are plenty of places I want to show you. Wait until you see the view from the old lighthouse. And we have to take at least two days to see Balboa Park. And that doesn't even count an evening at the Old Globe Theater."

"I'd like that. But right now there's something I'd like to see even more."

"Anything—what is it? If it isn't open, I'll break in."

"My bed," she replied frankly.

The statement could have been open to interpretation, but not when combined with the look, the touch, the steamy ambience between us. It took me a flat twenty minutes to roll to a stop half a block from the Plaza. I'm not claiming it as a record, but it's proof I didn't loiter.

She unlocked her door and entered her suite as if in a daze. Dropping her purse on the floor, she turned to me with a look of confusion. "Matt, this is stupid. I'm so sorry I . . ."

"Hush," I told her, taking her in my arms. "Talking is nice—we'll do some more of it later." I kissed her hard. I felt a shudder, but I sensed it came from awareness of me and not revulsion. I steered her through the connecting door into the bedroom. The band of light from the open door cast a gentle glow throughout the small room.

As I began undoing the buttons of her outlandish-looking Chinese jacket, she pushed me away. "Please! I'm not like this at all."

"It comes with the service. Part of my job is I have to boff all the female clients."

She stared at me with wide eyes. "What? How can you be so crude! That's not funny."

"I guessed that's what you must think of me. You say

you're not like this, implying you must think I am. Let me just tell you something. I'm here because I care one hell of a lot about you and I think it's reciprocal. That, my darling, is a very nice situation to find yourself in—man or woman—and it doesn't happen all that often anymore. If we didn't feel this way, it wouldn't amount to anything more than recreational sex, which is what all the sad little magazines for all the sad little people have coined it. They recommend it, but for me it's dehumanizing, and thanks, but no thanks."

She threw her arms around me and tried to speak between broken sobs. "Oh, Matt . . . I wish . . . I could. It's only been . . . three days since . . . my mother . . ."

I held her as a child awakened from a bad dream, rocking, stroking, waiting for the awful-awfuls to go away. I didn't blame her for an attack of the guilts. All of us are subject to them with alarming frequency. They turn too many of our blue skies dark. And all to absolutely no purpose whatever.

Finally the convulsive tears stopped, and she began to respond to my attentions. This time she didn't try to hinder my attempt to remove her clothing. When I finished, she shyly turned down the covers and slipped beneath them. I joined her quickly. Her satin skin felt cool, and for a time we just lay there enjoying the feel of another body, pushing back the loneliness bit by bit. When I thought she was ready, I coupled with her gently, then began a slow, rhythmic climb to the release I could feel her fighting against and yet longing for so desperately. For a long time I didn't think she was going to make it, but then she began to buck beneath me, making small mewing sounds that grew into groans of anguished delight. One final keening wail lasted several seconds, then trailed off as her body went slack. I kissed her dimly seen face and tasted the salt of fresh tears.

"Oh, God, I don't know what I feel," she mumbled. "How can you describe what just happened without its sounding . . ."

"I have a feeling you were about to say the wrong word, so

shut up. Win once told me that a writer fella he met a long time ago said, 'Anything you feel good after doing is a moral act.' Guy's name was Papa, and Win says he occasionally wrote some decent stuff. Of course, that's a ridiculous statement as it stands, but in this case I think it's true. I know I feel awfully damn fine, and I hope you do, too. We certainly haven't hurt anyone. What do you think?"

"I certainly have to admit I feel pretty darn wonderful myself. I'm sorry about all that emotional garbage. It . . ."

"Pardon the interruption again," I said as I slid up closer to her side, "but your emotions are not garbage and expressing them is allowed, even healthy. In case you don't know it, what just happened here was, among other things, a reaffirmation of being. A celebration of life. Between two consenting adults who happen to push each others buttons pretty good, which is why it was so satisfying. After all you've been through, it couldn't have happened at a better time. And the sooner you get over having the guilts because you fell into a little happiness the better. End of speech."

"It was a very nice speech, Matt. Everything about you is very nice, I think."

We lay back, touching all along our lengths, talking happily, seriously, and, finally, sensually. The second time there was no gentleness, no slow building toward release. We met like two carnivores in heat; no longer tentative, but giving and taking hungrily and completely.

This time Susan slipped all the way down into deep slumber, snoring contentedly with her lovely face childlike in repose. I dressed quietly, but I don't think rockets going off would have budged her. The elevator operator looked at me a little funny, and I realized it was because of the huge facetious grin on my mug. I hummed merrily all the way home.

It was pushing 5:00 A.M. when my head finally made contact with my pillow. All in all, it had been one hell of a fine night. I fell asleep making plans for a lot more just like it.

CHAPTER 12

*O*f course I'd known there'd be a price to pay. Eight o'clock came five hours early, and it took an extra cup of Louis's coffee to get my heart started. So it was with a full complement of his half-raw hen fruit properly stowed that I entered the office to face the music.

Win ignored my existence until I was properly seated in my chair. "I thought I made it abundantly clear you were to report to me upon your return."

In spite of his glowering demeanor I felt like laughing. "It was very late. You'd gone to bed."

"Nonsense! I made a point of waiting up for you. I happen to know the car returned prior to eleven o'clock. I sat here with the office door open, anx . . . prepared to confer. What did you do? Sneak in the back door?"

"The car returned about eleven, but I didn't. Our client turned out to be . . . ah . . . very demanding. I couldn't shake her until five this morning."

"Am I to understand you went to see Miss Neal late last night? After completing your assignment?"

"You understand only half right. When I called to cancel

last night, she came on very tough; it was either take her along or maybe lose a client. It all worked out fine. If you'll just relax and listen to my report, you'll see."

His handsome, craggy old face went through several changes, beginning with anger and proceeding to mere irritation.

"When time permits, we will discuss the fact you didn't see fit to inform me of this alteration in plans, though you passed within a few feet of this door on your way out last evening after making the change. For now, suffice it to say, my instructions are never optional. I specifically wanted your account last night because I have a decision to make that will be based, in part, on that report. Please give it now—as much of it as you may recall, that is."

I imagined me prodding him awake at 5:00 A.M. for a report. I vowed next time to give it to him as directed; then we'd soon see how optional these things could be.

"That's road apples and you know it. You'll get the whole thing, and it'll be just like being there, as always. But not until you say, Good morning, Matt."

He sighed in resignation, fully aware I could be almost as stubborn as he. Also, he could see I was riding high, and he still seemed a little off balance at finding out Susan had tagged along. The subject had never been broached, but I'm sure one of his greatest fears was that one day some tender young thing was going to set a hook in me I couldn't shake.

"Good morning," he growled.

"Close enough! Thank you. Good morning to you, too, sir." I gave him the works: words, deeds, and even thoughts when I was aware of them. I'd been aware of them quite a lot last night. Admittedly I edited the part about getting stalled at the gate, though I had a sneaky feeling Susan would regale him with the story the first chance she got. Naturally, the report didn't include anything beyond the track.

The worst he could muster was a mildly pained look when I was finished. "It seems to have turned out fortuitously, having the client on hand. Apparently it added a degree of credibility you'd have never attained otherwise." It was as close as he could get to backing down; it meant we wouldn't be having that nasty talk later, after all. By now he was half convinced I'd stayed up most of the night working.

"Was it necessary to offer them seventy-five thousand dollars of Miss Neal's money? You are aware of my attitude toward prevarication."

"Look, the world's chock-full of people I'd never consider lying to, but those two aren't on the list. I needed a wedge. Susan came up with a good one, and I ran with it."

"I only hope they don't attempt to importune our client as a result of your charade."

"If they try, I'll importune them. But that pair knows better than to harass someone who's not in hock to them. People like them don't make trouble—not so much as a speeding ticket. Their careers depend on an absolutely clean slate. Whatever else they are, they're pros."

"Which brings us to the question of just what else they might be. Your instincts prompted you to choose the shock approach. Were your instincts true? Your report is inconclusive in that regard. Surely the confrontation resulted in some personal conclusions. I'd like to hear them."

I'd known that was coming, but I still wasn't prepared. "As I said, they're pros. Maybe not big time, but they didn't get where they are by kissing babies. My best guess would be that they make out very well catering to the local high rollers, but they are also connected. Local reps for the mob, handling bets on everything from horses to high school football. They operate semi-openly; it's not much of a secret in any town which bars can lay off a bet for you. Hell, look at the way they described their high-stakes poker setup to us openly, and who some of their regulars are. Guys like them are allowed to coexist with the law in every large community. At least the law knows who they are, that they'll keep it clean, and they'll even help discourage competition. They consider themselves a new breed of cat—I guess they are. More businessmen than racketeers. Brooks Brothers suits, a computer network to handle the action, and I doubt either one has carried a gun in years. I don't say they're above collecting their debts, but it's not like the old days. Now it's more likely to be a letter to your wife or employer than it is a broken arm. Of course, if that didn't work they'd find something that did. But, incredible as it sounds, they have managed to achieve a cloak of respectability. Some of them are even active in politics. That's why I really can't see those two risking everything they've got going for themselves by becoming involved in any way in the murder of an influential member of the community. A murder where the investigation might be wide enough and deep enough to suck them in—it makes zero sense. The stakes just aren't high enough."

"Then why their extreme response to your suggestion they might share some guilty knowledge with Harold Herbert?"

"Maybe I didn't tell that part of it very well. My guess is they were mad because I'd sandbagged them into talking to me in the first place. By then Paul knew I'd foxed him. They were concerned, too, that we even made the connection between them and Harold. The last thing they need is to have the name of Nolte popping up in newspaper accounts of a murder."

"So you stand ready to discount all possibility of malfeasance on the part of the Noltes, then?"

"Don't put words in my mouth. Those two would malfease anyone right out of their socks. And violence wouldn't bother them either, if the stakes were high and enough safeguards were in place. I suspect they're violent enough on a personal level, but as a part of normal business routine, no. There's not enough chips on the table for them to stick out their well-barbered necks for Harold."

"There 'aren't enough chips,'" he corrected me automatically.

"Good, I'm glad we agree." I grinned. I didn't seem to be able to stop grinning that morning.

"You do that merely to vex me, I know. Find out if Mr.

Herbert is still being detained. A call to your friend Gloria should suffice."

"Nope! She's off Saturdays, and I wouldn't want to burn her out with another call this soon." I sat staring at the phone for half a minute, grabbed it, and hit the numbers for the SDPD.

The switchboard girl answered. "San Diego Police Department."

"Homicide, please."

"Thank you."

I listened to the faint buzz of an extension ringing. A voice I thankfully didn't recognize said, "Homicide, Duffy."

"This is Judge Detweiller's clerk. I have a warrant I'm supposed to deliver to an Inspector Dixon immediately. I was told he'd either be in his office or at city jail. The name on the warrant is Herbert. Which place is he?" The sound of the little "beep" every five seconds let me know the call was being recorded, as were all incoming calls.

"He never mentioned anything to me about any warrant on Herbert. When did all this happen?"

"We are not a wire service, Officer Duffy. Suffice it to say, the matter was presumably important enough that the Judge had to delay the start of his golf game in order to come in and draw the document. It would be appreciated around here if these demands could be anticipated during the normal work week."

"It's the lousy class of crooks these days—they're inconsiderate as all hell," he responded sarcastically. His trained caution now displaced with anger, he told me, "The Inspector left here half an hour ago to take another shot at Herbert over at the jail."

"Thank you." I hung up feeling pretty smug. Duffy would want to know what the warrant was about the next time he saw Dixon. It would drive Dixon nuts, listening to that recording. At least I hoped it would. I'd pitched my voice a couple of octaves higher and altered my entire speech cadence, as best I could.

"The poor bastard's still on ice as of half an hour ago. Dixon just went over to start in on him again, so he figures to be there for a while."

"Excellent! You have a gift for mimicry. You sounded exactly like the typical minor functionary. Now, I believe you have worked with Dirk, instructing him in various techniques of stalking a suspect. Is he prepared for an assignment of considerable importance?"

"Dirk tail somebody? Sure! It never occurred to him to follow a guy from the front, which is usually best for a single tail job. Other than that, I couldn't teach him a thing. He's better at it than I am, and I'm pretty damn good. His size helps—I'm too visible. The amazing thing is, he's got these great instincts. He almost seems to know what a guy's going to do before he does it."

"I am gratified to hear it. Please bring him to me."

I found Dirk outside clipping hedges and brought him in. He got that awed look on his face as he always did in Win's presence. It made me want to reach over and tweak Win's nose, just to put things back into perspective.

"Matt declares you to be an able stalker," Win stated.

Dirk looked ready to hang his head, say, Ah, gee, shucks, and start scuffing his toe into the carpet. It was more than I could stand.

"'Stalk' isn't quite the word you want, Win. He's likely to sneak up and throttle Harold. Try 'tail,' 'gumshoe,' 'keep under surveillance.' 'Stalk' is wrong—check your dictionary."

Win gave me a look designed to do to me what a microwave does to a roast. Ignoring the interruption, he went on to instruct Dirk. "This is fortuitous, because I want you to *stalk* a man named Harold Herbert, whom you heard discussed last night in Mexico. I anticipate his imminent release from custody. It may very well prove useful to have a record of his activities immediately thereafter. Matt will provide specific instructions. Phone in as circumstances permit."

Outside in the hall, I made a few suggestions. I told Dirk where Harold would be exiting if and when he was released. I described him with enough detail to insure that Dirk wouldn't be likely to wander off after the wrong guy. "And keep your eyes peeled for Dixon," I warned him. "Don't let him spot you, whatever else you do. Take my car. Harold rode in the house car the day of the funeral and may remember it. Log the details—times are always important—also addresses, car licenses—don't ever trust your memory. Food will become a problem if you're stuck there for a long time. Better have Louis whip up something to take with you."

"Never mind the food. I often go for days without eating. It's good for you." He remained standing there, something obviously on his mind.

"Question?"

"Not about the job," he told me hesitantly. "About last night. It was really fun. But Susan—Miss Neal, I mean—she's not like most girls, is she? You know what I mean. She's . . . kind of special, isn't she?"

"After they kiss you, it's okay to call them by their first names. Girls come in all types. Just like guys, only softer. She's by no means unique, but you're right—she is special."

"I like her, Matt."

"She likes you too. Thinks you're handsome and should have been a bullfighter. It's a good thing you feel that way, because you're going to be seeing a lot of her around here. She may even become a permanent fixture."

He beamed with pleasure at the idea and hurried out the door to change out of his scruffy gardening clothes. I knew our only concern would be pulling him off the job. When Win asked him to do something, the task became an obsession until completed. I shuddered at the memory of my arrival, when Win had assigned him the task of whipping me into shape.

Back at my desk, I told Win, "The bloodhounds are loose. What do you expect to get out of this?"

"I have no preconceived notions, but certainly Mr. Herbert's actions may prove suggestive. He will be very near the ragged edge of exhaustion after a day and a night of interrogation. His normal judgment may well fail him. If he were to meet with Nick Barber, for example, I'd be pleased to know of it. We may hope for a ringing endorsement of our hypothesis that Mr. Herbert acted in collusion with someone else. Failing that, I'll settle for whatever tiny morsel of datum Dame Fortune grants."

"While we're waiting on Dame Fortune, what am I supposed to be doing?"

"There are some letters to be attended to."

It was my turn to sigh. I snatched the top letter from the "In" tray and handed it to him.

"Matt," he inquired softly, ignoring the envelope in his hand, "may I inquire whether you are allowing yourself to become emotionally involved with our current client?"

There it was, just like that. You never could tell what gyrations were going on inside his skull. And he said I had an instinct for phenomena. "It's entirely possible," I admitted. "But there's a problem. It looks like Dirk and I might have to fight a duel over her."

"Dirk? Preposterous! Another of your witless jests."

"Nope—straight scoop. She kissed him good night. His eyes are still glazed over—didn't you notice?"

"Good grief! Both of you? The woman must be Circe incarnate." He frowned. "What was it Johnson had to say about a relationship with a woman? 'It was demeaning, expensive, and ridiculously brief'? That's not right; bring me Boswell's *Life of Johnson*. I'll be absolutely useless for anything else until I've looked it up."

I could feel a long, boring lecture on the way. The reference was just an excuse to jaw on the subject of the perfidy of women. The only way I knew to avoid it was to beat him at his own game. I didn't get the chance very often, but something had clicked and, besides, this was my lucky day.

"Win, it just so happens I've heard about this guy, Boswell, and from what I've heard, he wasn't much for taking Johnson's advice. I figure if it wasn't good enough for him, why should I listen? Stop me if I'm wrong, but isn't he the guy who spent a bundle running after half the dolls in London? And when he got too old to run he ambushed 'em—right?"

His look of utter exasperation was beautiful to behold. "Incredible! The sum total of your knowledge of literature could undoubtedly be engraved on the proverbial head of a pin, still you possess the one particular fragment needed to nettle me. How on earth do you manage it? I'm certain you've yet to read a single word of Balzac, but no doubt you stand ready to advise me of his imbroglios."

I just sat there grinning, enjoying myself thoroughly. He was right—I'd never read much literature, but in order to squeeze through even high school you get a certain amount of such junk thrown your way. With a memory like mine, some of it was bound to stick. There was plenty of odd crap stored between my ears, covered with dust, but there for me to take out and play with whenever I wanted to. But I'd never spotted anything with the name Balzac on it.

CHAPTER 13

We finished with all the priority correspondence by three in the afternoon. Then we worked back through the slush pile, answering some we wouldn't have normally fooled with while we had a case on, just to keep busy. I'd tried Susan's room at the Plaza when we broke for lunch, but there was no answer. I caught Win glancing at the wall clock with increasing regularity. Having nerves of steel, I restrained myself from checking my wrist more than once every five minutes.

Until Dirk called in, we wouldn't even know whether Harold had yet been released. It was possible he'd opened up to Dixon and that the case was closed. Dirk would stick until he rotted if I didn't eventually go down and drag him home.

The buzz of the phone erupted like a shot. Win had his hands free, so he beat me to it. "Yes," he snapped into the mouthpiece.

"That you, Mr. Winfield?" It was Dixon's unctuous voice. Win and I exchanged worried looks. The only reason for the call that I could think of was he'd nabbed Dirk.

"It is, Inspector." Win's tone was neutral.

"I need to talk to Doyle. He there?"

I nodded in response to Win's raised eyebrows.

"He is available. I'll see whether he wishes to speak to you."

Of course I was already listening on my extension, but we weren't even giving that much away to Dixon. "Miss me, Inspector?"

"For once in your miserable life just shut up and listen, Doyle. I'm at the Plaza Hotel. It looks like you and your boss are minus a client. One of the maids found Susan Neal dead in her room less than an hour ago. I want you down here to make the formal I.D."

I just sat there staring at all the little round holes in the mouthpiece, too numb to feel a thing.

"So? Doyle? You there, or what?"

"Yeah, I'm here." No one would have recognized my voice. It sounded brittle and tinny, like an old recording. "How was she killed?"

"Read the papers like everybody else. I can't reach her stepfather, and we need something for the record. Hell, you know how it is—we know it's her, but we can't accept the word of a maid who saw her once or twice in the hall. So you're elected—coming?"

"On my way." I managed to cradle the phone in only three tries. Win was watching me with a clinical frown.

"There's no need to put yourself through this, Matt."

"Yes, there is. It's the last time I'll ever see . . ." I had to stop and reach down and pinch the hell out of my thigh to take the center of pain away from my throat before I could go on. "It's a chance to be at the scene—I can't pass it up. Dixon doesn't know it, but he's doing us a favor. Besides, when the lab boys dust, they're going to find my prints all over the place. It will save them time and me trouble if I prepare them. They may also develop the theory she was the victim of a sexual assault if I don't set them straight." It was a rocky performance at best; my voice had worked its way up to alto by the time I finished.

"You were with her last night." He said it as if it were the saddest thing he'd ever heard.

"Yeah. Maybe sometime I'll feel like talking about it."

"I'm truly sorry, Matt," he stated with simple eloquence. "In your shocked state it's little wonder you missed the implication of a fact the Inspector inadvertently gave us just now."

Not really caring, I asked, "What'd I miss?"

"This case may well be concluded. The good Inspector just informed us that Harold Herbert could not be reached. Obviously, he's no longer in custody."

The situation slowly penetrated my stunned brain. "And Dirk's right on his heels. If he headed straight for the Plaza Hotel . . ."

"Precisely! We would have him. I'm almost tempted to say, 'Do have him,' for who else had the slightest reason to kill that innocent girl?"

"Except Harold," I agreed grimly. "He had lots of reasons." I shoved myself to my feet, jamming my chair back into the wall. Normally it would have brought a howl from Win, who can't abide an imperfection on the walls or ceiling.

This time all he said was, "You look dreadful. I don't think you should drive down there."

"What do you want me to do?" I croaked. "Want to dictate any more letters?" I regretted it before it was even out of my mouth. I suddenly noticed he looked pretty crummy, too. "Sorry, strike that. But I need to stay busy, keep moving—you know me."

"Yes, Matt, I know you." He nodded gravely. "Go, as you must."

I rushed outside, sucking up all the air I could find. It wasn't easy. There was some problem with my throat.

I took a swing by the jail to make sure Dirk wasn't still staked out. He wasn't. So presumably he hadn't missed Harold.

There were three official department vehicles outside the hotel, plus an ambulance. Everything looked normal in the lobby until I spotted a detective named Bostwick behind the desk. He was working a pencil while a nervous little guy in a dark blue suit worked his gums. The Prussian general at the bank of elevators remembered me. Nothing was said, but I could tell he'd made the connection. He gaped at me, no doubt toying with the thought he might well be eyeballing the murderer.

The mob scene began when I arrived on the twelfth floor. A uniformed patrolman challenged my right to exist. I gave him my name; he relaxed and allowed me to proceed. I was almost sorry he did. Outside 1218, men and equipment littered the hall. Open police lab kits and camera gear formed a maze, forcing people to pick their way in and out carefully. Two bored-looking ambulance jockeys leaned against the wall beside an immaculately made-up stretcher. They gazed down at it fondly, obviously wishing they could park their butts on it. They wouldn't, of course; it wouldn't do to have wrinkled sheets when they placed Susan. . . .

I inhaled down to my toes, reminded myself I was supposed to be a professional, and that there was only one way to do Susan any good now. So I ducked inside.

I nearly stumbled over her. The lovely, witty, sensuous woman who'd made every cell in my body hum barely twelve hours before lay sprawled on her left side, arms and legs akimbo, effectively blocking the narrow entryway. A guy with one camera around his neck and another poised to shoot barked at me to either get it in or get it out. I stepped gingerly over her outflung right arm and got it in. She might have been taking a nap if not for the dark, ugly weal at the right base of her skull, about where the trapezius muscle attached. Someone had arranged her hair in order to better expose the bruise. She looked frail in her robe, and the hair that had glowed with ever-changing highlights was dull. I wanted very much to bend down and brush her hair back to cover the terrible blemish on her neck.

Dixon was perched on the arm of a chair with his back to me, waving his arms angrily at someone. I sidled over to the far side of the room, hoping to buy some time before he spotted me. I let my eyes rove, taking in and storing details. There was no sign of any struggle that I could see. Bright sun streamed in through the oversized west window. To me, the room looked exactly as it had when I left that morning, with a single obscene exception: A lone white carnation lay on top of the coffee table that paralleled the sofa. I stared at it hypnotically, knowing I'd never lay eyes on another one without experiencing a sick feeling of revulsion.

Dixon rocked to his feet. Without conscious thought, I backpeddled out of the room. A thin young lab man with horn-rimmed glasses was fussily dusting the dresser top in her bedroom. "All the prints match, or are you coming up with multiples?" I asked without much interest.

He continued working. "Can't be sure about most of the partials, but so far all the good ones look like a match. Too bad—this glass top takes a beautiful print."

"How long've you been with the department?"

"Be three years in January."

"Ever come up with a print they were able to use?"

He looked up at me for the first time and smiled ruefully. "If you mean as corroborating evidence against a known suspect, yes. If you mean, have I ever identified a criminal and solved a case through prints, no. But I keep hoping."

It was a question I always asked lab dicks. The answer never varied. If a husband brains his wife with a poker, calls the police, and confesses, maybe the prints come in handy later after the guy's lawyer tells him to dummy up and the confession gets scrapped because somebody said a naughty word to the killer. Other than that, the only crooks I ever heard of who were traced by prints were in books written by guys who never met a real cop. Dumb as real crooks are, they've all heard of gloves. You can even get flesh-colored rubber ones now. The ads say they're thin enough to pick up a dime. Considering the current crime stats, they must be a hot seller.

Another guy walked into the room and asked me, "Are you the one's supposed to be doing the inventory so we can figure out what's missing?"

"Not me."

"Then what the hell *are* you doing here?" he demanded.

"Kibitzing, waiting for Dixon to get free. What's an inventory going to prove?" I asked him. "You can't know what she started out with."

"Someone back in New York may have helped her pack, and we've got standardized lists we can compare it to. Based on lots of variables like age, ethnic origin, financial status, stuff like that. You'd be amazed how accurate it works out most of the time. We know how much luggage she arrived with, and that helps."

It always helps to play dumb; it allows the other guy to play smart. It's a role we all cherish, playing smart, and one we seldom get a chance to act out. We were buddies for life.

He went over and started chinning with the print man, and I ambled back out into the front room. Dixon spied me and bulled his way over.

"What were you doing in there, Doyle?" he barked.

"Waiting for you to free up. Looked like you were snowed under when I arrived."

"And how long ago was that?" he asked suspiciously.

"Couple of minutes. What's the difference? I didn't mind."

"The difference is, I don't like the idea of you snooping around the scene of a murder as if you owned the place." His voice was loud enough to turn every head in the room. "In case you've forgotten, you no longer have a license to snoop. Don't you think you're in enough trouble already?"

I couldn't stop my fists from clenching, but I did manage to lock my elbows in time to keep from decking him. I gave him a look of pure venom, saying, for his ears alone, "The only trouble I give a damn about is lying over there by the door. If it's illegal to want to find out who did it, you can save us both a lot of trouble and arrest me right now."

Dixon's cop instincts sensed danger. He backed up a step, out of range, cocked his head, and regarded me thoughtfully. "Like that, huh? You let this one get close to you."

"Unprofessional, I know. I don't suppose it ever happened to you."

Dixon was lost to me for a moment. "Yeah, it's happened to me," he said in a strangely mellowed voice. His big face had visibly softened, and I suddenly caught a glimpse of the man behind the perpetually angry Inspector of Homicide mask. He almost looked human.

"Take my word for it, Inspector, she was a very special lady."

"Then I'm sorry, Doyle, but I still don't want you to get the idea you can just stick your nose in. Come over here." We were both struggling to get back into character and not quite succeeding. We'd both just shared something, though I wasn't sure what. A brief flash of humanity perhaps?

He handed me a short form to sign, stating that the victim was known to me as Susan Virginia Neal. I hadn't known about the Virginia. There was so much I'd never know. I scrawled my name with a slightly shaky hand and gave it back to him. Dixon had noticed, but didn't say anything. I nodded toward the flower on the low table. "Guess it's the work of the Del Mar cat burglar. Must have gotten lost."

"Sure, that must be it," he growled. "Look, I can see this has rocked you, Doyle, and I appreciate you coming down. I'll give you this for free. I've got an APB out on Harold Herbert right now. There's not a doubt in my mind this is his work. That shifty bastard and his fucking carnations!"

"Thanks. Can you make it stick this time?"

His bloodshot eyes blazed. "Oh, I'll make it stick. He'll rot in a cell until I do. If I have to, I'll hold him on suspicion for seventy-two hours, walk him around the block, and arrest him all over again for littering. I've got a crack lab team going over this place; we'll find something before we leave."

"So, as of this minute, you can't pin it on him."

"You tell me if I'm wrong. We turned him loose not two hours ago, six blocks from here. He left mad as hell at the deceased because he knew she'd turned those letters over to us. I've gotten a report on the terms of his wife's will. He was out in the cold. Except now, with the daughter dead, it will all revert to him, except for a life annuity for Mrs. Herbert's son, and some charitable bequests. Our Harold's back in fat city. There's no lividity; the stiff—sorry—Miss Neal hadn't even cooled off yet when we arrived. Even without the M.E.'s report, I know damn well she was killed after his release."

I was stunned by the impact of a totally unexpected factor. "Mrs. Herbert's son? First I heard Susan had a brother."

"He probably wasn't a favorite topic of conversation," Dixon told me. "Born with the I.Q. of a kumquat, from what I understand. Went right from the hospital to a home for the mentally retarded and stayed there. Twenty-five now, I think."

I didn't try to evaluate this startling new information, just tucked it away and did my best to keep up the momentum of the exchange.

"You seem to be implying he killed his wife, too. What happened to that alibi you assured us was absolutely tight?"

"Not only is the alibi worthless, it's become an indictment. Turns out he skipped the meeting for half an hour. Plenty of time to get home, kill his wife, and get back. We know his wife was as regimented as a Swiss clock. He could count on her getting home from her Sunday night committee meeting at ten sharp, give or take a minute. Even her neighbor knew it, which is how she knew to watch for her. The clincher is, his wife was murdered during the time period he was out. You can take this one to the bank, Doyle."

I held my breath, hoping no one would interrupt us. He was opening up like a book, probably out of sympathy, and I wanted to keep him going. "You're forgetting the fact that his secretary places him in his office working up a complicated bid during that half-hour time period."

"Helga needed that putz to work up the bid proposal like I need another ulcer. We're not sure of the exact scenario yet, but I figure he foxed her too, because otherwise she'd have come forward by now. She can't stand the guy—that's why it nearly kills her to provide him with an alibi. She hasn't said a dozen words about the whole thing, but we know damn well she could have done all the work on the bid contract alone. Herbert gave her the figures and said he was going down to the gym for a quick shower. She told him she could have it done in twenty or twenty-five minutes if she hurried. He told her to rush it and left. She says he came back before she was finished. She noticed his hair was wet, and she still swears he couldn't have had time to leave the building, kill his wife, and get back that fast."

He gave me a self-satisfied look. "But this might cheer you up, Doyle. Here's the clincher. We came up with a witness—old man who lives out there near the plant and walks his dog right by it every night. He knows Herbert by sight. We have a statement from him placing Herbert running out to his car and tearing ass out of the parking lot at nine-fifty Sunday night. That's the result of something called hard work, in case you hadn't heard of it. We canvass neighborhoods, wear out a lot of shoe leather. Sounds dull, I know, but it works. You don't solve complicated crimes sitting on your butt in a mansion in La Jolla reading books." So the truce was over and he was already reverting to form.

"If you've got that, you should be able to get a grand jury indictment. So why'd you turn him loose?"

"The field report on the witness came in fifteen minutes after he was released. By the time I went out and double-checked the old guy's reliability and got a sworn statement, the report of this," he waved his hand around the suite, "came in. That's twice I've let him go; there won't be a third time."

"Thanks for the dope, Inspector, it'll give Win and me something to talk about between soaps. By the way, he said you were probably very good at routine procedural work. I guess he was right. And don't forget to tell the print guy to pull mine when he gets back to the lab. He'll want to eliminate them, as well as Susan's, so he can see what's left."

He just stood there, probably wondering whether he'd just been insulted or complimented. I had to admit Dixon wasn't as big a louse as I'd thought. We were just natural enemies. Official cops don't like private cops. But he'd let up riding me when he saw that Susan's death had taken a big chunk out of my hide. And he'd gone to some trouble to let me know the scales were about to be balanced. I might have added his name to my Christmas card list if it weren't for that crack about sitting on our butts in a mansion. Maybe it stung so much because it was too close to home.

The medics had gone and taken Susan with them. There was nothing left but a taped outline on the carpet to show where she'd fallen when she died. On my way out I stepped high, over the pattern of her right arm, just as I'd avoided the limb itself on the way in. I wasn't aware of doing it. Dixon saw it, though. A long time after he would tell me about it, and say it was about the saddest goddamn thing he ever saw.

CHAPTER 14

The five o'clock traffic made for a slow trip home. Watching the diurnal river of cars only made me fantasize what it would have been like to have joined the mainstream of society, going home to Susan every night after work. It was a very sad train of thought, but better to think of her and be miserable than not to think of her at all. I couldn't help noticing universally dejected looks on all the faces around me—was it my perception, or was everyone depressed?

My heart rate jumped the moment I started up the long drive leading to the house. My Chevy was parked in its usual spot. Rushing inside, I found Dirk standing stiffly in front of Win, looking thoroughly unhappy.

"Don't tell me you lost him," I pleaded. "I know you can track a flea through a swamp, so please don't tell me you lost him."

Dirk merely shook his head, looking slightly offended.

"I instructed him to terminate the surveillance," Win informed me. His voice was tight with suppressed fury. "Dirk, it would be best if you would kindly repeat a full account for Matt's benefit."

As soon as I began warming my chair, Dirk angled around to face toward me. He opened a small notebook and referred to it. The suspense was unbearable. I knew from the atmosphere it wasn't going to be great news, but whatever it was, I wanted it. I felt like tearing the book out of his hands.

"Arrived across from the jail at 10:13 A.M. and parked where you told me, Matt. Nothing happened until 1:10 P.M., when Mr. Herbert came out, talking to another man. They both got into a 1988 Mercury, the other guy driving, and I followed them to 1931 Carol Court in Del Mar."

"That's his house! Harold went home?"

"Yes. The other man's name is Allen Kent. At least that's the name on the car's registration. I thought it might be important, so I took a chance and looked. The car was left in the drive unlocked."

"Nice going," I told him. "Then what?"

"Ten minutes later, 1:46 P.M., Kent came out and drove away. At 1:59 Mr. Herbert opened the garage door and drove out. He'd changed his clothes."

"I'll bet! Okay, fine. Then what?"

"I followed him south on Pacific Coast Highway. He took the Torrey Pines Park turnoff and left his car just inside the park. He took off, walking along one of the nature trails, the one leading out to the cliffs overlooking the beach."

"Skip that! Where did he go then? What time did he leave there?" The time element was getting close. He should have been on his way downtown by then.

"That's just it, Matt—he didn't leave. I kept expecting him to. It looked like he was trying to come to some decision, and then I figured he'd leave. That's why I couldn't risk going to find a phone. Finally I worked my way up close to where he was lying. It was a sandy spot right near the edge of the cliff. He was sound asleep! That's when I took a chance and beat it down to the phone at the golf course half a mile away. By the time I called it was after four. Mr. Winfield told me to forget it and come on home."

Dirk was completely incapable of referring to him as Win.

"You have fulfilled your assignment with competence," Win told him moodily. "You mustn't mistake our chagrin for denigration of your efforts. In ancient times a disgruntled monarch sometimes ordered the death of the messenger bearing ill tidings. I'm afraid some vestige of that unfair attitude persists here within this room today. We commend you, though our demeanor may not bespeak it." Win was at his most pedantic when he was pissed off.

Dirk may not have been able to spell all the words, but he recognized a dismissal when he heard one. He leaned over toward me and said hesitantly, "Mr. Winfield told me about . . . what happened to Miss . . . Susan. I don't know what to say to you, you know I'm not good with words, but I want to ask you something. I don't like asking favors, but I am. When you find the man who did this, will you come and tell me? And if it works out you have to go after him, I want to go. This is the only favor I'll ever ask you."

"She'll always be special, Dirk. As for the favor, I'll keep it in mind. It all depends on how things work out. If I can—and Win okays it—I will. But you'd have to promise to obey orders."

"Thanks, Matt. I'll do whatever you say. And I'm sorry as hell for you. I mean . . . you know."

"Yeah, I'm sorry too. For both of us."

It was getting pretty maudlin around there, and I was glad when he left, though I appreciated what he'd tried to say.

"I believe that's the very first lie I have ever heard that man utter," Win observed.

"Lie?"

"Indeed! It was a bald-faced lie when he told you he'd obey your orders if allowed the boon of confronting the murderer. Given that opportunity, Dirk would kill without mercy or restraint."

"What makes you think I won't? Damn it, Win, she was

such a great girl. I mean it—neither Dirk nor I will ever forget her."

Win looked over at me forlornly. "Do me the honor to include me among your number. I, too, confess to being quite taken with Miss . . . with Susan." He appeared lost in reverie for a minute, then resumed his look of grim determination. "It will be but a hollow tribute, yet the only one we are in a position to pay. Let's put an end to this accursed case. We'll begin with your report from the Plaza Hotel."

When I got to the part about Martha Herbert's having a twenty-five-year-old son tucked away in an institution somewhere, Win showed his first signs of animation. He called Randy and gave him the task of running the boy to ground, explaining it would be far easier for a doctor to penetrate the encapsulated world of institutions and medical records than it would be for me. When I asked him why he thought it was even worth finding the son, he said he wouldn't know until he found him.

Then, beginning with my innocent-seeming interviews with the initial robbery victims, we set out to review every single detail of the entire case. We plugged away until after eleven, busily building theories that invariably toppled of their own weight. I held out for Nick Barber, but Win wasn't buying it at any price. Killing Martha for Harold, in return for future considerations, had looked good, but why schedule the murder at a time when Harold himself was without an alibi? And why kill Susan in such a way as to further incriminate Harold? We kept bumping our noses against the fact that the killer had to be someone who wanted Harold put away badly enough to waltz into a busy hotel on a Saturday afternoon and kill again. Or did Harold kill his wife—which every scrap of evidence indicated—meaning we had murderers to worry about? We were forced to admit that Dixon's evidence was totally conclusive. Why else would he have snuck out of the plant last

Sunday evening? It was all terribly confusing. My missing hours of sleep were coming back to haunt me, and, combined with the emotional devastation of the day, I admit I wasn't tracking very well.

Win finally called a halt, planning to resume in the morning if I was willing to sacrifice my day off. I told him the last thing I wanted was a day off. Halfway to my room, I realized I'd worked right through dinner. I considered staging a raid on the kitchen but couldn't generate enough enthusiasm to bother.

For one of the few times in my life, sleep eluded me. I remembered the look of horror on Win's face when he realized both Dirk and I were eager to serve as avenging angels if the wheels of justice came up flat. For a man who'd chosen the detective business to while away his twilight years, he certainly was saddled with an incredible reverence for life in all its myriad forms. I recalled the first time I'd made that discovery about him. It had been several years ago, when I was still a rookie on the club, and Dirk was determined to teach me every trick he knew. That particular day it had been knife-throwing. My previous experience stopped at a fair game of mumblety-peg, but I was nothing if not game.

Dirk met me near the exercise mat out behind the house. Without a word, he handed me a strange-looking knife. It was a flat, thin length of dark carbon steel, wider at the blade than the haft, but coming to a deadly sharp point.

He walked twenty yards toward a two-foot-thick palm tree. I followed. He nodded at the tree. I shrugged and took the knife by the blade and threw it with force. It caromed off the tree and homed right back in on me, damn near stabbing me in the right thigh.

Dirk smiled, picked it up, glanced along its length to check its true, then moved two steps back. His motion was barely perceptible. One moment the knife was poised near his ear; an instant later it struck, thrumming, in the middle of the palm tree.

He retrieved the knife and returned. "It's simple, Matt, but like everything else, there are rules. Watch! Slow-Mo. My elbow is pointing directly at the target. Never rush the swing, but do it with authority. You flipped it—big mistake. The wrist must be immobile. Your upper arm doesn't change position as you release, so the extended arm winds up pointing directly at the target. Follow through completely so your hand ends up alongside your right thigh. Throw from the same stance as if you were boxing: left foot forward slightly and knees bent just a little."

After three slow movements from start through finish, he let fly again. This time I went to retrieve it. You could have covered both scars with the palm of your hand.

"The rest is nothing but practice," he told me. "Remember the rules and it'll come. One more thing. You can only throw so the knife hits point-on from specific distances. The blade will turn once and land right at about five feet, twice at about eleven feet, and three times at about eighteen feet. Beyond that, don't even bother. It only works in movies. The range varies with the individual, so find yours and practice until the effort becomes as instinctive as throwing a punch. As a weapon, the throwing knife has a limited usefulness, but there might come a time it will mean the difference between coming back from an assignment and not. It has several advantages over a gun, believe it or not. Besides the obvious one of concealment, a man with a knife in him has an irresistible urge to drop what he's doing and remove it. This buys you time when you might need it the most."

He turned and walked away. It was the longest speech I'd ever heard him make before or since. I spent the next two hours doing my level best to kill a tree that had never done me any harm.

After dinner that evening I'd entered the office. Win smiled up at me from his chair and told me, "I have been informed by Mr. Bomande your training is coming along splendidly."

"Yeah, today he even showed me how to kill a tree. In case I'm ever assaulted by one."

"Kindly explain yourself, Mr. Doyle."

"We were practicing out back with throwing knives. The target we used was one of those big palms." I was amazed at his obvious distress.

"Never do a thing like that again! Put up a target, use the side of the house if you must, but never inflict another wound on any living creature on these premises—do you understand? That includes trees—especially trees. All life is sacred. Good God, man, are you a barbarian? I'll call the nursery in the morning. I hope there is something they can do to preserve the tree. I believe there's something they apply to the wounds to prevent insects from entering, or some such thing."

I remembered sitting there with my jaw hanging. Ever since I'd arrived, all everyone seemed to care about was turning me into a walking weapon. And there the old fart who was behind it all sat throwing a tizzy about some scratches in a tree! It was the first of many paradoxes I was to discover about Carter Winfield.

I lay there wide awake, trying to grin at that long-ago day and at how much had happened to all of us since. Later I came to realize all the conditioning and weapons training was merely to ensure my own well-being and survival. Win worried himself sick that I'd someday fail to return from an assignment he'd sent me on. Not that he'd ever admit it.

It was all a valiant attempt to fill my mind with pleasant thoughts, thus displacing the gloomy ones in residence. It didn't work very well. Before I finally drifted off, there was more than ample time to conduct a detailed study of the effects of feeling totally miserable and frustrated.

CHAPTER 15

Morning came ahead of schedule again. My window view revealed nothing but a gray wall. The heat of the Santa Ana had broken, replaced by the usual low coastal fog that would drift five miles out to sea by noon and roll right back in at night. You could get the same effect by living inside a huge, inverted, galvanized steel bucket.

I delayed my morning ablutions when I heard the start of a five-minute local news spot on my TV. Harold had been arrested and was being held on suspicion of murder. They'd been waiting for him when he returned from his nap on the beach last night. Nobody was about to buy that for an alibi, of course. Dixon certainly wasn't going to upgrade his opinion of us when we stepped forward to supply Harold with an out. The real icing on the cake was that Dirk had never even had a license, being a convicted felon. The more I thought about it the more ludicrous it became. Two accused felons—Win and me—had dispatched a convicted felon—Dirk—to track an accused murderer—Harold Herbert. Now we were in the impossible position of being able to prove his innocence of at least the latest murder, but of being afraid to open our mouths. The whole thing was entirely too much for me. If we stepped forward they wouldn't let Harold out—they'd toss us in with him. I considered crawling back into bed and pulling the covers over my head, but it didn't seem like much of a long-term solution to me.

I couldn't get the least bit enthusiastic about my morning romp with Dirk but opted for sticking with routine as my only hope for salvation. He was waiting outside on the grass, running in place, wearing his usual gamy track suit. Mine was no joy to be near, I'll admit, but his made it advisable always to occupy the upwind side when running beside him. He took off as soon as he saw me coming, and I stumbled along after. The chill, clammy air was a tangible, hostile wall hovering a hundred yards in every direction.

We took it easy down the rough wooden steps leading to the beach. The weatherworn planks were loosely set in the sandstone and had a habit of dumping you if you stepped too far forward. Dirk hit the sand at the bottom. Suddenly he froze. I could see his body go rigid, alert, like a guard dog scenting trouble. He turned slowly, looking toward the cliff to the right of the steps. I paused, still four feet from the bottom, wondering what was going on.

The first thing I saw was the gun. It appeared from one of the countless shallow potholes worn into the soft cliff near the bottom by wind and rain and angry neap tides. The gun was attached to a hand, and the hand was attached to Carl Nolte. Paul materialized beside him. Together they duck-walked from the low cave, comically inappropriate in suits, ties, and gleaming leather shoes. Carl pointed the gun while Paul did the talking.

"Down the rest of the way, Doyle."

I graciously accepted the invitation. "You boys must have missed your plane to Vegas," I said, facing the pair from a spot beside Dirk. I silently willed him not to do anything hasty, noting the steady, businesslike way Carl was holding the gun.

At the same time, I prepared myself to back his play if my message was not received.

"We'll make the plane—don't worry—but first I keep my promise. I'm going to teach you not to come at me heeled and take advantage of my good nature." Paul shed his tie and jacket, never taking his eyes off me. "Nobody moves unless they want Carl to put a bullet in them. He's very reliable with that gun, I assure you."

So Paul was planning to take his pound of flesh from me. I relaxed a little, figuring nobody took his coat off in order to shoot someone. What the hell—I'd come to the beach for a little exercise anyway. And ever since yesterday afternoon I'd felt like tearing something apart. Paul looked capable of keeping me busy for a while, but that suited me fine.

"I thought you two civic-minded businessmen didn't believe in nasty, old-fashioned violence. And it's Sunday, too—what would your priest think?" I was fervently hoping Paul would retain his leather-soled shoes. They'd amount to ice skates in this sand.

He stepped back a pace and bent to remove his shoes. So much for wishful thinking. "This is strictly personal—not professional." He peeled off his socks, stood erect, and pulled the nastiest-looking sap I'd ever seen from his pants pocket. It was a slim leather bag containing, I guessed, twelve or so ounces of birdshot. It effectively extended his range about a foot and would be as lethal as an ax. He would be able to punish me cruelly without ever letting me get near him.

"This is a public beach, fellas," I reminded them. "What would your oh-so-respectable associates think if you ended up in jail on assault charges?"

Paul moved away from his brother and Dirk, beckoning me to follow. "Doyle, from what I hear, the cops in this town would pin a medal on me for what I'm about to do. But the fact is, I'm nowhere near here. You'd be amazed at how many guys are sitting looking at us somewhere else right now."

He glanced over at Dirk. "You're no part of this—just so you know. Relax and enjoy the show, then you can lug the remains home."

He turned back to me, working the cosh around in his right hand. Bending slightly at the knees, he began circling to his right. "The real secret's in the wrist, Doyle. Like golf. Lots of snap. In case you're wondering, I'm probably not going to kill you, but my guess is you'll wish I would before I'm through."

I stood there, flat-footed, trying to look terrified. My arms hung loose as I screwed myself around, following him in place. I'll admit looking frightened didn't demand a whole lot of acting skill. I knew, even if I managed to block a blow, the best I'd end up with would be a shattered arm. It was going to be all too easy for Carl to carry out his program unless I was very careful.

"Cheer up! You came out with your pal for a little exercise, didn't you?" The banter was designed to distract. Instead, it served to signal his intent. Lunging forward, he swung in a wide diagonal arc from my right shoulder to my left hip. I saw it coming and backtracked, but he followed, reversing the attack with a continuous figure-eight movement. The butt of the bag barely brushed my breastbone. The amount of pain generated was shocking.

His next target was my head. His method was simple and effective: to keep the momentum going, alternating sites until he connected. It was a no-win situation because Paul could maneuver forward a lot quicker than I could back away. I could have easily grabbed the damn thing, but all that would get me was a broken hand.

The odds weren't going to improve; I realized I had to make my move before he nailed me again. I waited, allowing my head to get out in front a bit. I didn't believe his statement that he wasn't going to kill me, because if it was true he wouldn't be going for all those head shots. Then he took the bait, aiming one at my ear with real enthusiasm. I dropped to the sand like a bag of cement. His forward momentum brought him within range before he could put on the brakes or bring his basher around in position again. Rolling onto my right side, I lashed out with both feet, hitting Paul at the ankles with everything I could muster. His feet flew away from me, and he impacted on his left shoulder with a gratifying groan. If I hadn't moved in time, he'd have landed right on top of me. The blackjack went flying as he instinctively tried to brace against the fall with outstretched hands. I snatched a handful of sand and threw it right in his face. It may not have been humane, but he'd forfeited all rights when he'd tried to brain me with that brute of a weapon.

As he choked, spit, and rubbed his eyes furiously, I scrabbled over and retrieved the evil-looking weapon. A glimpse of Dirk and Carl confirmed a presumption. Dirk had the gun stuck in his waistband; Carl lay face down in the sand, hands behind his head, arching his back to watch me.

I grabbed a fistful of Paul's hair and pulled him upright. "Talk to me. Try to make friends—fast!"

He stared hypnotically at the leather bag of shot now dangling from my hand. He had a deep appreciation of its potential; it was obvious he'd had practice. I slapped him on the left shoulder with it. It made a soft, sickening sound, surprising me that so little effort garnered such results. Paul moaned, his eyes popped, and he held his shoulder without ever taking his wild eyes off the lethal weapon.

"I said fast. It'll take me awhile to master that wrist snap you mentioned, but, as you said, I did come down here for some exercise."

"I don't know what you want me to say," he whined.

"Anything concerning Susan Neal's death will do, as long as it's straight. Every lie gets you a shot with your little sapper to the target of my choice."

"There's nothing I can tell you about that, honest to God, Doyle! I'm sick about it myself." His voice rose shrilly as I went into my backswing.

"An omission counts as a lie; remember that." I whacked him in the same spot, not as hard. He made the mistake of putting his hand in the way. There was a different sound this time—a sharp crack. Without looking, I knew he had at least one broken finger. Large beads of greasy sweat formed on his forehead in spite of the still chilly air.

"Don't blow this one, Paul. It's an easy one, but it's for all the marbles. Tie Harold Herbert to his wife's murder."

"He had nothing to do with it. He—wait, please!" he screamed as I went into my exaggerated windup. "Give me a chance and I'll tell you. Herbert was with me and Carl that night, right at the time it happened. I swear it."

"He was with you? Why would he go to all the trouble of sneaking out just to see you two? Make it convincing."

Paul was showing surprising potential as a tenor. "I guess we were riding him pretty hard by then. Told him if he didn't come up with something substantial by ten o'clock Sunday night, on account, he'd be laid up in the hospital for quite a while."

I turned him so his back was to his brother. "Very quietly, exactly where did you meet him? And God help you if you're stringing me."

"It was at Scripps Hospital parking lot. He left just as the ten o'clock news was starting on the car radio."

I grabbed an ear and pulled him across the sand to where Carl still lay face down on the beach. Either he'd lost interest or his back had given out, because he lay with his cheek deep in the sand, no longer even attempting to watch.

"Carl, I want the exact time and place you two met Harold Herbert one week ago today—if you did. Paul's given me his version. If it's straight, you should have no trouble duplicating his answer."

Carl twisted his neck and searched his brother's eyes. It wasn't easy, with his hands still locked behind his head. I suspected Dirk had made quite an impression on him and he wasn't about to risk upsetting him. "South parking lot of

Scripps Hospital. Ten P.M., give or take no more than five minutes either way," he told me flatly. "Mr. Doyle?"

"Yeah, Carl."

"My brother acted foolishly, coming here. He has this problem with his temper. I told him it was dumb, risking something like this for nothing. What I'm saying is this: Don't make it any worse than it is now—let's all pick up our marbles and go home. Don't hurt my brother anymore and it ends here. I can promise you that. Hurt him anymore, or me, and we all lose—everybody here." He spoke softly, unemotionally, as if remarking upon the dreary weather conditions.

"Suits me, after you finish telling me all about last Sunday night."

Carl was in a mood to volunteer. "We told him we'd be at the parking lot between nine-thirty and ten, not to fail to show unless he liked hospitals. He made it just under the wire with eight grand, which wasn't much, but it bought him some time. That's everything we know. Herbert couldn't have done it if the newspaper reports are accurate and she was killed at ten and he was gone from his office only half an hour. He wasted a good ten minutes crying about how the five hundred a day was killing him."

"Five hundred a day?"

"Interest on the seventy-five thousand."

"Killing him is right. Remind me never to hit you two up for a loan." I was stalling. Something hadn't sounded right. Then I had it. "How could you possibly have known Herbert was gone from the plant for only half an hour? That little detail has never been released."

"Relax," Carl said. "We knew because he wanted us to cover for him in case his secretary opened her yap about his not being right with her in his office. Said we might end up being the only thing between him and a life sentence."

"What did you tell him?"

"We told him to stick it where the sun doesn't shine. We'd deny ever seeing him that night unless he paid us off."

"Sweet pair, you two. Okay, Carl; last question. Tell me all you know or even suspect about who *did* kill both women."

"Paul gave it to you straight. We were planning to drop by with Herbert's note and see the girl, just on the off chance she'd actually be willing to pay it. Everybody in town is talking about the nut who's killing women, but there isn't so much as a whisper as to who. Guys who might be expected to know something about such things don't have a clue what's going down, believe me."

"Say I do for now. Get up and take baby brother somewhere and get his finger set." Paul was totally engrossed with the second finger of his right hand. It had already swollen to a lovely shade of hot red. His face was still caked with sand. Carl got to his feet slowly, rubbing his left kidney area, casting an inquiring look toward Dirk. Dirk patted the gun wedged into his sweat pants and shook his head. Carl didn't seem inclined to argue the point, so he gathered Paul's clothing and shoes, walked over and gave Paul a shove on the back to get him started down the beach.

I watched the pair shuffle away, then started up the steps.

"Aren't we going to run?" Dirk complained.

I gave him a dirty look. "Now that takes guts. You just stood around and watched me nearly get my head torn off—now you're bitching because I won't run. You run—I've had my exercise for the day."

Dirk shrugged, removed the gun from his waist, checked the safety, tossed it to me, and turned away up the beach. He soon disappeared, stepping high in the soft sand until he reached the hard-packed strip that paralleled the sea. I wished I'd seen him disarming Carl. No doubt Carl did too.

I trudged back up the rough steps, feeling hollow and a little shaky from the after effects of my flood of adrenalin. After adding the bag and automatic to my growing private collection of memorabilia, I showered the sand from my hair, changed, and went down to breakfast. Dirk arrived just as I finished, breathing deeply and looking smug.

"I don't suppose it ever occurred to you," I asked him acidly, "to make your move a little sooner?"

"He looked too competent, Matt. It would have been very risky, right up until you went down and dumped his brother. He forgot I existed for a split second then. Besides, I wasn't worried."

"If I were in your shoes I wouldn't have been, either. Next time you feel like a little workout, I'll bring that toy of Paul's along and chase you with it. Afterwards we'll see how frisky you feel."

Randy peered up from his plate curiously. "Muggers on the beach," I explained.

Win was waiting impatiently in the office; no pretense of preferring to read today. "Good morning, Matt. Thank you for agreeing to forgo your day of rest. You may take time off when we've cleared away the brush and put this damnable case to rest."

"Good morning. I'll hold you to that. Right now I come bearing gifts. Dirk and I had a reunion on the beach this morning with two old friends." I reported in full.

"It would seem you underestimated them," Win said. "They must be quite mad. You say you sustained no injury?"

"Just a welt the size of a silver dollar on my breastbone. Did you know Dixon's got Harold back under lock and key?"

"No, but I considered it a foregone conclusion. It has nothing to do with the case and is therefore of no interest to us."

"That's not the point. I'd love to hear your thoughts on how we go about telling the Inspector he's got the wrong guy. He'll go positively insane when he finds out we had a tail on Harold. And have you forgotten we couldn't get Dirk licensed because he's a convicted felon? He's working for you, and your license has been pulled. Talk about a can of worms. Meanwhile, Dixon is dead certain he's got the murderer, and from the 'evidence,' as he sees it, how can you blame him? But here we sit with proof of Harold's innocence on both counts. Can't you see what a hell of a mess this is?"

Win glared at me. "I simply cannot understand this absurd preoccupation with helping Inspector Dixon and freeing Mr. Herbert? The former is a witling and the latter a scoundrel. We owe them nothing."

"Here we go again, folks. My preoccupation is with staying out of jail. I've already got one hearing coming up in a week. Withholding evidence is what got us in the soup in the first place."

"Evidence of what?" Win groused. "How may we be adjudged to be withholding evidence of a crime? Our knowledge of one man's innocence does nothing to impugn another."

"Don't split hairs—negative evidence is still evidence. What if they indict him? And they will. We can't just sit here and let the guy rot in jail, much as the idea appeals to me."

"He will not be indicted. It will effectively remove all onus from Mr. Herbert when we turn the guilty party over directly to the District Attorney. With suitable press coverage as an added fillip for Inspector Dixon."

"So you really plan to jam this one down his throat, too? Maybe you even like the idea of letting him waste his time on Harold and end up looking like a baboon?"

"The day he arrested you and suspended our licenses, he ceded all claim to our aid and consideration. If he has elected to waste his time tailoring the facts to fit the man, we can scarcely be held accountable for his lack of mental acuity.

"Now, I want you to accompany Randy to a place in Vista called the Burnwell Center. It's a nursing care facility for seriously developmentally disabled patients. Randy has managed to trace Donald Neal there."

"What does Randy need me for? For that matter, why is either one of us going?"

"Randy is going because, in the inbred society of medicine, no one would give you the time of day, but they'll talk to Dr. Bruckner. You're going because I want to completely rule out the possibility—remote, I admit—that Donald Neal might be our nemesis."

I stared at him in utter disbelief; he'd finally lost it. "Look, maybe I didn't make it clear to you before. The guy has the mind of a toddler. I doubt he can even dress himself, much less engineer three breakins and two murders."

"How do you know that for certain?"

"Inspector Dixon said . . ."

"Precisely! You have the word of the same man who probably thinks the Diet of Worms is a weight-loss fad. I have read of cases where patients who were thought to be of very low intelligence were either deaf and dumb or shamming for some deep-seated emotional reason. Humor me on this. I want you both to go and observe this young man with your minds open and your acuitive faculties functioning fully. If your trip does nothing more than serve to put my mind at rest on this point, it will be worth it."

At least it was something to do. Randy was waiting for me in the hall—I had the rare sight of him in a suit instead of his ever-present lab coat. We made the trip in half an hour. Randy hadn't been able to learn much on the phone the day before because anyone can say they're a doctor over the phone. This morning he was prepared to back up his claim.

The complex was maybe fifteen or twenty acres, surrounded by high hurricane fencing. Randy's I.D. got us in the gate. There were half a dozen unmatched buildings sprawled more or less in a circle and connected with enclosed walkways. Some were obviously older than others, which explained the haphazard layout.

Randy worked his way from the receptionist, through two members of the medical staff, and finally to the assistant director. We weren't going to get any higher, because the director was in Europe attending a conference. I'd taken advantage of the half-hour ride up to give Randy a little coaching on how to handle himself and he proved to be a surprisingly apt pupil. I was afraid he'd balk at my instructions about inventing an excuse for our visit, but he seemed to take it all in stride. Like the rest of us in the house, whatever Win wanted was all right with him.

The assistant director's attitude quickly changed from uncooperative to chummy as Randy verified that both the boy's mother and sister had been killed, leaving Donald Neal an orphan. He then advised the doctor in charge that some provision had been made for the young man in his mother's will, but that certain contingencies existed. Nothing to worry about, mind you, but it would be necessary for Randy to see the patient and submit a report to the court verifying that his condition was chronic and irreversible.

At my suggestion, Randy had seen to it by then that the man was so impressed with him that he never thought to ask to see a court order. Noticing copies of the *New England Journal Of Medicine* on the shelves behind the assistant's desk, Randy merely asked in passing whether he'd happened to read any of his recent articles on genetic brain syndrome. He had; after that, Randy was hand-feeding him.

We were personally escorted to Donald's wing. I tuned out all the chatter about the effects of electrolyte imbalance on organic brain syndrome and took in my surroundings. I noted a gaily painted corridor and crisp-looking nurses and orderlies moving purposefully along. An occasional door was standing open to reveal what I took to be visiting family members, usually grim-faced, standing looking down at something or someone I never got a clear view of.

When we paused in front of Donald's door, our guide told us, "Donald is quite a favorite among the staff. They've nicknamed him 'Scooter' because he sits on his butt and pulls himself along over the floor."

"You mean he can't even walk?" I asked.

"Physically he could, with some help or a walker, but it wouldn't occur to him to try. Don't look so horrified," he told me, noting my expression. "He's content—he enjoys a variety of foods and often watches the sun work its way across the wall of his room all day. There have been days I've come in here and envied him."

He opened the door and we went in. There was Scooter, sitting cross-legged on the floor, using his arms to move forward in pursuit of a toy truck he'd pushed a few feet away. It was all the more difficult to accept because he was a hell of a nice-looking kid. And not only was he nice-looking, but I recognized him as surely as I would my own brother, if I had one. I nudged Randy to let him know I had seen enough. He made more gobbledygook with the assistant on the way back to the office, then made me stand around another ten minutes while he read Donald's medical records.

On the way home in the car I was preoccupied, but came out of it long enough to ask Randy what made Donald the way he was.

"Perhaps the most tragic of all birth defects," he said. "He was apparently a perfect child in every respect at the time of birth, but, as rarely happens, the umbilical cord became wrapped around his neck as he descended into position for birth. By the time his head emerged and the problem was observed, it was too late. The oxygen supply to the brain had been impaired too long, resulting in irreparable brain damage."

So Win could stop picturing Donald as a homicidal maniac, conning the doctors and sneaking out to slay his family. But I'd give him something else to think about; though what exactly it meant was beyond me.

When Randy and I walked into the office, Win seemed abstracted. He listened to the medical report from Randy impassively, obviously accepting it at face value. Win dismissed him, then turned to me with a questioning look.

"I expected nothing else," he commented, by way of explanation. It was a thing he rarely bothered to do—explain his actions. "Have you anything to add?"

"One thing," I said matter-of-factly. "I recognized Donald."

I was treated to another rarity; his mouth fell open and he looked utterly dumbfounded. "I don't understand."

"I recognized him. If he could stand he'd be well over six feet; he has pale brown straight hair and the long thin fingers of a natural-born musician. He's all but a double for his father, taking into account the thirty years' difference in their ages. No question in my mind; count on it."

Win's eyes turned inward thoughtfully for a few seconds. "Don Burns is the boy's father?"

"Yes, any odds you want."

He accepted the fact without any quibbling, knowing if there was the slightest doubt I would have said so. "It adds a new dimension. It makes me suddenly more curious about Mr. Burns's courtship of Martha Herbert and his subsequent emotional flare-up when she returned from an extended vacation with Harold as a husband.

"I'm glad I sent you along; I often am. Now, since your Sunday is being devoted to bringing this increasingly sordid affair to a close, I ask you to undertake another task. While I attempt to digest the possible ramifications of this latest datum, I want you to go downtown and find out everything you can from the staff of the Plaza Hotel. It is all but inconceivable no one saw anything useful. Had the police unearthed anything, they would not now be so entirely convinced of Mr. Herbert's guilt. So it remains for you to succeed where they have quite obviously failed. Bring me something, anything—a glimpsed irregularity, the faintest notion on the part of anyone—anything!"

"Terrific! I'll only be the third or fourth guy to grill everybody. Your faith in me is touching. Also desperate." I left again, totally unenthusiastic over the assignment. On the way downtown I thought of half a dozen approaches, not one of which was worth a damn. I still hadn't settled on an angle by the time I walked through the huge glass doors, so, as usual, I allowed circumstances to dictate.

The sour-looking old duck behind the desk watched me approach. "May I help you, sir?"

"I'd like to see the manager. Is he available?"

"On a Sunday? I'm afraid not," he told me.

"Sorry—how foolish of me. How about the assistant manager?"

"Mr. Atkins is busy checking time cards and cannot be disturbed."

"This will be the exception that proves the rule. Tell him it's Detective Doyle and it's official business." I let the grouch have a fast glimpse of my license. It was time to go for broke. Nine out of ten will accept the rest on faith. He was the tenth.

"I didn't see any badge, officer."

"Badges are for the troops. Like stripes are for enlisted men. I outgrew a badge a long time ago when I got promoted out of my monkey suit." If Dixon ever got wind of this, I'd make the Bird Man of Alcatraz an overnighter by comparison.

He still smelled fish, but he reluctantly shuffled over to a door behind the desk and knocked tentatively. It opened a few inches. He whispered through the crack as if it were a confessional, then returned to the counter. "Mr. Atkins will see you in a moment." He pointedly turned his back and began fiddling with some forms.

Eventually the door opened all the way, disgorging a stout, balding, self-important-looking little twerp. He looked vaguely familiar, so I decided to take a chance. I met him halfway, hand extended. "Thanks for another minute of your time, Mr. Atkins. You do remember me, don't you?"

He nodded uncertainly. "With all the rest of the officers here yesterday, weren't you?"

"Right!" It was even technically true. "I know you've been all over this before with another detective, but until the case is closed . . . you understand."

"I read where you got the guy already."

"Getting him and keeping him are two very different things."

Atkins sighed, looking back at his office with longing. "There was an officer here already last night with a picture of the one you arrested. Nobody here recognized him."

"That's exactly the problem. But never mind; I want to go over everything you told us yesterday while it's still fresh in your mind."

He looked exasperated. "What's to go over? We keep telling you, none of us saw a thing. What's the point in pestering us to death about it? Don't you think we'd tell you if we knew anything? This whole thing is awful, public relations-wise. I'd do anything I could to help convict the man, believe me, but I don't know a thing."

"Just bear with me, please—this is how it's done. Sometimes people know something and they don't realize it, or they don't recognize the significance of it. I'm looking for even the tiniest, unimportant, odd incident that took place here yesterday in the early afternoon. Something so insignificant it would never occur to anybody to report it."

"Not a thing—I'm telling you. You've got to get the picture: This place was a mob scene. People checking in, people checking out, suppliers, salesmen. A typical Saturday."

"And yet the fact remains the killer had to get to the twelfth floor. I happen to know you are very cautious about whom you allow into an elevator and give free run of the place."

"We do a good job, yes, but there were long lines at the desk, the elevator call panels were lit up like Christmas trees—we can't always be sure. Besides, who says he took an elevator? If he was nuts enough to kill that nice lady, he'd be nuts enough to climb twelve flights of stairs. Nobody pays any attention. People rarely use the stairs, except children who want to play on them. He wagged his head in anger at what was obviously a pet peeve.

"Okay. Thanks again, Mr. Atkins. I'll want to talk to

some of the other staff, but I won't interrupt hotel routine any more than I have to."

"See that you don't. And not a word in front of the guests—please!" He watched me stroll over to the stairway. From the look on his face, it was apparent he considered me somebody's idiot child.

I spent the next two hours validating his opinion. I chatted with maids, housemen, bellmen, even the full-time hotel plumber. Plenty of them gave me an earful—especially the plumber—but nothing I could relate to the murder. I never got an impression anybody was sitting on anything either. Susan had been well-liked, and there was universal outrage at the crime. It's true I was the recipient of some interesting private theories concerning the murder, but they were interesting only because they pointed up the particular psychoses of the theorists.

I reentered the lobby via the marble stairs, which I'd discovered turned to steel from the second floor up. Atkins was standing near the elevators, shaking his fists in the face of the ancient operator I'd ridden with the first time I'd picked up Susan.

"Never you mind your fancy excuses, Dick," he growled at the man in the red uniform. "You know damn well it's your responsibility. You should have had it taken care of before you came on duty."

"How could I?" wailed the equally angry old man. "You think I wear this clown suit in the street? This is the way I found it when I came to work. It's not my fault someone screwed around with it and tore it, is it?"

I was halfway out the door when I froze. I executed an aboutface and trotted over to the two antagonists. Each was trying to outglare the other. "What's all this about, Mr. Atkins?"

The assistant manager tilted his head back to include me in his glare. "Nothing at all, just a minor personnel problem. Grooming and deportment," he added archly, returning his glare to the elevator jockey.

Infuriated, the old man turned to me seeking justice.

"What do they expect me to do? Buy a new uniform? I get minimum wage and all the tips go to the bellhops and maids. You'd think I was the sneak that done it instead of the poor guy it was done to."

"Show me," I told him.

He gave me an injured look and turned his back. The seam was split wide open where the right jacket sleeve joined into the back. Alarm bells jangled in my head, and I could feel my heart pounding. It always happens when I hit pay dirt.

"You say you leave your uniform here in the hotel, Dick?"

"Down in the locker room. Next to the laundry in the basement."

"Let's have a look."

"Officer, this man is on duty," objected Atkins. "He cannot possibly leave his post; besides, I haven't finished disciplining him."

"We'll only be a minute," I assured him, shoving Dick toward the stairs.

"The board is lighting up—we need this elevator!" Atkins's plea followed us around the corner.

Once we were out of sight, Dick chuckled. "Bet the little fart doesn't even know how to run it, neither."

The basement was considerably less elegant than the rest of the hotel. Dim lighting revealed a vast maze of tools, parts, piles of junk ranging from old plumbing fixtures to beat-up furniture. Dick threaded his way to a bank of battered steel lockers against a clammy wall. A sloshing sound emanated from around the corner, accompanied by the powerful odor of bleach. Dick opened the door of the third locker, revealing a rumpled pair of pants and a loud sports shirt, both hanging from a single hook. "This here one's mine."

"I'll bet you didn't work yesterday, did you, Dick?"

"Naw, they like for the younger fellas to work the real busy days, so I get Fridays and Saturdays off. Fine with me," he added defensively.

"You don't keep this locked?"

"What for? Nobody's supposed to be down here. Only one locks his is Jerry." He pointed out number 7, which did indeed sport a two-dollar padlock. "That's only because he keeps a bottle so he can come down here on his break and sneak a couple of shooters. As if the rest of us would steal any of his rotgut anyways."

Methodically, I opened each of the lockers—except Jerry's—and inspected the contents. Dick watched me with increasing discomfort. Of the twenty lockers, thirteen were now in use. My search revealed nothing remarkable.

"Are you sure that's your jacket?" I asked Dick.

"I'm sure. It's got my name inside with that iron-on tape. I'd know it anyway, from the way the one pocket bulges, where I always carry my keys."

"How about the pants? Anything different?"

The question threw him. "Pants! They wouldn't've put on the pants. One of them idiots must have spilled something, and had to finish their shift wearing my jacket. Don't know why they had to tear it up, though. All the uniforms are exactly the same size. You can see mine's too big for me. I been here fourteen years and you think I could ever get them to buy me a small? No, sir; act like every day might be your last. But I'll find out who did it, don't think I won't."

"I hope you do, Dick. It was a lousy trick. I might even be able to help." I opened the locker next to Dick's and removed an identical red uniform with gold braid. Holding the pants up at my waist, I could see they'd be short. I put the jacket on. It was a very snug fit, and I felt the slightest movement would tear it. I thought I knew what the motion was that had damaged Dick's. Now all I had to figure out was who was wearing it.

"How come you're so interested?"

"Good practice, Dick. I love this kind of puzzle the way some guys like crosswords. Do me a favor and check all your pockets carefully. You may not have used all of them yet today."

"Pants, too?"

"Please. And go slow. If you find so much as a piece of lint, I'd like to see it."

Dick worked his way patiently through four trouser pockets and three jacket pockets, carefully piling his pitifully few possessions on the bench in front of the lockers. "That's all there is—nothing here that don't belong," he announced.

"Is there a watch pocket in those pants?"

"Nope, I checked 'em all."

"No, you missed two, as a matter of fact." I stepped up to him and reached inside his jacket. My hand delved gently into his right hand-breast pocket—empty.

"I ain't never used them," he complained.

The one on the left was empty too—almost. My middle finger brushed against a tiny island of satiny softness where there should have been only rough fabric and stitching. Dick eyed me strangely as I attempted to extract the tidbit. I finally sensed I'd imprisoned it between my second and third fingers, so I withdrew my hand.

Dick tried to catch a glimpse, but I quickly transferred it to my own pocket.

"What'd you find in my pocket?" he demanded.

"Can't tell yet. Feels like a bit of paper. Candy bar wrapper, or a piece from a cigarette pack, maybe. I'll have the lab boys check it out. With any luck, it'll pinpoint your thief for you."

"Fine with me," he muttered as we climbed back up to the lobby, "but you'd think you guys'd have better things to do, all the crime there is today."

I thanked him and waved at Atkins, who was frowning at me from behind the desk. Outside, I broke into a dead run for my car. In my haste to prevent Dick from getting a good look at what I'd extracted from his pocket I'd barely seen it myself. But I'd realized exactly what it was before I got it out. I'd known absolutely the instant my fingertip brushed against it. Nothing else in the world feels quite like a flower petal.

CHAPTER 16

*L*unch was nothing but a bad memory and dinner still hours away by the time I made it back to the big house overlooking the sea. I'd come to think of it as home, never tiring of the thrill of coming upon it suddenly, sunlit and gleaming amid the intensely green grounds and lush tropical plantings.

I jollied Louis into permitting a minor raid on one of the three big refrigerators. Munching happily on a cold turkey sandwich liberally spread with cranberry sauce, I kibitzed over his shoulder. He was rapidly dicing a chunk of evil-looking dark meat.

He turned to me and announced proudly, "This is going to be a real treat, Matt—Paté a la Louis."

"Maybe," I observed doubtfully, "but it looks like liver to me." He was obviously on one of his tangents again, either the result of thumbing through his books or watching some cooking show on the TV in his room. Louis sometimes got delusions of grandeur, probably from all the years of hanging around Win. He was wearing a T-shirt outside his pants, no shoes, and apparently he'd forgotten where his razor was. I made a note to make a run into town for dinner.

Win had sworn off the book dodge for the duration, which indicated an incredible amount of dedication on his part. He gave me his full attention from the moment I opened the door to the office. I made the most of the few steps to his desk, depositing my booty before him with a flourish.

He studied it in silence for a full thirty seconds. "I've always considered flowers to be vastly overrated," he finally mused. "I would never have imagined one small petal from the most mundane of blossoms would one day provide me so much satisfaction." When he looked up at me, his expression was absolutely beatific. "I trust this bracteole comes complete with an illuminating history."

"That's your job." I laid it all out for him. By the time I ran down, he'd lost much of his glow.

"So now we know how the killer blended into the woodwork so effectively at the hotel, but not much else," I reflected. "This doesn't even begin to put a name to him. In fact, I'll be damned if I can see how it helps much at all. And I rolled in here as if I were bearing the Holy Grail."

"No name, not yet," Win admitted, "but let's not be too quick to disparage your bounty. It's our first direct clue, a positive link to the assassin. It is suggestive. As an example: Could Nick Barber have worn that man's uniform?"

I considered it. "I could wear it in a pinch; so could he. The results would be laughable, at best. Pants would be too short by inches. Waist would be a problem, but he could fake it. Jacket would be tight in the shoulders, but I got it on, so he could too. It would explain the torn seam. But either one of us would attract a lot of attention; we'd both look like a blivet."

"A blivet? I fear I'm not familiar with the term."

"You wouldn't be. A blivet is ten pounds of shit in a five-pound bag."

"Coarse, but uniquely descriptive. Needless to say, Mr. Donald Burns would have had no trouble wearing the jacket?"

"No, except that he'd be showing one hell of a lot of ankle and wrist. At around six foot six, he'd really be a sight."

Win was in a mood to debate. "Perhaps, yet the facts belie the claim. We already know someone wore it to gain access to Miss Neal's suite."

"Okay, but why didn't somebody on the staff spot him for a phony? It's a big hotel, true, but they all know each other. It was a hell of a chance to take. Frankly, I don't see how he pulled it off."

"Oh, I think we may assume he was seen. The uniform wasn't for the benefit of the staff, you see. It would merely serve to underscore his duplicity. I'm inclined to accept your Mr. Atkins' theory concerning the stairs. Hotel employees earning minimum wage are not so motivated or in sufficient hurry to use the stairs. Our culprit could therefore count on quite excellent odds of reaching the twelfth floor unseen other than perhaps by an occasional guest. The uniform's primary function was to render him invisible to *guests*. Wisely so, because most of us do not see people when they are menials dressed in livery. If the attire was ill-fitting, it would arouse only slight notice. And, finally, the uniform served to gain him access to room 1218."

"I'll buy all that. But where does it get us?"

We bounced it back and forth right up until dinnertime. If we accomplished anything constructive, I missed it. Win must have felt the same way, because he told me not to bother coming back after chow.

I skipped by telling Louis a bare-faced lie and ate in town. Afterwards, Louis, Randy, Dirk and I swapped nickels playing poker. By the time I turned in, my net take for the day was forty-five cents and one carnation petal. And I'd recognized a good-looking young six-footer with the mind of a backward three-year-old. And the abraded spot where Paul had caught me with his lethal toy was beginning to hurt like hell. It had been a long day. But I've had worse.

Monday morning I woke up feeling frisky. There was no good reason for it, other than the fact I'd gotten my first full eight-hour sleep in three nights. Dirk and I did our usual prance along the beach, and I was pleased for a change not to find anyone waiting in ambush.

There was a full house at breakfast, except Win, of course. Randy was sitting, sourly pushing odd little turban-shaped things around in a bowl when I arrived. "Kadota figs," he explained when he saw me gawking at them.

"It's all your fault," Louis told him miserably.

"Your fault?" I asked Randy. "What did you do, sign an exclusive contract with a Turkish market?"

"All I did was provide Win with a couple of books he asked for on nutrition. What else could I do?"

"You might have considered reading them first," I suggested rudely. "After all, there are all kinds of nutrition books, featuring everything from berries to booze. Surely you could have come up with one that didn't promote these damn things. I couldn't stand Fig Newtons even when I was a kid."

Louis had vacated the dining room; now he returned bearing a bowl on a saucer. I sneered at the contents and shoved it away. "Never mind the figs. Double my order of hen fruit, bacon and toast likewise, and we'll stay friends."

Louis gave me a stricken look. "I'm sorry, Matt; the only other thing I'm allowed to fix is oatmeal with wheat germ."

"What's the matter? The birds on strike?"

"Oh, no, I have plenty of eggs. But I am not to serve them because of the . . ." He looked to Randy for help.

"He means because of the cholesterol. You know how Win can be when he goes off on a tangent. Seems we can only have eggs twice a week, lest our cholesterol count get too high."

"That's not all," wailed Louis. "Mr. Winfield has told me I can't serve meat very often. Only when I ask him and he tells me to. I don't know what to do. Nobody likes fish."

The truth is we all liked fish just fine, but not after Louis finished incinerating it. Brisket or filet of sole, it was all the same to him.

"Pretty damn nervy, if you ask me," I agreed. "Especially considering the fact that he eats almost nothing himself."

Louis looked me in the eye, which he hardly ever does, and pleaded. "Matt, will you please talk to him? Tell him you can't do your work on a diet. You'll just become weak and someone will kill you—tell him!"

"Why me? I thought cholesterol was an antibiotic. It should be Randy—he's the doctor. You think he's going to be impressed with a lecture on nutrition from me?"

"No, Matt, Louis's right," Randy jumped in. "You're the only one who can make him change his mind and you know it. And it's true—both you and Dirk do need to eat a high caloric diet. You're both very active physically. I'm the only one around here who needs to watch his weight—I'll admit I'm getting pretty sloppy. But I'll do it on my own. It's ridiculous to force the rest of you to starve just because I'm sedentary in my work. Talk to him. You're the only one he really listens to, Matt."

I stood up and saluted. "If I don't come back, tell mom I died game."

When I breezed into the office, Win was staring off into space with a frown on his face. I marched up to his desk, leaned over it with my hands braced, and announced, "I quit!"

That got his attention. "Please, I'm deeply engrossed in this confounded problem confronting us, and I may finally have a line worth pursuing," he told me with a frown. "This is no time for any of your nonsense."

"No nonsense, it's simple. A big part of what I work my tail off for around here, besides the modest salary, is bed and board. Until today the board was pretty unreliable, with the possible exception of breakfast. But I just came from the dining room where I got sent away with an empty belly. I ordered a simple, nourishing meal of bacon and eggs and I was told that my only choice was a bowl of something that looked like road apples, but didn't smell as good. That's why I quit."

"A modest change in the dietary habits of the inhabitants of this house will . . ."

"Call off the order or I walk. Dirk and I couldn't be any healthier if we were horses. Louis only picks and tastes, he never even eats a meal, as far as I know. And his body type will never gain an ounce. You don't eat when you do come to the table—you make designs on the plate by rearranging the food. That leaves Randy. Nature and his life-style have conspired to make him a fatty. He's sworn to do something about it and, since he's a damn fine doctor, he should be able to manage it. That's about as logically as I know how to put it. Now, if you have instructions for me, I'd love to hear them, but I'm too weak to do much more than sit here all day with you and read books. We could have a great time—I could tell you my life story. I respectfully suggest you call Louis and tell him to break out the rations. I will return to the table, take on my required quantity of fuel, and come back so we can get to work. Or I can drive down to the nearest greasy spoon and eat while I check the classifieds under job opportunities."

He was trying his best to maintain a look of anger on his face, but I detected the beginnings of a grin. I knew him so well. He'd have himself a good laugh, but not until I was out of the room. The truth was, he did get carried away sometimes, but it never took him long to realize it.

The phone call to the kitchen was made. I thanked him for his consideration and returned to the dining room. A chorus of enthusiastic cheers greeted me—which was, after all, only my due.

Win seemed unusually animated when I entered the office for the second time that Monday morning. "Matt, I want you to return to Neal Pharmaceuticals right away. Bring Peter Durning to me."

His request surprised me; it wasn't at all the one I'd been anticipating. "If you've got Pete pegged for the murders, I want to submit a minority opinion. I'm giving written guarantees he couldn't spoon himself into that elevator jockey's uniform—couldn't come within eight inches of buttoning the pants. And good luck on getting him to walk up twelve flights of stairs."

Win smiled tolerantly. "It is not my intention to promote him as a serious candidate for our quarry. My interest is based rather upon his qualifications as an expert on the subject of that avaricious company and its denizens. He was apparently well-disposed toward you. Given that and his affection for Susan, he may reasonably be expected to endorse our efforts to bring the killer to bay. Thus I wish to avail myself of his wealth of knowledge without delay."

"His tongue requires frequent oiling. Better send Dirk out for a fifth of Seven High Bourbon."

"Thank you for reminding me. I tend to forget the social amenities these days. I shall do so at once."

"I thought for sure you'd decide to send me to the plant for another reason—to scout up a picture of Nick Barber to flash around down at the Plaza Hotel. I admit it's not much of an idea, but it's the best I came up with."

"God help us if we find ourselves so devoid of wit we must resort to routine police procedures. Our right to exist as private detectives would then become indefensible. Go! Bring Mr. Durning to me."

I headed north toward Sorento Valley. This time I didn't sneak in; I marched right through the front door as if I owned the joint. Snaggle-Tooth had to let me know she was displeased with me for not remembering to sign out last week. To save time I let her get it out of her system, then asked her to kindly inform Pete that I was growing old standing there. She did so in slow motion, then allowed me to sign in again with obvious reluctance. We were not destined to be friends, but it was a loss I thought I could live with.

This time Pete's outer office was occupied. A well-fed matron with a cherubic face asked me if I was Mr. Doyle. No beauty queens for Pete; he wanted results, not style. A husky voice intruded through a crack in the inner door before I could reply. "Matt, you just git your tail in here, boy."

There was no sign of any bourbon yet, but then it was only nine-thirty in the morning. The florid-faced old warrior of the drug wars screwed his puss into a deep frown as he mangled my hand in his. "What can I say, Matt? This whole thing is worse than any nightmare I ever heard of. Never dreamed that crazy son of a bitch would go after Susan, too. I'm just as sorry as a man can be, boy."

"So am I, Pete—thanks. My boss thinks we can do something about it. There are still a lot of unanswered questions. He's Carter Winfield, and he'd like to talk to you right now. It's important. Could you break away for a while?"

"You work for Carter Winfield? He wants to see me?"

"I do, and he does, yes."

The old stump of a man regarded me with an owlish look. "My hunches are usually pretty good—I had a feeling there was more to you than you were letting on. Winfield, huh? Isn't that something! A great American—a great man. There was a time I'd hoped to be able to vote for him. Naturally I'd consider it quite an honor to meet him—but I didn't think he saw people much anymore."

I could never get over being surprised at hearing older people speak of Win in such reverent tones. Of course, they'd never had to live with him. "He's not much of a social gadfly, it's true, but I think you'll enjoy his company. He's just another guy, like you and me, except he knows more words."

"Why would he want to talk to me? It's all over but the shouting, isn't it? Harold's in custody and charged. What's the deal?"

"I'd rather it came from him—he's waiting."

"What the hell then—let's go!" He made the considerable effort required to separate his broad butt from the chair. "Janet," he instructed his secretary on the way out, "try and keep a lid on this bughouse, will you? I'm leaving for a little while. If it turns out longer than a little while, I promise to call and let you pester me."

"How're things going at the store these days?" I asked him in the car.

"What do you think? It's a damn zoo! Nobody's sure who's on first. Management's all lathered up, jockeying for position instead of doing the job. Harold was no bargain, but at least he occupied space and left the rest of us to do the work. With him gone, too, there's suddenly a power vacuum. Everybody's all stirred up."

"Sounds jolly. Assuming Harold's out of it for good, who's in line to take over?"

"That's the worst part of all—I am, God help me. Matt, I just can't get geared up for it. Not that I have much choice. I've been putting off moving offices. Helga's still occupying Harold's old office. Lord knows what she does all day."

"Dear Helga. What a charmer."

"She's a little nutty and we kid about her a lot, but it's the best kind of nutty. You know the type: lives for the company, works like a dog, and never a complaint. If you want to know the God's truth, we ought to let her run the place. She practically has, ever since Scotty died."

"Helga has? What about Martha Herbert? I thought she ran such a tight ship."

"Sure, Martha was the admiral, but Helga was the skipper. Remember, Martha was a housewife when Scotty died. Didn't know beans about the nuts and bolts of operating what amounts to a damned complex, cutthroat business. She'd helped out in the beginning, before we got successful, but she was way out of touch by the time she had to step in. Helga had been Scotty's secretary. You know how it is, a good secretary gradually takes on more and more of the burden. Scotty was primarily interested in research, so Helga inevitably became the power behind the throne. When Scotty died, she trained Martha, which is why Martha became a fanatic about schedules. I've never known either one of them to be a minute late for anything—you could set your watch by the pair of them."

"Sure is a weird little duck, isn't she?"

"Very, but I'll let you in on a little secret. Every executive prays for a Helga of his own to make him look good."

We'd arrived. I ushered Pete into the office and made the introductions.

"It was kind of you to come on such brief notice, Mr. Durning," Win told him warmly.

"My pleasure, sir, but everybody calls me Pete unless they're mad at me."

"I assure you, Pete . . ." Win paused as he caught sight of me poised above my chair, about to land. "Matt, I'm afraid I'll have to ask you to return to the plant. The time has come to force events on every front."

"Return and do what?"

"That which you do best: listen, stir things up, go wherever your excellent instincts dictate, observe. I will attack the problem from the angle of logic and deduction, with Mr. . . . with Pete's help. Your forte is intuition, an uncanny knack of precipitating events. Unleash that force; let's see where it leads."

"Yeah, I get it. You brains—me brawn. The only thing that comes to mind is to ask Nick Barber where he spent his Saturday afternoon."

"Then do so. I, too, would like to know. Let's hope he responds a bit more rationally than last time."

"He will, unless his memory is even shorter than his fuse." I headed for the door, then paused. "Aren't we forgetting one of the unbreakable rules around here?" I asked. I was referring to the firm understanding that Win was never to be left alone with anyone, regardless of how innocuous they seemed.

"I forget nothing; Dirk is stationed just outside. Please ask him to enter." He explained to Pete, "In case we require anything." Then back to me. "Don't neglect to take Mr. Smith along."

Mr. Smith was his euphemism for my revolver. Due to a nasty incident a couple of years back, he had become absolutely paranoid about my going into the field on a capital case without it. I ducked out the door. Dirk was standing at parade rest two steps away and was on the move immediately. I had to grin, but, for all he knew, Win was alone in there with the killer. Come to think of it, for all I knew he could be right. "You can use my chair," I called to his back, "but sit up straight and don't get too used to it."

I clumped upstairs to my room for "Mr. Smith," disappointed at not being invited to sit in on the conference with Pete. It was typical of Win to chase me out on some flimsy pretext, in case he did extract something we could use. If he did unearth any nuggets, one thing I knew for sure—he'd sit on them until they hatched. Reporting worked only one way around there. How he loved to play the omniscient mastermind—the rat.

The training lab was empty except for Nick, seated behind a small desk, apparently grading some test papers. "Where are the kiddies today?" I inquired innocently.

His head came up with a jerk. "What do you want?" The words themselves were belligerent, but actually he merely looked startled.

"It's time for that little talk I mentioned on Friday." I secretly willed him to stand so I could try picturing him in the red uniform better.

He discarded the red marker he'd been using to slash angry marks across the papers and considered me with care. "Look, I came on too strong before. No good excuse for it, except this place is driving me buggy. When you needled me I thought it was a good chance to work out some of my aggression. Not one of my brighter moves—you're a pro, and I should have known better. Even so, I don't see why I should put up with a cross-examination from you." He said it matter-of-factly, without emotion.

"One reason would be, it's the easiest way to get rid of me. Why don't we start with you telling me where you were last Saturday, from two to three in the afternoon."

He looked genuinely blank for a few seconds, then the coin dropped. "Susan Neal!"

"Good guess. Where were you?"

"Why in hell would you try tying *me* in with that?" he protested.

"Same reason I'm trying to tie you in with her mother's death. The two murders are hardly coincidental. Maybe you're waging a one-man war against matriarchy in the business world. I don't know. Third time—where were you?"

"I may as well tell you and get you off my back." He shrugged. "Haven't got anything to hide. I drove to Phoenix for the weekend to talk my wife into giving it another go."

"Wives are lousy alibis."

"Mine should be an exception. She's about to be my ex-wife, anyway. And she's so pissed at me and this company she can't see straight. But I don't get it. I thought Mr. Herbert was picking up the tab for both murders."

"You and Harold are pretty good buddies, aren't you?"

"I'll admit I'd like to see him beat the rap, but not if it means I have to take his place."

"When I was here last week you were the only person who knew I was a detective, except Harold. He was the only one here who knew me as anything other than Susan's fiancé, and he had good reason not to broadcast it. Yet he told you. I find that fascinating."

My broadside didn't jolt him as much as I'd hoped. "He and I were pretty closely involved in some planning, that's all. The old-timers around here have given him a bad time since day one. We knew we could negotiate a more favorable price in the sale to Trans-United if the numbers could be beefed up first. I proposed a very aggressive saturation sales promotion I thought would work and he liked it."

"Quite a coincidence; making all those plans that were quite impossible to implement as long as Martha Herbert was alive. Suddenly she's dead."

His neck got red and his jaws got tight. "You've got it all wrong. The planning only began after her death—at least, my part about the sales campaign—not before."

I shrugged, grinning. "Sure. Like I said—coincidence. Then Susan began making waves and she got it too. Curiouser and curiouser."

"Look, I'm not going to insult your intelligence by pretending Martha Herbert's death tore me up any. I had nothing to do with it, but if asked, I might have offered to hold the coat of the guy who did do it. As for the daughter, I'd never even met her. I'm telling you, I was in Phoenix from Friday midnight—I drove direct from work—until Sunday afternoon late. Now that's all I can tell you, so how about letting me get back to this piss-ant job of mine?"

"First I want you to stand up."

"Why?" He didn't look anxious to comply.

"So I can visualize you in a red uniform with gold braid." I gave it my best Clint Eastwood implied-threat manner.

Nothing! No reaction other than a puzzled frown. Disappointed, I spun on my heel and left. It hadn't convinced me of his innocence so much as it made me admire his nerves.

I paused in the hall outside, wondering what else I could do to stir the pot. A few people recognized me as I worked my way toward the opposite end of the building. Some averted their eyes sheepishly. Others offered me condolences, still under the impression I'd been Susan's intended. The role was now intensely uncomfortable. One way or another, they all managed to ask whether Harold was really nailed for good. I told them the police had, through some oversight, neglected to take me into their confidence. Which is about as honest as you can get.

Don Burns's weathered-cowboy face hove into view. At the sight of me he stopped in midstride and faced me with an angry look. "What are you doing here, you lying bastard?"

The confrontation surprised me, because I'd labeled him as such a nice guy. No one likes to have his labels come loose. "Just doing my job, Mr. Burns. What's stuck in your craw?"

He glared down at me. "I don't like sons of bitches that lie in their teeth. You can turn your ass around and crawl out of here right now."

My reply came spur-of-the-moment. I don't say I'm proud of it, but he'd succeeded in ruffling my feathers, and besides, I'd been sent there to stir things up and observe results. "Speaking of crawling, I had a nice visit with your son, Scooter, yesterday. Scooter's a good-looking kid."

The results were open to interpretation. His angry glare intensified. "That's none of your fucking business, you bastard." He look ready to strike me for an instant. Finally he snapped out of it and brushed by me without another word. It would be up to Win to find it suggestive; to me it was inconclusive.

When I arrived at Harold's office, I found it locked. Not expecting an answer, I knocked.

"Who is it?" demanded Helga's flat, atonal voice.

"Matt Doyle. We're old friends—remember?"

There was no reply. I was getting set to knock again when the lock clicked and the door opened. She was dressed as before: full black body stocking, skirt, shirtwaist, and vest. She was only shoulder high, and her monkey-face was screwed up with agitation. Or maybe she was trying to smile. Who could tell?

"I keep the door locked because there is so much work to do. People keep bothering me," she explained. "You're the one who made the police arrest Mr. Herbert. I knew you would, the first time you walked into the office." She'd tilted her face up as close to mine as possible, and I was catching some spray from her mouth. She needed a stronger gargle.

"You give me too much credit. Actually, the cops thought that one up all on their own. But if it makes you happy, fine. I'll be your hero if you'll do me a tiny favor."

"What is it?"

"This is not for publication, Helga. Nothing said in this room is fodder for the ladies' room wireless, promise?"

"Don't be a fool. You think I'd waste my time gossiping with those geese? Tell me."

"Okay. Without making any firm accusations, I think Nick Barber may be involved in the murders, too. You know him?"

She turned her broad back to me and remained silent for some seconds. "I know him. He's been here to see Mr. Herbert several times lately. Mrs. Herbert detested him—I can tell you that. She fired him from his job and was going to send him back on the road in the worst territory she could find. That's all I know."

"It's enough to make him a prize suspect. Along with Harold," I added, just to keep her happy. "Here's how you can help. During my tour I was told all employees have to take a psychological profile test. I want a look at Nick's. I just had a chat with him over at the testing center. He was alone, so I tried shaking him up, but suddenly he's become one very cool customer. It occurred to me there might be a handle somewhere in those test results I could use to pry him open. Maybe have a top criminal psychologist evaluate his outline with an eye toward violence potential, something like that. I'd like to give it a try."

I thought for a while I'd struck out. She began pacing back and forth across the office with fierce strides, ignoring me completely. After a full minute of this, she went quickly to her desk and snatched up the phone. Pecking out a triple-digit number, she soon began dictating crisp orders for Nick's complete personnel file to be released to me. She hung up.

"Thanks, Helga. I really appreciate it."

"I'm the one who should thank you. And I do," she told

me solemnly. I was her hero; she was convinced I'd been instrumental in putting Harold away.

The material was waiting for me when I arrived at the personnel office. A raven-haired Barbie doll handed over the manila envelope reluctantly, confiding nervously, "Do you know it's against company policy for those records to leave this office? They're very personal and confidential."

"I could call Helga Metz and tell her you've changed your mind about following her orders to let me borrow them."

That was low. She swallowed dryly a couple of times, and her hands trembled slightly. "That's certainly not necessary. I only meant for you to be very careful with them."

I promised. Next stop was the cafeteria, where I snared a quiet corner table and spread out the contents of the bulky envelope. Not bothering with the tests themselves, I found the shrink's comments and studied them with intense interest. Whoever wrote them thought Nick was a cinch to be a high achiever, though he left himself an out by mentioning the possibility of discipline problems. The personality profile showed plenty of aggression, but seemed to treat it as a positive sales trait. Much of it didn't apply, but I came across one promising paragraph: "Subject is incapable of compromise with himself and his goals. Will go to extraordinary lengths to achieve desired ends. May become more than problematic at some level of his career."

I liked it. Demotion to a guy like Nick would be like a knife in the gut. I replaced all the sheets back in the envelope and left, remembering to sign out with Snaggle-Tooth as ordered.

Outside, the sun was beginning to burn through the morning coastal yuck. I was sitting behind the wheel before I saw the note pinned beneath my wiper blade. I opened the door and snagged it. It contained only two typewritten lines and no signature: "I know who killed them and why. You'll find the answer under the middle heparin vat behind the plant."

Sometimes it happens like that. Apparently I'd kicked

over the right rock somewhere along the line. Of course it smelled to high heaven of a setup, but what can you do? Ignore it? Not likely. But what you can do is proceed very, very carefully.

I dashed across the parking lot and around the corner of the building. Not a soul in sight. I patted the .38 on my belt. My heart was pounding thirteen to the dozen as I approached the putrid-smelling tanks. I forced myself to slow down, scanning frantically in all directions. No sign of life. I spotted the small folded square of paper thirty feet away on the barren ground directly under the middle tower. The hair on my neck stood up and saluted, and I hated the whole deal. Why two notes—one on my windshield and another one here?

Trap or not, the bait was there, and I meant to have it. I stood frozen a full ten seconds, studying the roofline of the plant. It was the only real vantage point for anyone planning to pot me. I fully expected to see a head pop up any second, but nothing moved. Suddenly, hoping to frustrate any sniper, I dropped into a crouch and covered the last ten yards at top speed, ducked under the cross-bracing into the shade of the vat, and grabbed the paper.

Something splatted into the dust dangerously near my foot. Then came the screeching sound of metal on metal. Cursing, I hit the ground and rolled. I was caught flat on my back when the whole vile mountain fell on me.

Somehow I managed to retain consciousness, hands shielded my face instinctively, pinned there now; my mind barely able to grasp what had been done to me, the knowledge devastating, worse than any nightmare, the thought of countless slimy tons of rotting hogs' lungs drowning me in a sickening, viscous sea totally overwhelming, the stench as bad as the weight, seeming to infect every part of my body; I fought to control the rising tide of panic threatening to immobilize and destroy me, the crushing weight terrible but not quite as final as sand or dirt, slightly compressible, minute movements barely possible, able to use my hands as shields, partially freeing nose of the terrible filth, even succeeding in inhaling a thimbleful of air before it turned to more slime, trickier then, tried turning over onto my stomach, managing to swivel hips a little but no chance of lifting either shoulder free of the ground; absolute agony now, thrashing face around wildly, anything to free it from its fetid mask for even an instant, defeat, acceptance, abandonment of plans for turning over and crawling forward on elbows and toes, not possible! I kicked insanely at the gelatinous crap entombing me, more in anger than in hope, gained a few unexpected inches—painful—lifted my knees as quickly as the enormous forces arrayed against them allowed and frantically repeated the process, moved some more, repeated, little result, realized I had to force myself to pause a couple of seconds after lifting knees to allow the void under my feet to fill so I'd get greater thrust, very hard to do; air now the critical factor, brushing across my nose and mouth constantly, inhaling tentatively, mostly getting nothing but a snootful of the repulsive juice, yet an occasional wisp of air, enough to keep from going utterly mad, lift, wait, kick, roll head from side to side searching for air, endless drill, no idea how much distance covered as a result of kicking, judging by the beating my backside was taking, some progress was being made, thighs screaming now from the restricted yet powerful movement required—least of my worries, cupping my hands into what I hoped was an air pocket and gulped desperately, out of control now, mouth filled with streams of indescribably foul liquid, little glops of semi-solid matter, results explosive, only enough sanity left for one more kick, opened my mouth a slit to scream, a few precious atoms of priceless air, closed mouth, no remaining sense of time at all, three minutes, three days, almost out of it, the last lucky pocket of air nothing but a curse, only prolonging what should have been ended by now, head striking something suddenly, fingers fighting to find it, explore it, identify it, tracing a rough metal upright—could only be the tower leg—renewed kicking wildly, ignoring horrible cramping pain of thighs, forgetting to wait now between thrusts, fingers clutching steel greedily, thoughts drifting, hard to focus, drifting, forgetting, no more air, too long, nothing left but anger, clutching base in a death grip and pulling, trying to jackknife torso into sitting position, keep fading out, coming back and gripping higher and pulling and kicking, brain numb but some lower command center determined to die standing upright, still no air, rarely aware of impending death but quest for air continues atonomically, quivering legs have little left to contribute as my hands continue their upward struggle, all happening with minimal conscious direction from me, no more interest in the program, just something to do until the message center shuts down, knees manage to lock, no point, time to sink back down into putrid oblivion and to hell with the whole damn . . .

"Holy shit! Look, Dick—somebody's in there."

The voice came to me from very far off. I opened my eyes for the first time since the mountain fell on me. There was nothing to see, and it hurt like hell so I closed them, but in the meantime my hands, apparently of their own volition, reached up and broke free from the horrible sea. Frenzied now, I began pawing at my face. The huge mass of sludge ended at my eyebrows. By tilting my head back to force the crap away from my nose, I was able to breathe. I just stood there reveling in the delight of it. After a lot of choking and retching my brain kicked back into drive. On tiptoe, I pulled myself snug against the girder and freed my mouth. Eyeing the two men standing near the back door, I croaked, "How long have you two idiot children been outside here?"

They stared back in silent awe. "About three or four minutes," one answered sheepishly.

"Well, so far you're a bust as far as Good Samaritans go. You any idea what I've been going through down there while you two stood around gawking?"

They shrank from my baleful glare. Finally one told me, "Hell, buddy, how'd we know anybody'd be under there?"

Good question. "So now you know. If one of you doesn't

throw me a rope damn quick, I'll be right back down there. The only other way out is to climb the girder, and I'd never make it."

Even as I stood there, I could see the level of the gelatinous mound receding. This meant its circumference was widening as it settled. That's how close it had been; if I had not hit the girder I couldn't possibly have reached the ever-widening outer reaches of the spill.

They woke up and began scrambling. I was shaking with a mixture of utter exhaustion and ice-cold fury. Next thing I knew, my reluctant heroes were arguing just inside the open back doors.

"You guys deciding whether to let me out for Christmas or what?" I screamed. My legs had been seized by terrible cramps, and there wasn't a damn thing I could do about it. I'm afraid it did nothing to improve my disposition.

"There ain't no rope around here. All we got inside is that metal strapping they put on crates." He spoke chidingly, as if it were rude of me to make unreasonable demands.

I believe it was as near to hysteria as I've ever come. It required a major effort on my part to swallow a caustic remark, among other things, and force myself to survey the situation calmly. There was a hose hooked up to a spigot at the far corner of the building.

"Would one of you fine gentlemen kindly go and bring me that hose over there?" I inquired politely.

They both raced for it, fought to unscrew it, and hurried back with it between them. The one doing the tossing made three attempts to reach me without success. My mobility was still severely restricted, and I could see he was most reluctant to approach too near my mountain of putrescence. I didn't say a word, just fought back the nausea and nerves, nursing a secret hope that these two clowns ended up on the clean-up crew. On the fourth try I snared my end as it rebounded off my skull. They dug in their heels and tugged tentatively. I slowly began emerging until I was nearly awash; then Frick and Frack eased up for some unknown reason and I immediately began sinking.

"Pull—damn it!" I shrieked as I went under.

They did, bless their stunted little hearts. I reappeared, surfing down the slope of the pile. I released the hose in time to avoid letting them drag me all over the grounds. Staggering to my feet shakily, still in two feet of the shit, I high-stepped my way to freedom. The two of them watched in open-mouthed wonder, backing away to maintain some distance. I actually couldn't blame them; I was certainly no treat to any one of the senses.

When the full reaction came, it was a beauty. My legs went on strike, and I sat down abruptly, trembling violently. The truth was I'd never been so completely terrified in my life. I've been shot at, and occasionally hit, and I've seen and heard a knife scrape along my ribs, but nothing in my experience had ever hit me like this. I sat there, helplessly retching a dozen times or more, until there was nothing left to expel but the memory of the noxious material I'd had to swallow. That was going to take a long time; probably a lifetime.

It was quite a while before I recovered enough to stand, pick up the hose, and stumble over to the outside tap. I screwed it back in place, turned it on full force, and began at the top. The cool water was balm. I shucked my vile jacket, then did the same with my shirt, tie, pants—all were beyond redemption. I'd have liked to include tee shirt, shorts, and shoes. I considered making a run for my car in my birthday suit, but decided there was something I really had to do first. I retrieved my belt, hosed it off, including the gun and holster still clipped to it. After fastening the belt back around my waist, I forced myself to go back to the malodorous clothing and extracted my keys and wallet.

Having regained my composure enough by now to begin tracking, I asked my two reluctant saviors if they'd seen anyone around the back of the plant, or anywhere near the back doors when they'd come out. They both shook their heads mutely. It didn't matter; I knew where to find my would-be murderer.

Looking something like an angry reject from a Fruit of the Loom ad, I stumped through the rear doors of the plant. Frankly I didn't give a rat's behind how I looked at that point; all in the world I wanted was to fasten my twitching fingers around Nick Barber's big neck. And there was nothing in me but pity for anyone ill-advised enough to try and stop me.

My reluctant benefactors followed me down the brilliantly lighted corridors. I guess they just loved a parade. People reacted in various ways as my procession passed. Some hugged the walls with their faces registering myriad emotions—none to my benefit. Others dove into the nearest available doorway. Though I never looked behind me, the growing level of murmurs and buzzings were a clear indication of my growing train.

The door to the training lab was locked. I stepped back and gave it one bone-bruising kick just beside the lock. It exploded inward noisily. My shoes still squished as I stamped in, leaving small damp spots on the tile to record my passing. I was betting Nick had returned to the lab as cover; if not, I was going to look and feel pretty foolish. As if I didn't already.

And so he had, but, unlike my timid rescuers, he'd succeeded in finding a rope. One end was lashed around a water pipe that ran along the ceiling. The other was looped around his bull neck. He hung suspended a foot off the floor, turning slowly from side to side.

One glance was enough—his darkened face was swollen almost featureless. There was no mad scramble to cut him down; none was necessary. I crossed over to the desk where he'd been working and spied a sheet of paper protruding from his typewriter. Doing my best to tune out the swelling tumult from my entourage, which was rapidly spilling into the room and reacting in various noisy ways, I bent and read the note without touching it.

It was short and to the point:

I have no regrets for my actions. I killed Martha Herbert for the good of the company I love as much as for what she did to me. Her daughter had no rights here. You will find the torn bellhop uniform I wore when I killed her in the basement of the Plaza Hotel.

I know Doyle found out, so I chose this over spending the rest of my life in prison. Of course he told others. I had the satisfaction of killing him for it.

That was it—no signature, just his name typed at the bottom. I looked around. At least fifty people were milling about, staring alternately at Nick's corpse and at me. I saw a chair lying flat a couple of feet from the body.

"Somebody call the police," I suggested. "Ask for Inspector Dixon in Homicide. Until he arrives, I suggest whoever's in charge seals off the room, and the rest of you get the hell out of here." I then marched in a direct line for the door. There was no one in my way. I felt a little like Moses crossing the Red Sea, except, of course, he had a robe.

Now that my fury had dissipated, I suddenly felt profoundly foolish parading around in my skivvies. I vowed I'd switch to wearing boxer shorts. Though the front entrance was closer, I opted to return the way I'd come. The urge to run was pressing, but I managed to keep it to a brisk walk. Since I no longer looked as if I were insane, and had ceased growling, there were a few brave souls demanding an explanation. I told them the new drug wasn't ready to market yet, the side effects were too bizarre.

Outside, I yielded to the urge and dashed to my car. My driving may not have been up to my usual high standards; when I arrived home I screeched to a stop as near the front door as I could get and sprinted inside. Louis was in the hall. When he saw me, his eyes popped and he just stood there staring in wonder. I stuck my head in the office. Win and Pete were still at it. Dirk sat slumped in my chair, looking bored.

Being indoors for long periods during the day was a heavy burden for him. The jug of bourbon rested on one corner of Win's desk, at least the half that remained. All three occupants stared at me in mute amazement, so I grinned back and went on in.

"Sorry to interrupt, but I have news from the front."

Pete's first inclination had been to laugh, which made me like him even more, but he'd thought better of it after taking a closer look at my condition. My entire backside was caked with dried blood, marking the damage sustained during my tunneling expedition. Between shock and anger, the symptoms of my tattered hide had been masked, but now messages were beginning to come through loud and clear.

"Good grief!" Win exclaimed gently. "You're in a terrible state. Go up to your room at once—I'll send Dr. Bruckner to attend to you." (It would never do to call him Randy in front of company.) "Whatever your report, it can surely wait."

"Not this one! It probably looks a lot worse than it is. Just a slight accident over at Pete's place of business."

"What happened, boy?" Pete asked sharply.

Win winced at Pete's preempting him, but gave me the nod to tell him. I gave it to them from the time I found the note on my car until I was dragged from the mountain of rotting hogs' lungs at the end of a hose. At that point I got interrupted.

"Jesus!" Pete exploded in horror. "That's the most disgusting thing I ever heard of. I have no idea how a thing like that could happen."

"Easy, Pete; someone suckered me under there with a note they knew I'd have to check out. He was waiting in the one spot I didn't consider—the narrow platform around the vat. All he had to do was pull the linchpin and release the whole mess right on me. It should have worked. He thought it did, and he was damn near right."

"Do you have any idea who it was?"

"Yeah, I was about to get to that." I noticed Win wrinkling his sensitive sniffer furiously. "I know the stink is god-awful," I told him, "but it'll only be for another minute. Do I answer his question? He'll hear it the minute he hits the plant anyway."

"Mr. Durning has elected to employ our services." Win said. "By all means, satisfy his curiosity."

I turned back to Pete. "To answer the who, it was Nick Barber. I've been pretty sure of him all along. When I finally broke out of that mess, I went inside to have it out with him. I'm not sure now what my intentions were, but I'll admit I have never wanted to kill anybody so badly in all my life. Fortunately, I didn't get the chance—I found him dangling from a rope, right there in the training center."

"He's dead?" Pete was nearly shouting. "He killed himself?"

"Right on both counts. He left a message behind telling the world he died happy because he got me first. The note also included a confession to both murders."

"Holy hell, boy, when your boss tells you to go out and stir things up, you don't screw around." Pete heaved himself upright, tossed off the half-inch left in his glass, and looked down at Win. "Our deal still stands. You, or should I say Matt, solved the case. That fellow Barber would probably have gotten away with it if not for your involvement. As interim president of Neal Drugs, I had the right to hire you. I have done so and will damn well see to it that Harold Herbert pays your bill the day you submit it, whether he likes it or not. He'd be a fool to mind, since it's his bacon you saved."

Pete turned to me, smiling broadly. He reached out to shake my hand while pointedly holding his nose with the other. "You remind me of myself when I was young, Matt—tough to kill. Good damn work! Even if it was one of my own employees, at least it's finished. I guess this is one time brawn won over brains, huh?"

"Dirk will drive you back to your office, Mr. Durning," Win told him, apparently oblivious to the dig. Like hell he was. "I've enjoyed our little chat a good deal."

Dirk leaped to his feet, delighted to be released from his dreary tour of duty. "I wouldn't suggest you use my car," I warned him. "The driver's seat may have to be replaced and the rest fumigated." I started to follow them out, heading for my room and a long, hot shower.

Win stopped me. "Please remain, Matt."

It was my turn to stare. "You're asking me to stay? Like this?"

"I'm not fond of the idea, but there's no helping it. Take your seat. Perhaps if you could move it over near the door . . ." he suggested, indicating the remotest possible point from his desk.

"I'll pass on the chair. It may be a while before I get to like the thought of sitting again."

"Of course. Forgive me, Matt. My mind is a maelstrom." He picked up the phone and pushed Randy's extension in the basement. "Please come to my office at once; bring the necessary medicants for treatment of severe cuts and contusions. Whatever you think . . . of course it's Matt. Come!"

"Wouldn't it be better all around if I hit the shower first? There's no big rush now. And congratulations on figuring out a way we can get paid. That was clever."

He was regarding me vacantly. When he sees right through you like that, you know something is driving him nuts.

"Your forbearance please," he muttered as if in a daze. "It's imperative I receive your full and complete report at once. Begin from the moment you arrived for the second time this morning at that monument to mendacity."

I would have given plenty to ask why, but Randy came in and began clucking over my battered hide, so I just plugged my memory into automatic and began. Stripping my underwear was the worst part. I was appalled when I saw how little remained of the back of my shorts. It explained all the giggles I'd gotten while storming through the plant. After Randy finished with my back, he had me stand while he sat on a chair. I guess it gave him a better perspective on the pounded steak that used to be my butt. I kept right on reporting, even when he made me stand on the chair so he could work on the backs of my legs. As he progressed, a part of my brain monitored the pain levels. The heaviest damage seemed to be centered around my shoulders and the back of my lap.

I finished before Randy did. Win's entire mood had changed; he now sat there watching me with a bright gleam in his eyes and asked me to repeat the exact text of the suicide note. I dumbly obliged, at a complete loss to find anything in my own recital to justify his increasing exhilaration. You might have thought he was simply glad the case was over, and he'd just snuck under the wire in getting Pete Durning to underwrite the rest of the investigation. You might have thought he was just feeling smug, because all there was left to do was submit a bill as large as our combined greed totaled and wait for the check. You might have—if you didn't know him better.

He was becoming impatient by the time Randy finished by zapping me with a tetanus shot. "Do you think you could possibly manage to rejoin me in an hour?" Win asked doubtfully, noting with obvious dismay my macerated hide. "If it weren't absolutely imperative I wouldn't ask it."

"Sure, I'm probably better off if I keep moving anyway. But I want tomorrow off—I plan to hurt a lot."

"Excellent! Unless I'm entirely mistaken, tomorrow will be a free day for both of us. Of no consequence whatever. If we are to solve this vexatious case, it will be tonight or never. I rather think it will be tonight."

I gaped at him, shaking my head in wonder. "I thought it was solved. As a matter of fact, I know damn well that it is. Weren't you listening?"

"Oh, indeed—intently," he replied. "Now go, please, both of you. I need a period of quiet to arrange my thoughts. One hour, Matt." Even as he spoke, he'd leaned back with his eyes closed and made steeples with his fingertips.

Randy and I left, closing the office door quietly. I climbed the stairs one at a time at a papal pace, dreaming of a shower and clean clothes. The shower turned out to be something less than the orgy of pure delight I'd envisioned. It hurt like hell, but my only other option was to continue smelling like the inside of a sewer pipe, so I grinned and bore it. The puddle at my feet was dull pink, so I suffered through a long dose of cold water to help discourage the bleeding. I waited five minutes before patting myself dry. There were a reassuringly small number of bloodstains on the towel when I finished. I rummaged around in the bottom drawer for some older clothes and climbed into them gingerly. The next chore was to remove everything from my wallet and wipe each item clean and dry with tissues. After that I cleaned and oiled my pistol. By then it was time to slip on a jacket and tie and report back down to the office.

One quick glimpse of Win's smug face spoke volumes. He looked like a Cheshire cat who'd just finished the world's richest bowl of cream.

"Where's the bourbon Pete left behind?" I demanded.

"Louis has removed it. Do you feel the need for some stimulant to blunt the discomfort of your wounds?"

"Nope, but you look about three sheets to the wind to me. I thought maybe it was the bourbon."

"Alcohol depresses, befuddles, and ultimately slays the brain. You know full well I'd as soon imbibe hemlock. No," he purred, beaming at me, "on the contrary, the emotion you note is satisfaction. I might say the extreme satisfaction of putting to rest at last a most irksome case."

"I guess it's put to rest, all right. When Nick's farewell message mentioned the uniform, that made it signed, sealed, and delivered as far as I'm concerned."

"Do you know what a black star is, Matt?" he asked.

"Sure, there's Richard Pryor, Eddie Murphy, Sidney . . ."

"Perhaps I should have been more specific," he interrupted. "Restrict the term to its scientific connotation."

"You tell me—I guess I played hooky that day."

"Very well. A black star is a terrestrial body invisible because it exists only in darkness, neither reflecting nor emanating any light whatever. The very existence of these stygian spheres may be extrapolated only by calculating the actions of those adjacent masses that are observable. It may be noted that these visible bodies behave in specific patterns that would be unaccountable otherwise; therefore astronomers are able to state empirically the presence and exact location of a so-called black star."

"Is this leading up to something, or do you just get chatty when you're looped?"

He merely smiled up at me with the tolerance a great man would show toward a fool. "Our murderer is a black star—invisible, but discernible through precise observation and careful consideration of all the data. It does me but little credit to have required this much time to reach such a conclusion."

If he was attempting to come off modest, it was a bust. "What does that make me? If you're right, that leaves me still in the starting gate. What makes you think Nick wasn't our boy?"

"Of that I'm positive; the facts proclaim it. Mr. Barber was merely the third unfortunate victim of a cunning and decisive killer. I never found him a satisfactory suspect. From the very first day you delivered your sham report on the robberies I've sensed an unseen malevolence lurking just beyond my sight."

His contemplative expression suddenly gave way to one of determination. "Call the District Attorney, Mr. Homber. It's imperative I speak to him immediately."

"Hold on, I know you want to gig Dixon again by going over his head and making him a laughingstock, but this time I'm not buying it. He was almost human the last time I saw him at the Plaza, and let's not forget I've got a hearing coming up in a few days. Rubbing his nose in it again is just going to make things a lot tougher now and in the future. Would it kill you to go through chain of command? He may never be a friend, but we don't need him as devoted enemy."

Win frowned, as he always did when his orders weren't carried out post haste, but he finally managed to swallow it. "As it happens, timing is critical and it would be expeditious to deal with Inspector Dixon directly. Call Neal Pharmaceuticals and get him on the phone; if he's not there, find him."

As I dialed, I told Win, "Forgive me if I sound testy; it's only because someone has recovered my chair in ground glass. Let me put it another way—I've already got a big enough pain in the ass without playing the goat while you gloat. Before you tell Dixon whatever it is you're going to tell him, would it kill you to tell me?"

He gave me a wounded look. "I sympathize with your painful injuries, I assure you, but I hesitate to deny you the satisfaction of reaching your own conclusions, of utilizing your own considerable gifts of acumen." Noting the furious look on my face, he quickly added, "Retain your extension and attend to my conference with our nemesis. I'm sure that will give you all the clues you need."

It was his cute way of saying, "Figure it out yourself, dummy." My business with the phone was being performed gingerly. I was doing my best not to involve any more of the muscles in my shoulders than necessary. It took a bit of time to work my way up from the girl on the switchboard all the way to Dixon. At last I heard his impatient growl on the line and was instantly sorry I'd insisted we go through him.

"Doyle, what the hell's the matter with you? Don't you even know better than to skip the scene after you discover a stiff? How you ever got your big mitts on a license I'll never figure. And I don't care if it was just a suicide—from what I hear you're in this thing up to your neck. The guy even names you in his suicide note, for Christ's sake."

"I was up to my neck and way beyond in something else out there—did anybody happen to mention that to you? Trust me—having me hang around would not have been any treat. I had to get back home and take the worry out of being close."

"Yeah," he chuckled with delight, "I'm real sorry I missed that. Might have had to add a charge of indecent exposure to your list. Listen!" he said sternly. "You've got one hell of a lot of explaining to do. What's all this about a bellhop's uniform? Withholding evidence again, and you haven't even made it to court on the first charge yet. Plus I understand you were charging around here waving a gun, which we both know you are no longer licensed to carry. All this is going to look bad when you go to trial, Doyle. And . . ."

"Inspector Dixon," Win cut in icily, "if you could possibly cut short your infantile litany of imaginary grievances against Mr. Doyle for a moment, I wish to make you a proposition."

"Winfield? Don't bother trying to pull the VIP crap on me. I know Doyle only does what you tell him to, so you're in this as deep as he is."

"Cease your interminable bluster, sir, and at least attempt to speak to the point. My offer is simple and straightforward. I am willing to deliver the murderer, along with sufficient evidence to convict, in exchange for a few minor considerations. Does such an offer interest you?"

There was a slight pause. "What in hell are you babbling about? Doesn't Doyle tell you anything? It's a wrap! Some lunatic named Barber had a beef with Mrs. Herbert and ended up killing the daughter too."

"Inspector, must you leap from one inane conclusion to another like a demented cricket? Don't you ever pause for thought? Either decide now to trust me, or prepare yourself to pay the penalty for still another blunder. Mr. Barber was nothing more than an additional victim."

"Bull! I don't know what your angle is, but it won't wash. Everything fits like a glove—this Barber even tried to wipe out Doyle. When he wrote the note he thought he'd succeeded. And he's got no alibi. He told people here he was going to see his wife in Phoenix over the weekend. I checked. His wife's in a home for battered and abused wives in Phoenix—there's no way in hell he got anywhere near her lately. He had to string himself up because he knew from what Doyle told him he was in for it. The whole series of events is about as obvious as you can get. And the DA will have a field day with you two in court. Without licenses, you stumble onto something that would convict a man of two murders"—his thin voice was rising in outrage—"and instead of reporting it, you go running to the killer and *tell him!* Now you've got the gall to try and dodge the bullet by—"

"A simple 'no' will suffice," Win cut him off. "I only make this offer out of courtesy to my associate, Mr. Doyle; at Susan Neal's suite he thought he detected some small shred of intelligence and human decency in you. No doubt he was mistaken. It is my personal opinion you are taking money—whatever amount the people of this city pay you—under false pretenses. I'm going to hang up now, call the District Attorney, and arrange to deliver the felon directly into his hands.

"Actually, I'm grateful for your refusal. This will be much more adventageous to us," Win went on in his most imperious tone. "As you've pointed out, it will be that very office that will shortly find itself in the untenable position of having to prosecute us due to your petty mendacity. I merely sought to spare you the embarrassment and adverse publicity that will surely follow. Given your total preoccupation—well documented in the press, by the way—with Harold Herbert, I fear this is going to prove quite humiliating for you, personally. But doubtless you're immune to such petty considerations." Win caught me grinning at him; he winked back.

There was a satisfying hollow silence in my ear with the phone stuck in it. Dixon had seen us pull many a bluff, but one thing he knew he could take to the bank—Win was no liar. It wouldn't be the first time my boss had made an elephant appear on center stage, and there was no way the Inspector could afford to miss the show if he did it again.

"How sure are you about all this?" Dixon finally asked grudgingly.

"I believe I have stated it as a certainty."

"I'm listening. I trust you half the distance I can toss a piano, but you have been known to get lucky once you get your teeth into something."

I placed my hand over the mouthpiece and chuckled. That was Dixon's idea of a compliment; he was trying to make friends, just in case. Win simply waited him out, knowing he'd succeeded in hammering the policeman into submission.

"That crack about taking money under false pretenses was uncalled for," Dixon complained, no doubt embarrassed at having to cave in, "but we can talk about that later. Just what 'minor considerations' did you have in mind?"

"Nothing onerous. Nothing, in fact, which you do not already owe us, and which we will receive in any case. Reinstatement of our licenses and cessation of all charges. I am tempted to include an apology, but will forgo it; as with love, unless given freely, it would have no worth." Win was having a swell time; he knew Dixon was hooked. Hooked, hell—he'd swallowed it.

"Agreed. I'm still listening. You can start with a name."

"First, Inspector, you have a small but vital role to act in the denouement. Please announce, clearly and for the benefit of everyone around you, the fact that you've developed the gravest reservations concerning Mr. Barber's suicide. You might mention such inconsistencies as the typed, unsigned suicide note. You understand? It's absolutely critical that everyone get the strongest possible impression of your dismissal of the suicide theory.

"You must also state your firm intention to obtain a court order first thing in the morning for the purpose of conducting a thorough search of Mr. Barber's residence."

"He's dead—I don't need a warrant."

"No matter, our quarry won't know that."

"This doesn't make sense. You've got to tell me who we're

after—otherwise how will I know to get it across to the right guy?"

"I think we may rest assured the culpable party will make it his business to observe your investigation closely. The announcement you are about to make will spread throughout the plant like a fire storm. Since I have no knowledge of your level of skill as a thespian, I have decided not to rely on it."

"It's just like you to make it too complicated," Dixon complained. "If you're right, and the killer's still running loose around here, I'm giving him a free ticket to anywhere. The minute he knows this little scheme failed, what's to stop him from catching the next plane to Rio? Just give me the damn name and let me get the cuffs on him quick."

"It can't be done that way, Inspector. You would only have to remove them later, and justice would never be served. I have evolved a logical sequence of events which must be followed exactly. Time is of the essence; your role must be played well before the employees leave for the day. Either trust me or not—as you wish."

"That's all you want me to do? Run around here letting on I'm not fooled, and mentioning that bit about the warrant? Then what happens?"

"Then you await my call."

"What the hell does that mean?" Dixon's voice was getting very hoarse. He'd swallowed it up until now, but he was choking on that last one. "How long do you expect me to just 'Await your call?' A day—a week—a year? If you've got something, the law says you turn it over. Why don't I just come over there and . . ."

"And make an ass of yourself," Win finished for him. "There is certainly no law in existence requiring me to report each and every hypothesis I formulate concerning a crime. In answer to your question, the call to you will come within the next eight to ten hours—or it won't come at all. I strongly advise you to accept my offer; it's almost certainly the only opportunity either of us will ever have to bring to book an extremely dangerous and cunning killer."

"I can stand on my head for ten hours as long as I know there's a payoff, but it sounds to me like you're just fishing."

"Inspector, you know me well enough to credit me with a certain meticulousness in my selection of words. An hypothesis is considerably more than a wild idea. Add evidence and it becomes a provable fact. I'm all but certain I'll have that evidence within the time frame specified."

"Hey, Dixon," I broke in, "better give me your home phone for later. I tried to call you once and found out you've got an unlisted number. What kind of public servant is that?"

"In your hat, Doyle!" He spit out the number, then broke the connection. And—judging by the sound—quite possibly the phone.

Win sighed. It wasn't that he hadn't enjoyed it, but talking to Dixon, or any other baboon, is a trying experience for him. "The stage is set for the final act of this ignominious inquiry. We shall require the home address of Mr. Barber."

"It's in his personnel file. I left it in my car." I began moving instinctively—big mistake. The sudden stresses on my shredded hide caused me to freeze with a grimace. I couldn't stop the groan from escaping. I finished standing in slow motion.

Win frowned at my predicament. "I sorely regret the exigencies at hand force me to commit any more of your depleted reserves tonight. But my sole alternative is to send Dirk alone, and there are good and cogent reasons why I hesitate to do that. We confront a clever, resourceful, and . . . ah, unusual villian. Without disparaging Dirk's abilities, I would prefer having you on hand to insure success."

"Don't give it a thought, boss—my only mistake was sitting too long. Are you telling me you want me to take Dirk along? I thought we decided that was out, that he'd break ranks and tear the guy apart."

He favored me with a look of tolerant amusement. "I don't think we need concern ourselves about that. It will require the two of you at a minimum to watch the house adequately and detain any visitors. You are certainly in no condition to engage in a physical confrontation."

"I'll have to admit you've got that right. We better get started. I'll need to have a good look around before dark." I stood in place, patiently, looking down on him.

"Yes, Matt?"

"It would help if you told me who I'm supposed to ambush," I told him evenly. "Whatever you got must have been spilled by Pete. The least you could do is tell me what it was."

"Mr. Durning 'spilled' nothing more than some bourbon; I can still smell it in the carpet. A full and complete report of our conference would yield nothing of any merit whatever."

He looked up at me with that mischievous twinkle in his eye. "You aren't seriously telling me you still haven't unraveled this conundrum for yourself? Yes, I see you are. Well, in that case, just return with whoever happens to call."

I stomped out the door, slamming it hard enough to give his sensitive damn ears a real treat.

CHAPTER 17

Dirk and I found 1431 Ocean Walk Way by four-thirty. It was a small, wood-shingled cottage in the Mission Beach section of San Diego, on the bay side of the two-block-wide isthmus stretching south from Pacific Beach.

I surveyed the house and the area immediately surrounding it from the parked car. The yard was nothing but sand; no trees, no shrubs. The street was incredibly narrow. The homes were set back barely enough to permit a sidewalk and a meager ten-foot-deep front yard. The postage stamp grounds in front were to allow for the maximum depth of beach behind. Since the beaches remained public, each house was enclosed within some kind of privacy fence. Nick's was overlapping weathered boards. A back gate led to the narrow beach and the waters of Mission Bay. The only waves that would ever hit this stretch of beach would be those thrown up by ski boats; the entrance into Mission Bay was too narrow to admit any of the Pacific's restless activity, and the tidal range was seldom over four feet.

"It's no good out here," I told Dirk.

"Not enough cover for a mouse," he agreed. "Right here from the car is our best bet, then?"

"Nope, can't even see the back door. And what if he recognizes the car and just keeps going? Whoever it is knew my car today, remember—he left me a note on the windshield. For all I know he may be familiar with the Continental, too. We'd better assume he is; I drove it to Mrs. Herbert's funeral. Damn that cute boss of ours. I could plan this a whole lot easier if I knew who the guest of honor was supposed to be."

Dirk couldn't stand it when anybody bad-mouthed Win, even me. "It's the only fun he has, Matt."

"Don't kid yourself; he has more fun than a bus full of kids on a picnic. He spends all day every day doing exactly what he wants most to do in the world. The guy gets more kicks from books than most guys I know get from girls." I glanced over at Dirk and grinned. "It's possible he didn't tell me because he doesn't know. He figured a way to set a trap and put out the bait, but maybe he isn't sure himself who's going to fall in. I don't say it for a fact, but it's possible."

"Either way, he's smarter than any cop, isn't he, Matt?"

"Yeah," I told him as I started the car and pulled out into traffic. Dirk was all for him. So was I, most of the time.

"We'd better grab a bite to eat somewhere close. It might turn out to be a long night." Dirk had reluctantly agreed to let me drive the "house" car when I explained it helped me to keep moving. I couldn't afford the luxury of allowing my body to stiffen up just yet, and experience had taught me the only way to delay the process was to keep on trucking. But I was amused to notice that Dirk was driving too, glaring at every other vehicle in sight, and moving his feet on imaginary pedals.

"Shouldn't I stay behind?" he asked, glancing back at the house uncomfortably.

"Relax, there's no need. I guarantee you he won't try barging in there in broad daylight during the rush hour."

We settled on a burger joint half a mile south. Dirk eyed the menu with grave misgivings, finally risking his life on the diet plate—a scoop of cottage cheese ringed with canned fruit.

He ate the cottage cheese and played with the fruit while I inhaled a double cheeseburger and a large order of fries. I hadn't realized it until we sat down, but I was starving.

Across the street I could see the dilapidated skeleton of the big roller coaster marking all that was left of the famous Mission Beach Plunge amusement park. Built right on the beach, it had once been a favorite fun spot for both the locals and the tourists, and the pride of the city. Now it was a favorite hangout for dopers—buyers and sellers. It happens, even in America's Finest City.

I elected to leave the car three blocks away. From there we hoofed it back to Nick's house. "Disguised as a doctor?" Dirk nodded at the satchel in my hand.

"Yeah, and Dr. Doyle is about to operate. If you're a good kid, I'll let you watch."

A block short of the house, we deserted the sidewalk and cut over to the public beach. Behind the house, we walked boldly up to the gate. At a sign from me, Dirk easily vaulted the fence, though it was a good six feet high, and opened the gate from the inside.

Twilight was about over when I squatted painfully to examine the lock on the back door. Opening my kit, I selected one of half a dozen large brass rings strung full of keys. Each bore a taped label on its head. The third one I tried worked.

"Shouldn't we have left that back gate open?" Dirk suggested once we were inside.

I considered. "Better not—wouldn't look normal."

The place was certainly no palace. Four rooms and a bath, and too much furniture. It was obviously the lair of a newborn bachelor. One of my minor concerns was the possibility of a live-in girl friend, but a quick look around eased my mind on that score. Irrationally, I found myself wondering who'd do the stack of dirty dishes in the sink now.

"Our target will be coming in the back door, too," I told Dirk. "He won't be turning on any lights. Pick a spot somewhere near the door, but be careful of the moonlight through those rear windows later on. Your job will be to secure the door as soon as he's well into the kitchen here. I'll be over there beside the arch leading into the living room. Wait for me to hit the switch. My gun will be available if needed, but it's up to you to bundle him up. And bundle up does not mean tear his head off and hand it to him. Think you can resist the temptation?"

"What's the difference? If I accidentally strike too hard, I mean?" He wasn't begging; he was merely asking. He really wanted to know so he could decide.

So I told him. "The difference, my friend, is twofold. If we don't deliver the bastard in one piece, Win and I may never see our licenses again, and I'll very likely do some time on that withholding-evidence charge hanging over my head. Win and I are both in a deep hole, and we need this guy—in good working condition—to dig our way out."

"I'll be careful," he promised.

"Please do. Now, that's it for talking or noise of any kind until our guest arrives. You're part of the woodwork until I turn on the light."

There were no lights on the beach behind the house except for the faint twinkling signs and outside lights of the hotels far away across the bay. The dark inside was nearly absolute and would remain so until the moon ascended. It was one of those weird occasions when time actually seemed to stand still. A comfortable position was an impossible dream: my sudden lack of mobility allowed my tortured body the chance it had been waiting for to seize up. There was absolutely nothing to do but wait.

My mind raced. I tried shutting it down, but that only made it worse. Thoughts of Susan crept from the dark around me, and finally I welcomed them. My trick memory allowed me the sad-sweet experience of reliving every moment and rehearing every word of our brief time together.

After that, I reran all the old brain games I could think of:

presidents, states, state capitals, and finally, old song lyrics. When I burned out on that, I let Susan's memory take over again. Between the all-but-unbearable burden of her murder, and the fresh horror of my own near death only a few hours before, I began entertaining macabre fantasies of revenge. That would never do. I ordered myself to repeat, "You are a professional," one hundred times. Then I began to worry about Dirk's good intentions eroding away in the dark like mine. His thoughts would be on Susan, too, right now. He'd never broken a promise to me or let me down before, but he'd also never let a woman get inside his space before. Win's change of heart in letting him come along still puzzled me. It was true I wasn't in condition to trade punches with the guy, but I could still point a gun and even put a slug in his leg if necessary. I was a lot more worried right now about how I'd stop Dirk if it came to that. He could easily kill a man with a single blow, and only he would know until the blow was struck. That was it, then—there was no way to stop him. I'd have given a week's pay to hit the light button on my watch, but experience had taught me better. What if it read only nine o'clock?

I was guessing it was well past midnight when I heard the faint sounds of a door being tested. Startled, I suddenly came to full alert and looked through the windows on either side of the door. The bright, eerie light of a three-quarter moon flooded the night scene, its intensity magnified as it glanced off the smooth waters of the bay behind the house. A trace of a fleeting shadow brushed the window on the left.

All I heard was a soft rubbing noise—a metallic scraping. With a shock it dawned on me that whoever it was had been attempting to force the lock open with a thin wedge of some kind, the same way he'd gained access in the original burglaries. It couldn't be done! The back door opened outward; the bevel on the lock was on the inside. The guy was a complete putz—he'd never get in. And he damn sure couldn't just kick the door in, as he'd done at Martha Herbert's. Any sign of a break-in would defeat his whole purpose.

The door gave a sharp rattle; it sounded loud as automatic weapons fire after the long-standing stillness. He was clearly registering frustration. None of his previous breakins had shown the slightest aptitude, I realized, cursing my ignorance at not allowing for his limitations.

My body felt sixteen feet tall, maybe three inches thick, and fastened together with used paper clips. There was no way I could risk nearing those windows, so I tottered into the living room, down a short hall, and into the back bedroom. Willing it to silence, I released the brass lock on the window facing the bay. Though he might draw the line at taking a crack at the front or side windows, surely he'd try all the ones at the rear. There were only three: one on either side of the back door, and the one I'd just unlocked. I hadn't realized how bad off I was until forced to carry out this simple activity. My equilibrium was shaky at best, and I felt like the Tin Man just before Dorothy got to him with her oil can. Suddenly I was very glad Dirk was on the scene. It would be embarrassing to pull a gun on a killer, tell him to freeze, and then faint.

I cautiously backtracked as far as the door and fumbled for the light switch. My gun in one hand and my other poised on the switch, I held my breath and waited. A black silhouette appeared on the windowpane. The lower section of the double-hung window shifted. I distinctly heard a sigh of relief being emitted, along with the soft sound of wood-on-wood as he raised the lower casement.

A medium-sized cardboard box appeared on the sill, then was lowered down onto the floor inside. A featureless black figure followed the box. First the right leg draped over the sill, followed by the left, and then a torso arched low under the window and was in the room. I'd gotten a fleeting impression of grace and power in a compact body; nothing at all like Don Burns, who was the one I'd been expecting.

I had no way of knowing what Dirk was up to. His eyes and ears are better than mine, so surely he knew what was going on. But I'd told him to remain in the kitchen, and he had a way of taking things too literally sometimes. Or he could be sound asleep. It was touchy. I couldn't continue just standing there until the murderer bumped into me, still I wanted him far enough away from that open window so he couldn't turn and dive right out of sight. When in doubt—move out! I thumbed the light switch and tried to steady the revolver in my hand.

It was lousy staging. The naked overhead bulb blazed to life, piercing my widely dilated pupils like knives. I instinctively raised my left hand as a shield, trying to squint under its shadow. In the center of the room—frozen in midstride—stood Helga Metz, clutching the box. She was dressed in the familiar black body stocking and sneakers. Her physique was that of a very fit welterweight wrestler.

Helga's recovery time was better than mine. She heaved the box at my head and quick-stepped toward me right along with it. My instincts betrayed me. They dictated I fend off the incoming box, which was the least of my worries. Helga got off a beautiful NFL-quality punt, scoring a goal between my legs. She smiled, pleased with the results. I screamed piteously and collapsed like a house of cards. The overhead light turned into a strobe.

I lay on my side, curled tightly into the fetal position, busy gasping and whimpering softly. Her right foot shadowed my nose and I could see her happy, simian face from the corner of my eye. At last I'd found what it took to make her smile. I ordered my hands to strike out and grab her at the ankles, but the command didn't get through. I kindly asked my mouth to scream, "Dirk!" All that came out was a pathetic mewing sound. Apparently all roads to headquarters were blocked. I spotted my gun under the edge of the bed, less than four feet away. All I could do was stare at it with longing. Academic, I decided. I couldn't grasp it if someone handed it to me, much less pull the trigger.

"You have no idea how much I've wanted to do that to you, Mr. Doyle," she gloated down at me. "And now, while you're still nice and relaxed, I'm going to do something else that I will enjoy even more. Unfortunately from my standpoint it will be a mercy to you, because it will end your pain—along with your stupid, miserable life." She circled around in order to get behind me. The last I saw, she was still wearing the same maniacal smile.

As I lay there utterly helpless, wondering whether or not my benumbed brain would register the blow that killed me, Dirk made his belated entrance. He dove through the open window, did a tuck and roll, and ended up nicely poised on the balls of his feet. He stared down at me curiously. I gave him complete instructions. It sounded like, "Wo bu dom fa."

Dirk gave up on me and switched his attention to Helga. She stepped right over me as if I were a felled tree. He looked confused and uncertain, which terrified me. She moved closer, her thick body somehow assuming the deadly grace of a jungle cat. She was no longer just another dumpy, middle-aged woman. My worm's-eye view revealed an impressive swell of calf and thigh bulging with her every movement beneath the skintight fabric.

Fear served to partially neutralize my agony, enabling me to form nearly intelligible words. My voice was high-pitched and tiny; the thought flashed through my mind that this was what I'd sound like in the unlikely event I lived to be one hundred. "Put her away!" I squeaked. "If you don't, we're both dead."

Helga was only two short steps from him. "Surely you aren't afraid of me, are you, young man? Can't you see I'm twice your age and only half your size?"

The questions were meant to distract and, though Dirk of all people should have known better, they worked. Pretending to take another normal step, she hopped forward and launched another ball-buster kick with the smoothest motion I'd ever seen. Only Dirk's own incredible reflexes saved him from being drop-kicked into an instant eunuch. He barely managed to twist enough to take the monstrous blow on his right hip.

"Wrap her up, you idiot!" I croaked. "She's meaner than

a snake and a lot faster. She killed Susan. If I could reach my gun, I swear to God I'd plug her."

He'd been standing there, frowning and rubbing his hip. I don't know whether it was the shock of the pain or my pleas that finally got through to him, but something put that hard, nasty gleam in his eye I'd been praying for. Pretending to look at me, Dirk suckered her into committing to another field goal attempt. He sidestepped it and snagged the lethal foot, using her own swift momentum to betray her. Lifting her foot high in the air, he upended her neatly. Helga made a one-point landing on the bare planked floor. There was a satisfactory-sounding dull thud as her head bounced once, then she lay still.

"My gun—under the bed," I pleaded.

Dirk retrieved it for me. With concentration, I managed to free my right hand from sick duty and grasp it. Until that moment I had been in complete terror of the bloodthirsty and deadly woman even as she lay stunned on the floor. I fully expected her to leap to her feet and take us both on. Having seen her in action, I got little enough reassurance from the gun.

"Go into the bathroom and rip up some towels. I want her tied up as securely as you know how. Pretend she's a Bengal tiger—and don't loiter." The pain was washing over me in great waves now instead of the constant agony of a few moments before. It wasn't necessarily any better, just different. Helga was conscious; her eyes were fluttering. "Just lie there and behave, Helga. I'm pretty sure I'm over my hang-up about shooting a woman now. If you'd care to test the theory, I'm willing."

She rolled her head around and peered at me with fearless contempt. I zeroed in on her broad nose. She stayed put. Dirk returned with half a dozen strips of frayed terry cloth. He studied the situation for a moment, then told her to roll over. She didn't move.

"Do as the man says," I suggested, "or I'll put a bullet in

one of those muscle-bound legs of yours. I'll try not to hit your knee, but I'm still pretty shaky so I can't make any promises."

Regarding us both like a dowager queen eyeing a pair of bugs, she gave a shrug of utter indifference and rolled over. Dirk sat astride her quickly and gathered her hands together. When they were lashed to his complete satisfaction, he reversed direction. "These too?" He indicated her ankles.

"Especially those," I told him. "Those damn gorilla legs of hers should require a weapons' permit."

He tied two of the strips end to end, securing her ankles with two feet of slack so she could still hobble. When he was finished, he came over and offered me his hand. "I'm sorry, Matt—I thought the smart thing to do was go outside, watch the window and back door, and cut off any escape." He was obviously distressed at my condition.

"Never apologize for saving a man's life," I told him, accepting the aid of his outstretched hand. "I know I have to do this, but I also know damn well I'm going to hate it."

He slowly coaxed me to my feet. A series of low animal moans escaped my lips. There was an overwhelming urge to walk crouched over to ease the pain, but I forced myself to maintain an upright position.

"If you're okay, I'll go for the car," Dirk offered.

"No, I'll go. I need to work this out." The three-block walk to the car was entirely level, and the sidewalks were smooth. It was the roughest quarter mile I ever covered.

I pulled up in front of the house. Dirk immediately appeared from the shadows on the north side. He held the box under one arm, and the other was firmly attached to the bun at the back of Helga's head. He overcame her resistance to forward movement by the simple expedient of pushing on the bun. This gave her the option of either moving ahead or falling smack on her ugly face.

"You get to sit in back with Godzilla," I told him.

Half an hour later, we marched into the office. Incredibly enough, it was barely after eleven. Helga led the parade, mincing along like a reluctant geisha. Win made no attempt to mask his relief at the sight of the three of us. There was nothing in his expression to clue me as to whether or not it had been a fishing expedition after all. Dixon and two other plainclothes cops were sitting in a row facing Win. Shock and disbelief registered on each of their faces as they turned and saw who our guest was.

"If this is your idea of a joke, I'm not laughing," Dixon growled.

"Hardly," purred Win. "Permit these gentlemen to examine the contents of the box you have there, Mr. Doyle. After they have done so, please favor us with your report."

I placed the carton on my desk and stood back while Dixon and his pals pawed over the contents.

With a lovely look of confusion on his face, the Inspector turned to one of his spear carriers. "You satisfied this is the crap taken from those homes in Del Mar?"

"It is, or it's a good job of setting us up. I can't say for sure until one of the victims looks it over, but it fits: golf medals, chess set, busted watch, and a few old coins. It looks like a good bet unless, like I said, these guys are pulling something." The plainclothesman gave Dirk and me a long, hard look with his steely gaze. Maybe I was reaching the end of my rope—I don't know—but I just couldn't help it—I laughed in his face.

"Cute, Doyle," Dixon grumbled as he stumped back to his chair, turning it ninety degrees so he could see both me and Win. "I'm listening," he said. His chins hid the Windsor knot in his tie and his fundament overflowed the chair. He looked for all the world like a petulant child.

I summarized the evening, but without all the detail I would have given Win. Dixon wouldn't have understood if I'd begun describing the expressions on people's faces and what I thought they were thinking. But I gave them everything that counted, and it didn't take long.

Dixon sat there staring at Helga when I'd finished.

"Where did you get this stuff?" he roared at her. "And who put you up to breaking into Barber's to plant it?" It was right then and there I decided my first impression of him had been the correct one. If brains were string he'd have trouble coming up with enough for a gnat necktie. He may have been a whiz with the flasks and beakers, but his knowledge of human nature was rudimentary at best.

She stood there with a faraway look in her eyes and the faintest ghost of a smile on her face. There was no sign she'd heard a word any of us had said. Dixon might as well have been speaking Urdu to a stump. He jumped to his feet as if he thought maybe a good shake would bring her around.

"Please resume your seat, Inspector," Win told him. "Perhaps you would find it helpful if I were to briefly outline, for your edification, this woman's odious career as a triple murderer."

The old boy was really lapping it up now. I left Dirk stationed behind Helga and worked my way through the crowd to my desk. It was going to be quite a show, and I was looking forward to it.

"You may be spared, Mr. Doyle," Win said politely. It was always Mr. Doyle when there were guests present. "Have Dr. Bruckner attend to your needs and go to bed. You are thoroughly exhausted, and quite obviously suffering considerable discomfort."

"Nothing doing! I'd pay admission to see this and you know it. I won't die—don't worry about it."

Dixon glared at Win angrily. "You don't seriously expect me to believe she's the murderer? That she waltzed right in and strung Barber up like a side of beef?"

"I dare you to challenge her to Indian wrestle," I told his back. "I'll take her—any odds you name."

"Unless you intend to spend the entire night railing at me," Win said evenly, "I suggest I be permitted to continue. Withhold all questions, please; most of them will be answered by the time I'm finished."

"I'm listening," Dixon said again.

"Thank you. As you know, all of this truly began with a series of apparently inept burglaries. I became intrigued after Mr. Doyle interviewed the victims. He thought it an exercise in futility and did it merely to pique me. But I recognized the situation for what it was: a carefully structured framework to utilize the ploy of Poe's *The Purloined Letter*. The thefts were patently unsupportable on any other basis. The carnations were a red flag to me. All was an effort to create crimes and a supposed criminal in order to hide the greater crime to come.

"The murder of Martha Herbert was, of course, that crime. You must try to imagine her chagrin"—he indicated Helga with a nod—"when Harold Herbert was suspected of the murder. After all her painstaking preparation to preclude that very thing. It must have been simple enough for her to dispatch her first victim. It is well known that both women were compulsive about schedules. No doubt Miss Metz had ascertained that Mrs. Herbert was to be home no later than ten o'clock. Indeed she may even have had an appointment with Mrs. Herbert, probably to report on Mr. Herbert. What appears at first to be an astonishing feat of timing becomes quite simple when the facts are understood. There was a flash of brilliance in the simplicity of it. She had expected her alibi would shield Mr. Herbert, but no one, including Mr. Herbert, ever realized it was also designed to shield her. Even when his alibi was shattered by diligent police procedure, not one of us realized that she too was now left unaccounted for during the critical half hour.

"You and I must share the onus, Inspector, for not recognizing the import of this fact: The breaking down of that man's alibi left two people—not one—peccable.

"The completed bid—another detail we foolishly allowed to sway us—presented no real problem. Miss Metz had done hundreds like it over the past decade. Surely it was a simple matter to prepare a number of bids covering the relatively narrow range of possible agreements.

"You talked to Mr. Herbert again, apparently amid much sound and fury. You removed him from his office and took him away. In her state of paranoia, Helga mistakenly concluded he'd been arrested. Possibly she overheard such threats and accepted them as fact. Indeed, she informed others that he had been arrested. Her worst fears were validated when his confinement lasted through the night. The next day her erroneous conclusion drove her to yet another desperate act.

"In a valiant, yet damnable effort to clear him, she struck again. Susan Neal died for no other reason than to convince the police the killer remained at large. But this time the fates conspired cruelly against her; approximately one hour before Helga Metz slew her second victim, Harold Herbert was released. Instead of exonerating him, she made him a prime suspect in a second murder. Worse, he was again left without an alibi.

"We must grant she is a woman of swift decision. This morning Mr. Doyle confided to her his suspicions of Nick Barber. Nothing more was required to launch her into deadly activity. Luring Mr. Doyle to a near-fatal tryst, she waited until the ideal moment to pull the linchpin and release a foul mountain of death, burying him alive. It required no great feat of agility to scale the iron ladder and await him on the opposite side of the platform. The moment the deed was done, she doubtless descended, leaping clear of the noxious pile before it had spread too widely.

"From there she proceeded to the training lab to set the stage for a final solution to the threat to Harold Herbert's freedom. It very nearly worked. If not for Mr. Doyle's tenacity, it probably would have. My best guess is she incapacitated Mr. Barber with her most trusted weapon—one swift and deadly blow delivered at the base of the skull. This was her most hazardous enterprise, for she could not afford to kill him with the blow. It must have been a challenging feat, maneuvering an unconscious man into a noose seven feet above the floor. No doubt a search would reveal a stepladder nearby. Such a feat is certainly not beyond a woman of her extraordinary prowess, with adrenalin at full flow."

Win turned and spoke to Helga directly for the first time. "You are a resourceful and determined nefariant. You're also a stupid and gullible woman. In a very real sense, you are as much a victim as those you killed."

She never batted an eye.

Dixon was sitting hunched over, staring fixedly at the carpet. His nervous habit of tugging on his right earlobe had brought it to a nice shade of pink. "I could drive a Mack truck through the holes in this case," he groused. "Let's start with the biggest one—a small detail we call motive. Why in hell would she do everything you say she did for a guy everybody knows she hates?"

"Why do you think I told her she was a victim as well? I daresay Harold Herbert may be relied upon to provide your motive," Win mused quietly. "I should think the moment he learns the truth, you'll find him a willing, even enthusiastic, witness. In the event he fails to grasp the full implications, ask him if he really wants Miss Metz back at his side, unfettered, his constant companion, expecting him to live up to his covenants. Remind him of her ever-increasing proclivity toward violence. I think not. When he seduced her, I believe he only did so to neutralize the spy in his camp, his wife's monitor, and to gain her support of his plan to effect a merger. Much as I detest metaphors, I'm tempted to say it must have been like shooting fish in a barrel for Mr. Herbert to show her the love and affection she'd never known, thus converting her into his most loyal ally. Little did the foolish man know he'd created not a lovebird but a bird of prey." For a guy who hated metaphors he was suddenly laying them on pretty thick.

Apparently Helga had been registering after all; Win's last remark caused her to smile down at him haughtily. She began singing softly to herself, swaying slightly to the music. Her face had taken on a radiant look that helped soften her brutish features.

"It figures—nutty as a fruitcake," Dixon muttered angrily. He directed his two men to remove her, read her the Miranda card, and wait for him in the car. She shuffled off between them, still crooning the indistinguishable tune.

"If one of you gets the notion to remove those restraints, forget it," I told their backs. "She's stronger than the two of you together, and she knows a lot more dirty tricks."

Dixon remained, crouched forward on the edge of his chair, rubbing his chubby hands together in agitation. "Jesus! You'd think all the years I've been at this, nothing would surprise me anymore."

"There is a slight matter of value received," Win reminded him. "Have we your word the specious charges pending against us are to be dismissed? And our licenses reinstated?"

"Yes, damn it! My word's good, and you know it."

"Thank you. May I suggest a point or two of interest? Mr. Barber's subsequent hanging will have masked, but not, I think, obliterated all evidence of the blow that stunned him. A second area of interest is the suicide note and the message left on Mr. Doyle's car. No doubt both were executed on her office machine. And now that you have her fingerprints to work with, you are likely to find a match at one or more of the crime sites; she is more energetic than sophisticated in her methods."

"Don't you ever run down? Since when do I need lessons from you on how to do my job? The one thing I just can't picture is Herbert whispering sweet nothings into that toad's ear, regardless of the payoff."

"In that respect you underestimate him. No, that does him too much credit. Put it that you overestimate him. He's a professional—a gigolo. No doubt he's quite proficient in his chosen field; it's certainly served him well. As with any of us, he encounters distasteful aspects to his work, but one does what one must to achieve goals."

"Yeah, I know all about distasteful aspects. That's what this is—sitting around here listening to you crow." Dixon twisted around so he could glare at me over his shoulder. "We got that uniform out of the Plaza basement, no thanks to you. I guess I don't have to tell you two what I think of creeps who walk around with incriminating evidence in their back pockets until they can wrap it up and sell it themselves. Because of you, my department was left pounding sand while you were out beating the bushes, knowing we were holding the wrong guy. Did it ever occur to either one of you that your grandstanding killed Barber? That if you'd obeyed the law he would still be alive? I swear I don't know how you two sleep nights."

"*How dare you, sir!*" Win roared. There was nothing old about his remarkable voice; he could still stop traffic when it suited him. "You transgress all boundaries of civility. First, through perversion of the law; now, with scurrilous accusations, you attempt to stop us from functioning. You strike out blindly, angry at us, for unearthing the existence of the uniform. Why? Your men had trampled that ground to dust already. Whose fault is it they were incompetent? Ours? We didn't 'remove' it. We merely noted it was a slightly unusual detail that may have occurred concurrent with a crime. The fact that the jacket had been torn in just such a way that an assailant delivering a fatal blow might have torn it was there for anyone with eyes to see. Did none of your men search those lockers? If Mr. Doyle had the sagacity to do a better job than your entire horde, don't decry him for it. Praise him! Look to your own if you would find the fault. Remember, you arrived with three unsolved murders and you leave with their killer—a fact I'll no doubt read about in the morning papers, with your name prominently mentioned. Mine will be conspicuous by its abscence. I expect no more from a man like you."

The Inspector was ready to blow. I could see his right temple from my angle; it was pulsating to the rapid beat of a straining artery. I prayed Win knew when to back off. I really wasn't up to another night in a cell.

My boss took his cue and beat Dixon to the punch. His voice was almost paternal now. "The truth is, there is a valid role in the community for both of us, Inspector. For ninety-nine per cent of the crimes committed, you are infinitely better suited to effect a capture than we are. Why must you feel compelled to deny us the remaining meager portion? There are rare occasions when police procedure doesn't serve. Some malversations fall beyond the net cast by your methods. This case was one. Procedure and experience, your excellent tools, led you astray. Given the apparent facts of the case, who could blame you?

"Mr. Doyle and I foundered as well for far too long a time. Our client was slain while we were in her hire. Do you think we're vainglorius about that? We expended precious time nurturing the theory that someone wanted to make Harold Herbert appear guilty. Then, we wasted more time . . ."

"The one thing I want to know," Dixon interrupted, "is how you knew to keep plugging away." Win had succeeded in molifying him somewhat; he'd dropped back down to just average angry. "By all rights Herbert was sewed up, but somehow you knew better—otherwise there was no reason for Doyle to go near the Plaza, or back to the plant either." He got to his feet and leaned over Win's desk. I didn't like it, but before I could react, Dirk silently appeared at Dixon's side. "How did you know that?"

I froze. If Win got carried away with his lecture and dropped the bomb that we had the Nolte brothers alibing Harold for one murder and Dirk tailing him at the time of the second, we might as well both go out and jump in the car with Helga. At the very least, it would strain beyond the breaking point Dixon's promise to drop the charges against us.

Win shook his head slightly, eyes half closed, as if in deep thought. "I fear there is no way I can explain my methods that would make any sense to you. I do not have squads of men at my beck and call, so I'm forced to depend on phenomena. Or call it intuition if you like; I'm afraid that's about as close as we'll ever come to an understanding."

"You're so full of it it's a wonder it doesn't leak out your ears," Dixon snapped. Then he turned back to me. "Doyle, God knows you're no prize yourself, but *this* guy! How the hell do you sit here day after day and put up with him? Doesn't he ever run out of crap?"

He turned back to face Win, getting his big, red face even closer, both knuckles resting on the desk. "Intuition, my ass. Don't you think I know what happened? You kept Doyle barging around like a bull in a china shop, hoping I was wrong about Herbert. Your motive was to make me look foolish, which seems to be your main hobby. And you lucked out because *he*"—Dixon pointed to me—"finally pushed the right panic button. Then you dreamed up this idiotic charade—with my help—damn it!—and it worked. But one thing I'm sure of—you've been improvising all along. You didn't *know* who was going to show up at Barber's house tonight. I heard Doyle's report; he was surprised to find Metz. If you knew, you'd have told him. You're a menace. I hear you were really something once, but now I think you've got a loose screw. The only talent you've got between you"—he was kind enough to include me with a gesture—"is colossal gall. If I had a man in my department who worked like you two, I'd kick him to hell off the force. You'd lecture me on how to solve crimes, huh?" He finished with an impressive volume and disappeared out the door. We listened to his angry stride punishing the tiles all the way out the front door.

"Better go check," I advised Dirk. "Part of his problem was severe nicotine withdrawal. You can bet he lit up before he cleared the porch. This could be the night it would appeal to him to try burning down the place."

When Dirk was gone, I looked over at Win with the best grin I could muster. "Phenomena and intuition, huh? For a minute there you had me scared to death you were going to brag to Dixon that we had airtight alibis for Harold on both murders. But I thought you had this thing about lying—and you told him 'phenomena and intuition.'"

"I qualified it. Go to bed—you look ghastly."

"I just wanted you to know I finally caught up. Once you'd convinced yourself Nick Barber was a decoy, there was no one else it could be but Helga. She was the only one I'd told about my suspicions of Nick."

"But you were taken unaware by her arrival and paid dearly for it. That was petty and stupid of me, particularly given your present condition. You deserve my apology, and you have it. It's a flaw in my character these days; I sometimes succumb to an urge to be cryptogrammic."

"So I've noticed. As for the apology, thanks, I'll have it framed." I began the long arduous trip to my feet. "I'll pound out a bill for Harold—actually, I'll dun Neal Pharmaceuticals—in the morning. How's fifty grand sound?"

"A trifle high, don't you think?"

"Not to me. That was one of my favorite suits I had to leave out there beside that pile of rotten hogs' lungs. Thanks to Helga, I'll probably never have children. Not that I want any at the moment, but it's the principle. And the way I expect to feel when I wake up in the morning, it may end up even more. Think of it this way: They'll give away more than that in free samples before midafternoon."

"That does tend to put it in perspective. Very well, I leave such details entirely to your discretion, as you know. Good night, Matt. Well done."

I wobbled out the door and up the stairs, one at a time, clinging to the banister. There was plenty of time after I crawled into bed to try to sort things out. Usually a "well done" from Win was only slightly less satisfying than winning the Irish Sweepstakes, but I was having trouble finding that warm glow that usually came with wrapping up a case. Part of the reason might have been the fact that I had more square feet of hurt than I'd ever had before in my life, but far more painful was the terrible price I'd paid emotionally. Now that it was over, my defenses were down and there was time to think and remember. Too damn much time. They say you can't actually feel your heart. They're wrong. Mine felt like a small, cold stone.

EPILOGUE

The following ten days were every bit as bad as I'd anticipated. The worst of it was the huge scabbed areas across my back and butt that cracked and started healing all over again every time I made a wrong move. And there weren't many right ones. Randy finally succeeded in concocting some goop that helped. Either he or Dirk applied it every couple of hours, accompanied by appropriate sarcastic remarks.

Things were peaceful in the kingdom. The check arrived from Neal Labs after a couple of weeks' delay. There was a letter included. It was from Pete. The reason for the delay, he explained, was a shake-up. Harold was no longer popular, it seemed, even though he wasn't being charged with any crime. Martha Neal's huge block of stock, and Susan's as well, had passed on to the employees of the company, according to the terms of Susan's will. Harold never had a chance. The first thing they voted to do was give him the boot. That left him the house and car and an unknown amount of cash. If he was smart, he'd find a way to make it last.

I was pleased to see that the letter had also been signed by Don Burns, now vice-president, according to the letterhead.

I took that to mean that he'd gotten over his anger at me and I was glad. I still felt guilty about throwing his son's name back at him when he'd cussed me out.

The police had eventually managed to dig up some history on Helga Metz. It turns out she was the youngest member of a famous family in her native Austria. They were, for some four generations, the foremost trapeze artists in Europe. It was the custom of the family to begin training each new arrival practically from birth, and so the troupe continued. Apparently, the act was altered to suit the available personnel.

Helga was the equal of any of her family, past or present, in strength and ability. Unfortunately, she was the ugly duckling of the family, and that counted heavily against her. So, though she was by far the better of the two sisters, she was relegated to the lowly post of catcher for her more attractive younger sibling. After increasing signs of hostility and isolation from the family, there came the horrible night more than twenty years ago when she'd dropped the hated sister to her death. She didn't fail to catch her, mind you; she caught her just fine, then deliberately dropped her. Everyone there knew exactly what she'd done. Her family shunned her. She emigrated to the United States and lived a peaceful, if somewhat isolated life. Until more than twenty years later, when Harold Herbert unsuspectingly re-ignited the banked fires of her violence to white-hot flame. The police had no trouble getting an indictment, and sources in the DA's office told me their case was solid. Not that it made the slightest bit of difference; Helga was slated for a rubber room for life. I wondered how many staff she'd coldcock before they learned to leave her alone.

As for me, I was developing symptoms of cabin fever. It suddenly occurred to me that I hadn't even started my car in nearly two weeks, so I grabbed my keys, happy to have an excuse to get out of the house, if only for a few minutes.

As I stuck the key in and turned it, a sharp explosion immobilized my senses. I sat there frozen, listening to the shrill descending scream that followed. As I struggled to regroup my shattered nerves, I saw the smoke leaking upward from under the hood and grill.

Dirk was there by the time I got out, and the others were on the way. Even Win appeared at the door, looking frightened. "Relax, everybody," I told them in an embarrassingly shaky voice. "I recognize the sound. Somebody's idea of a joke, that's all."

I lifted the hood and found what I'd expected. The charred remains of a device known as the Screamer was fixed to my ignition wires with alligator clips. But there was something else. Taped to the side of the block was a small metal cylinder eight inches long and maybe two inches in diameter. I removed it carefully, somewhat reassured by the fact that it wasn't hooked up in any way I could see and appeared to be harmless enough. Besides, if whoever it was had wanted to do the job for real, he wouldn't have used a joke bomb.

"What in the world are you doing?" Win shouted from the front door. It was about as far out into the world as he'd ventured in nearly a year. "What was that incredible racket?"

"Just an overgrown firecracker," I assured him, walking toward the house with my other surprise. "They're illegal as hell, and they've been known to do some real damage. But my guess is this is the interesting part of the message." I held out the cylinder so he could get a better look. "The noise was just to get my attention. It worked!"

We all went inside, where the debate began. Win wanted the cylinder opened on his desk in the office. Everybody else wanted to watch. I told them that was a swell idea because, if it did blow up, we could all go off together. Win demanded to know whether I actually expected it to explode. I told him no, but that I would find it personally embarrassing if I was wrong. The opinions flew back and forth for a while, but in the end I exercised my veto. "It's mine, so I will open it when and where I please."

With that settled, I walked back out the front door to a

point about fifty yards from the house. I checked to make sure I was alone, then proceeded to unscrew the cap. I'd opted for the outdoors because of the risk of poison gas. There was nothing inside except a sheet of heavy bond paper rolled tightly. I read it, shrugged, and walked back toward the house. I handed the note to Win; he looked it over, then read it out loud.

"In Chicago several years ago, you made a near-fatal error. You interfered with the work of certain businessmen. One of them died. But there were considerations. It was decided to let it pass.

"Two weeks ago you once again interested yourself in the business concerns of associates of those mentioned above. This was not prudent. But, again, there were considerations.

"This method of communication was selected to impress upon you the ease with which we can act. I must also convey the certainty that we will act if you ever inconvenience any of our associates again.

"You have two strikes against you, Mr. Doyle. You know the rules. Three strikes—you're out!"

No one had much to say for about a minute.

"An outfit like that," I told them finally, "you'd think they could afford stamps."

Win's mouth had tightened into a thin straight line. He walked into the office and took his seat behind his desk. I knew what was bothering him. He was in an absolute fury at the thought of someone trespassing onto his grounds and telling one of his employees what he could and could not do. It was outrageous and intolerable. Worse yet, he knew there wasn't one single damn thing he could do about it. To even try to establish contact would be to challenge these men to make good on their threat. And they were noted for promissory fulfillment. He just sat there for a long time, digesting the unpalatable edict. Every case we took from today on needed to be considered from a whole new angle. Limits had been imposed. Fences were up. He just sat frozen in a silent rage. I think I felt sorrier for him than I did for me. The stubborn glint in his eyes only served to ratify what I already knew: He'd never roll over and accept limits on his activities, not from anybody.

He looked up at me and nodded once, as if in agreement—then I understood. He'd found the same message reflected in my eyes as well.